A TOUCH OF MAGIC

Fae-Touched, Book One

Isabelle Adler

A NineStar Press Publication

Published by NineStar Press
P.O. Box 91792,
Albuquerque, New Mexico, 87199 USA.
www.ninestarpress.com

A Touch of Magic

Printed in the USA
First Edition
May, 2018

Print ISBN: 978-1-948608-87-9

Also available in eBook, ISBN: 978-1-948608-76-3

After returning to the straight and narrow, Cary Westfield hopes to rebuild his life as a stage magician. Only thing is, the success of his new show is entirely dependent on a strange medallion inherited from his late grandfather—an amulet that holds a rare and inexplicable power to captivate the wearer's audience.

Ty prides himself on his ability to obtain any item of magical significance—for the right price. When a mysterious client hires him to steal a magical amulet from a neophyte illusionist, he's sure it will be a quick and easy job, earning him a nice chunk of cash.

As it turns out, nothing is sure when greed and powerful magic are at play. When a mob boss with far-reaching aspirations beats Ty to the snatch, Cary and Ty form an unlikely partnership to get the amulet back. The unexpected spark of attraction between them is a welcome perk, but each man has his own plan for the prize.

All bets are off, however, when it is revealed the magical amulet holds a darker secret than either of them had bargained for.

Chapter One

CARY WESTFIELD WASN'T a terribly catchy name for a magician, so the playbill read The Incredible Mr. Mars.

Ty studied the vintage style poster near the theater's entrance, which depicted said Mr. Mars pulling a bewildered-looking white rabbit out of a hat. Despite the old-fashioned font and style, the poster was brand new. Mr. Mars was a relative newcomer to the live entertainment scene and had only been performing at the Garland Magic Theater for two weeks, but the shows had been consistently sold out. Granted, this wasn't the largest or the most prestigious venue in San Francisco; however, considering the act in question wasn't at all original or shocking, consisting of run-of-the-mill stage illusions and a bit of mind reading, it was quite a feat.

The mass appeal would have been something of a mystery had Ty not known exactly what was behind it. That was too bad for poor Cary Westfield—sudden and unwarranted success tended to draw the wrong kind of attention.

Ty followed the line inside. The usher took a look at his ticket and directed him to the back row. Ty took the aisle seat and waited as the lights dimmed. The darkness sharpened the smell of dust coming from the old upholstery, the whispers of the spectators, and most annoyingly, the glare of their cell phone screens. It would seem even the promise of magic couldn't tear some people away from their social media. The emcee announced the magician, and the show began.

Contrary to tradition, Mr. Mars didn't have an assistant. His tricks weren't all that complicated, but Ty had to give him credit for showmanship. He supplied a running commentary for the performance, which was both witty and charming and elicited laughter from the crowd. Smart. People always loved it when a show made them laugh, so they were more likely to forgive the lack of surprise and excitement. Not that Ty was in any way an expert on magic shows, but he was, in a manner of speaking, an expert on excitement.

The magician's looks didn't hurt either. His smooth tan skin and fine features made the gaudy stage costume appear elegant. Ty absently noted the lean figure and the fluid movements, but he wasn't there to admire Westfield's form.

As Mr. Mars struck another impressive pose, pretending to strain to recite the contents of some woman's purse, Ty slipped quietly into the shadows, making himself as inconspicuous as possible. Thankfully, the small theater had an appropriately small staff, even on a busier Saturday night, and no one spotted him as he made his way to the backstage passage. There was only one dressing room, and the lock on it was a joke. He let himself inside and closed the door softly. The runes tattooed into his fingertips with invisible ink prevented him from leaving fingerprints, so he could rummage freely without being encumbered by gloves. That shit always came in handy—bad pun intended.

The small room was cramped, serving both as a makeup nook and a storage space for various costumes and stage props. There was a vanity with a large backlit mirror. Ty looked it over, but saw nothing of interest besides a kohl eyeliner and a few mini-sized bottles of flavored vodka scattered all over the tabletop. Either the Incredible Mr. Mars needed some liquid courage before facing the crowd, or Mr. Westfield had a bit of a drinking problem.

It was more force of habit than curiosity. Ty didn't really expect to find anything of value lying around. He retreated to a far corner, where he spotted an oversized armchair under a pile of old sequined jackets, and settled there, taking out his SIG. The show was supposed to run for at least forty more minutes, but that was okay. He could wait.

IT WAS ANOTHER hour or so before the door swung open, admitting the magician. There was a noticeable sheen of perspiration on his forehead, and he was breathing rather heavily, as if he'd run a race. He looked at the door and frowned, testing the doorknob again, probably recalling he'd locked it before going on stage.

Ty moved before Westfield had a chance to retreat. The magician froze as Ty stepped in front of him, holding the gun to his face. His dark brown eyes widened, making his expression resemble that of the rabbit from his own poster.

"Sit over there," Ty said, nodding toward the armchair he'd been occupying earlier.

Westfield kept as much distance between them as the small room allowed as he slowly walked to the chair and sat down, never taking his eyes off the gun. Ty shoved the door closed again and locked it.

"Now," he said, taking a step toward the other man. "I believe you have something I want."

Westfield licked his lips nervously. His eyes darted to the door, but now Ty was blocking his only escape route. He was wearing a ridiculous top hat that looked like something straight out of a Fred Astaire movie, and even his scarlet cravat was soaked with sweat.

"I don't have any cash," he said quickly. "The register's at the front."

"Don't play dumb with me, Houdini," Ty said. "The amulet."

Westfield's tawny skin turned ash gray. There was no doubt he knew exactly what Ty was talking about, and he wasn't thrilled about the prospect of being parted with it.

"I don't know what you mean," he insisted, despite Ty's previous admonition.

Ty took another step toward the chair, watching as the magician shrank back instinctively.

"One last chance," he said. "Hand it over, or we'll see if it helps you stop a bullet at point blank."

Westfield pressed his lips together, his nostrils flaring. He looked ready to either burst into tears or lunge at him. Ty tightened his grip on the weapon, but apparently the magician wasn't that reckless. He slowly reached inside his shirt to reveal an embossed silver disk on a sturdy chain around his neck. There was another moment's hesitation as he removed the chain and tossed the thing at Ty.

Unfazed, Ty caught it with his left hand. Amateurs were the worst. Such a powerful thing, and this dude was using it to enhance his cheap parlor tricks. Worse, he was wearing it against his bare skin. No wonder he looked ready to keel over from exhaustion.

What was more surprising was Ty had sensed Westfield could actually perform real magic. Not that he could do so on his own; everything he'd done on stage depended entirely on the amulet he'd been wearing. But Ty could feel Westfield's inherent magical talent coursing through his veins, almost see the genuine spark underneath his skin. Westfield had the gift, the talent for true sorcery, and he didn't even know it, preferring to resort to hashed out illusions augmented by an external power he had no hopes of understanding. It seemed like a waste to let this kind of potential be squandered in ignorance, but Ty had more pressing matters than guiding a newbie magic practitioner on the path of self-discovery.

The round silver pendant, about two and a half inches in diameter and covered in swirling patterns, felt warm to the touch, even slightly too warm. Ty couldn't stop to examine it closely, but he had no doubt this was indeed what he'd been looking for. These things always had a certain feel to them, an unmistakable aura. Ty's talent for magic was nearly nonexistent (as Leland, his former mentor, had made painfully clear), but his sensitivity to its trace presence had been honed like a fine blade.

"Look, man," Westfield said pleadingly. "I know it'll sound lame, but it's kind of important to me, okay? It's not even that valuable, but it's sort of an heirloom. Can't we cut some sort of a deal here? I can give you way more than it's worth."

Oh, so suddenly the man *did* have cash? Ty almost rolled his eyes, but he didn't have time to listen to any more lies. Undoubtedly, Westfield knew the amulet wasn't a cheap trinket; he'd been consciously using it. But Ty was also certain he didn't have a clue as to its real potential. Otherwise they would be having this argument in a much grander place than the dressing room of a backwater theater.

"I doubt that," he said, pocketing the pendant inside his jacket.

"Come on! I got it from my grandfather. It's the only thing I have to remember him by. You must have had a grandfather, right? A family?" Westfield leaned forward ever so slightly, probably trying to gauge whether he could get any closer to swipe the amulet right out. Picking pockets wasn't Ty's forte, but he knew enough to recognize the telltale signs of someone intending to do just that.

The nonsense about family heirlooms was just a stalling tactic. In any case, Ty didn't have grandparents. As far as he knew, he didn't even have parents. At least not parents who wanted him. And family wasn't something he missed having, not in his line of work.

"Shut it," he told Westfield, taking a step back. As he was contemplating coldcocking the guy so he wouldn't try to follow him, there was a bang on the door.

They both froze, Ty with his gun arm raised, Westfield teetering on the edge of his seat, his black-lined eyes huge in his sweat-dampened face.

"Special delivery for Mr. Mars," said a muffled voice from behind the door.

"You expecting anything?" Ty asked, not taking his eyes off the magician.

He doubted it, though. Westfield looked genuinely startled. *Just don't be an idiot and try to tackle me*, Ty begged silently. He really didn't want to shoot him, not even to incapacitate, and had already made a mistake, talking with him for so long. He should have just knocked Westfield over the head and gone through his pockets instead of playing out all this nonsense, chatting about the guy's grandparents, of all things.

"Other than someone robbing me? No," Westfield said testily.

The thumping on the door became more persistent. Shit. Could he have competition?

Ty had had time to check the room out before, and he remembered there was a small window on the farthest wall, half hidden with drapes and a rack of old theater costumes.

"Stay quiet and do as I say," he said as he went to the window. He pushed the junk away from it and broke the murky glass with the butt of his gun. Thankfully, they were only on the first floor, and the window led to the back alley.

The knocking stopped.

"Get your ass over here," he hissed at the magician and gestured at the window. He could get the fuck out on his own, but he had a gut feeling whoever was after the Incredible Mr. Mars wasn't going to pull their punches like he had. For some reason, he didn't want the guy to get killed if he could help it. Maybe it was the huge doe eyes, though Westfield was definitely not his type.

"What? Why? What if it's...flowers? A present from a fan? A job offer? Why the hell should I listen to you? You've just mugged me!"

There was a loud and heavy thud on the door, as if someone was trying to break it in with his foot or shoulder, quickly followed by another.

"Sure, it's flowers," Ty said sarcastically, pushing the broken glass out of the window to clear the way. "Fine, suit yourself."

He wasn't about to force it. Pretty eyes or not, Westfield was welcome to deal with whoever it was on the other side of the door if he wanted to. Ty had gotten what he'd come for. It was high time to get the hell out.

"Shit." Westfield stared at the door for a moment and then darted to the window, apparently coming to the conclusion Ty was the lesser of two evils. "Be a gentleman and help me, would you?"

Ty snorted, holstered the gun, and laced his hands together to make a step for the other man to push off from. Westfield scrambled to climb out just as the old wood creaked and the door burst from its hinges. Ty grabbed the window frame and hurled himself out, feet first, not turning back to see who the unwanted guest was. He landed in a neat crouch in the alley and then grabbed Westfield by the hand, pulling him forward.

"Run!"

Westfield didn't have to be told twice. They ran for a few blocks, taking the back streets when possible and turning corners at random, until Ty finally pulled the magician into a dark alley and almost threw him against the wall, flattening himself against it as well and peering cautiously around the corner. No one seemed to have followed them, but plain eyesight couldn't always be trusted. It was time to bail.

"Now listen to me," he said in a low voice, turning to his inadvertent companion. "My advice—go spend the night in a motel or at a friend's. Whoever that was, they're probably gonna follow you home next, looking for that amulet."

"Who's 'they'?" Westfield asked. He was breathing heavily, and there was an almost hysteric note to his voice. Not that Ty could blame him, really. At least the guy had kept his wits about him enough to follow Ty without making any unnecessary fuss. "For that matter, who are *you*?"

"As for them—no idea. But you weren't exactly discreet about using that thing, Mr. Mars," Ty said, ignoring the second question. "If I could find you, others could have, too. Next time you're dabbling in magic, try not to flaunt it so blatantly."

"It's called 'sleight of hand,' asshole," Westfield snapped. Amazingly, he still had that stupid top hat on. It must have been glued to his head or something.

"Whatever." There wasn't time to get into pointless arguments. With the competition on his heels, whoever it was, Ty had to make the drop as soon as possible. "Just stay out of it for a while."

He backed out of the alley, keeping his eye on Westfield. It didn't look like he was about to tackle him, but in Ty's experience, desperate people were capable of anything, and watching the source of one's livelihood being stolen was a damn good reason for desperation. But the man was just standing there, watching him and trying to catch his breath. So when Ty stepped onto the street, he turned and walked away briskly, looking out for any possible pursuit.

There was none that he could spot, so he relaxed marginally and picked up the pace, shoving his hands into his jacket pockets. He didn't enjoy the part of his job that required him to actually rob people at gunpoint. He much preferred the other parts, in which he got to explore forgotten ruins and visit faraway places. But those parts were rare and far between. The harsh truth of life was that everyone had to do things they didn't really want to. People like him didn't have all their dreams and wishes handed to them on a silver platter. They had to hustle to make their way in the world. Sometimes other people got caught under the wheels, and there was nothing he could do about it, except to try to keep the damage to a minimum. Mr. Mars would just have to chalk this one up to experience, pick himself up, and move on to the next gig. If he was lucky, soon he'd realize he didn't really need any crutches—that he had magic enough within him. Provided, of course, that he managed to dodge Ty's competition.

But that was none of Ty's concern, was it? He'd done his job, and the mark's continued safety wasn't his responsibility. It was silly to even give it another thought. He'd helped the guy as much as he could, and if he was smart, he'd lie low until the whole thing blew over. Ty's next move was to drop the hot loot with his fence, getting rid of it so he could focus on the next job.

He definitely had no business thinking about the look of despair that had clouded Westfield's eyes as he watched Ty take off with his pendant. None at all.

Chapter Two

CARY STAYED IN place and watched as his robber cleared the mouth of the alley and disappeared into the street. Helping hand at the window aside, the man was still carrying a gun, and Cary didn't want to agitate him any further. Besides, he'd had the opportunity to gauge his opponent back at the dressing room. The robber was a large man—not really bulky, but tall and built of solid muscle, like an athlete. Cary could gather that much from having practically climbed on top of him to push himself through the window. Even if he hadn't been armed, there was no way Cary—with his self-admittedly fetching, but much leaner physique—could have arm-wrestled him.

He was so damn exhausted and frustrated about someone casually deciding to take his granddad's amulet. At gunpoint. And just as it was looking like things were picking up for him, too. The show was doing great, and he'd been considering changing the venue for something grander. Why was his luck always running out just when he got optimistic again? He felt like bursting into tears there and then, curling up on the dirty pavement amid the smelly trashcans and giving in to the utter helplessness that was nearly choking him.

It wasn't fair. The thought was childish, but he couldn't help it. He had always been such an utter failure in everything he'd done, and why should this be any different?

Cary took a deep breath to calm his wildly beating heart, fighting back the unwanted tears. The autumn air felt cool against his flushed cheeks, adding a little bite as he sucked it into his lungs, still strained from his panicked flight. Childish or not, he instinctively balked at the idea of letting his amulet be taken away. The robber had probably thought that Cary was shitting him, and most likely didn't care either way, but he *had* gotten it from his grandfather. Well, he'd found it in his grandfather's stuff after he died, but it was the same thing. It was something to hold on to—the only real legacy left after years of discord, and there was no way he was going to just give it up, even if it was out of sheer stubbornness. Whoever this guy was, he was in for a surprise. Cary had some tricks up his sleeve, none of which had anything to do with magic.

He took off the hat, the jacket and the vest, and hid them in a neat bundle behind one of the dumpsters. He hoped he'd get them back later, but if not, that was collateral damage. There was nothing else of value in his jacket's pockets aside from a deck of cards, which he moved to his pants pocket. Then he quickly undid the top button of his shirt, rolled up his sleeves, and tousled his hair. That was it. Now he wouldn't attract attention, and particularly not from people who, even if subconsciously, expected him to look the way he had before.

He walked out of the alley, looked to the sides quickly to make sure no one was waiting to jump him, and headed in the direction the robber had taken.

THE UNDERGROUND PARKING lot was mostly empty at this hour. It was also badly lit. Many of the overhead fluorescent lights were smashed or broken, creating sporadic pools of light on the gray concrete, with the rest of the space occupied by murky darkness. A faint smell of urine permeated the air.

Cary crouched behind a blue sedan, keeping to the wall and doing his best to blend in with the shadows. Following the robber had not been easy. He'd almost lost him a couple of times, as the guy was clearly trying to keep a low profile and avoid any unwanted attention. Cary had been lucky to spot him early on, walking down the street past the brightly lit shop windows. After that, it was only a matter of tailing him without the other man noticing, hiding in alleys and falling back every time he took a turn or crossed the street, keeping away from the lampposts, to the shadows that hugged the almost empty streets.

Once or twice, the guy had stopped and cast a look around, as if he sensed someone following. Each time, Cary ducked behind a truck or the side of a building, avoiding even looking too closely at his quarry for fear he might home in on the source of his apparent unease. But the guy never stopped long enough to catch sight of him, only hurrying along after a momentary pause, keeping his head low and his hands in the pockets of his leather bomber jacket.

When the man descended into the parking lot, Cary had been afraid he was headed to his car, and with no means to follow, that would mean he'd have to forgo any chance of getting his property back. But the guy had stopped in the middle of the yellow-painted section, and was just lounging there against one of the support pillars. Either he was waiting to be picked up, or he wanted to pass his ill-gotten prize on to someone else. Both options were equally bad. In his mind, Cary apologized to his granddad for having been such a useless dolt back at the theater. Apparently, no amount of deftness and dexterity would help if you froze like a deer in the headlights when someone shoved a gun in your face.

The guy's pocket buzzed, and he took out his cell phone. He swiped the screen and frowned at it.

Cary tensed. This was his window of opportunity. He was considering creeping around and advancing on the other man from behind in hopes of picking his pockets while he was busy reading his messages, when car tires screeched around a corner, and the guy straightened. Cary hid farther behind the hood of the parked car, peeping cautiously around the bumper. Shit, he'd been dawdling for too long and was about to miss his chance.

A large black SUV with tinted windows pulled to a stop in front of the robber. Four men stepped out, fanning around him. They were armed with some sort of stumpy shotguns. Cary knew absolutely nothing about firearms, but they looked like serious business. The robber must have realized this as well, because he slipped the phone back into his pocket and lifted his hands without being prompted.

So—definitely not whom he was expecting to meet. Wouldn't it be funny if he got robbed in return? Hysterical. Especially since Cary could then kiss his amulet goodbye forever. His luck seemed to be sliding further and further down the hill with each passing minute.

A man in a gray suit climbed down from the SUV's passenger seat and came to stand in front of the robber. To the guy's credit, he didn't flinch or even look too scared.

"You're not my contact, and I don't believe we have an appointment," he said levelly. The voices carried in the near empty parking lot, but neither of the participants seemed to care.

The suit smirked. He actually looked classy, not like those mobsters in fake Armani. Not that Cary had much experience with either mobsters or real Armani, but even he could tell the difference. The guy looked dangerous. He gave off a certain vibe that made Cary's hackles rise. He'd seen his share of dangerous people, and this one was by far more intimidating than his unlucky robber, with or without a gun.

"Let's just say AJ won't be coming today." The guy in the suit had a slight accent Cary couldn't quite place. "The merchandise?"

"I don't have it," the robber said.

Under different circumstances, Cary would have gloated at the guy having to squirm just as he'd done, but right now, things weren't going too well for either of them. A deep unease settled in his stomach—some nasty shit was about to go down. He'd had enough of that in his past life, and he really didn't want to be sucked in it again.

"Liar." The suit smiled. He was attractive, of average height and slim build, with dark hair and almost aristocratic features. Sleek and easy on the eyes, but it was like watching a poisonous snake about to strike. "Too bad. I was hoping to resolve this amicably."

One of his henchmen took a step forward, raising his weapon, and Cary's robber moved too, dropping to the ground and kicking at the armed man's knees. The bodyguard staggered and took a step back, but the robber had already rolled and sprung to his feet, diving behind the concrete column and whipping out his own gun from a holster hidden under his jacket.

Cary's heart hammered in his chest as he watched. The guy definitely had balls, but what could he possibly do against all these armed men? A gunfight was about to erupt in the parking lot, and that was bound to end badly for someone. He should probably get the hell out before he somehow got caught in the crossfire, and, considering the direction in which this bizarre evening was progressing, it wasn't out of the realm of possibility.

"Don't shoot," the man in the gray suit ordered. His guards halted, glancing between their boss and their target, waiting for further instructions.

Why weren't they shooting? The robber was surrounded. He had nowhere to run, and these thugs didn't look like they'd be squeamish about leaving dead bodies behind.

In the resounding, tense silence, a woman climbed out of the SUV. She was wearing a cherry-red silk blouse and a pair of black slacks that looked like they cost Cary's annual rent. Everything about her, from the perfectly arranged waves of her dark hair to the tips of her manicured nails, spoke of a high level of taste and an equally high level of income to match it.

Completely unfazed by the volatile tableau, she walked toward the column right past the armed bodyguards, her high heels clicking loudly on the rough concrete, and threw out her hand.

There was...something. Cary couldn't quite explain what it was, but he felt the air around the woman rippling without anything actually moving. He held his breath for a moment, but nothing happened.

"You gotta do better than that," the robber called. From Cary's vantage point, he was half-obscured by the column, but it looked like he was inching back, toward the row of cars behind him.

The woman twisted her palm upward, and the fluorescent lights overhead exploded in a shower of electric sparks and shards of glass. The robber ducked instinctively, his gun arm going up to protect his face. It was a momentary distraction, but it was enough for the bodyguard on the right to slam into him, jamming the butt of his gun into the side of his head. He dropped to the ground like a puppet with its strings cut. His gun fell out of his slackened hand and clattered to the ground.

Cary flinched and withdrew even farther into the shadows, watching in shock, but apparently, he was the only one who'd been taken aback by what had happened. *What in the hell?*

Obviously, it was magic of some kind, but he could hardly believe it. Sure, he knew his granddad's pendant apparently had some powers that defied his understanding, but that could very much be his imagination running rampant. Seeing someone else perform magic—not stage magic, but some truly dangerous stuff—was another matter entirely.

The armed henchman knelt to pat the unconscious man down, going about it quite professionally. At least, Cary hoped he was unconscious, because he really, really didn't want to be a witness to a murder, especially not one he couldn't readily explain to the authorities.

"Take all his jewelry," the woman instructed.

Cary could only see the henchman's back, so he couldn't tell what the guy had found when he straightened and handed something to his boss.

"Thanks, Letti," the gray suit said, turning to the woman. Through his stunned haze, Cary absently noted a strong resemblance in their features.

The woman shrugged. "I figured he could be useful to us in the future," she said. "Business is business."

The man in the suit smiled that unpleasant smile again and motioned to his bodyguards to get back in the car while the woman climbed inside. He then returned unhurriedly to the passenger seat. Cary strained to see what he was holding, but he couldn't risk being discovered snooping around. *But really, what could it possibly be?* The woman had said to take the jewelry. That must have included his amulet. The robber hadn't been waiting in the middle of the night for nothing, even if the wrong people had shown up. Still, Cary had to make sure. It would be silly to leave without checking, especially seeing as he'd been effectively incapacitated.

He waited, unmoving, until the SUV had driven off, and the parking lot was once again deserted and silent. Then he left his hiding place behind the sedan and approached the fallen man cautiously to crouch beside him.

He was covered in tiny pieces of broken glass, still breathing. Cary really didn't want him to end up dead—not after he'd helped him out of that dressing room with pursuit hot on their heels.

Could these be the same people who had come after Cary in the theater? Someone was hell-bent on getting the amulet. That was for damn sure.

But he didn't have time to think it over. He hurried to search the other man before he came to, reaching into the inner pockets of his leather jacket. He eyed the discarded gun nervously, but it was out of reach, and Cary was definitely not touching it.

Other than the phone and a receipt for filling gas from this morning, he found nothing. He shoved the phone back and was trying for the jeans pockets when the guy twitched and opened his eyes.

"What the hell are you doing?" he demanded gruffly.

Cary snatched his hands away and sat back on his heels, feeling heat creep up his cheeks. *Shit.*

"I wanted to make sure you were alive," he said. "Who the hell were they? What did she do?"

The guy sat up and rubbed his head where the bodyguard had hit him, grunting with pain. Cary winced sympathetically. The bump that was already forming promised to be quite spectacular. At least there was no blood. Not that he should care if the guy was badly injured, really. But for some reason, Cary was glad that he wasn't.

"Fuck, those bastards." The guy took quick stock of his pockets, much as Cary had done before, coming up with the same results. "Fuck."

"They took it, didn't they?" Cary said accusingly. He had no idea why he was still talking with the man, especially since he was pointedly ignoring Cary's questions, but right now, he was Cary's only remaining link to the amulet, slim as it was. "No honor among thieves, huh?"

"Rub it in, why don't you." He looked around and then stared at his left hand as if seeing it for the first time. "Fuck."

"What is it?"

"They took it too. My ring." There was a band of pale skin around his ring finger, standing out against the otherwise lightly tanned skin.

"Was it a diamond solitaire?" Cary asked testily. He rose to his feet, dusting off his pants, which were close to ruined.

The guy gave him a look.

"It's a magic ring," he said. He got up, supporting himself on the pillar. He didn't look as intimidating as he had in the stuffy dressing room. In fact, he was rather handsome with his broad shoulders and a mop of yellow sun-bleached hair, mussed from his recent exertions.

"Like in *The Lord of the Rings*?" Cary asked. *Get a grip,* he told himself. *Who cares what the guy looks like. He mugged you at gunpoint.*

"I wish," he said. "No, not like that. But it does negate any effects of magic directed at me. Just not its fallout." He grimaced.

Serves you right, Cary thought, but didn't have the heart to say it out loud.

"So now what?" he asked instead.

The guy shrugged noncommittally, but now he was eying Cary with a renewed interest.

"How did you manage to track me down?"

"Sleight of hand," Cary said, deadpan. The other man snorted.

"Well, it looks like it's all been for nothing. Sorry. But hey, it looks like you can safely go home now. They have what they want. You're hardly of any interest for them anymore." He took out his car keys and started walking (wobbling) toward the back of the parking lot, presumably to where he'd parked his car, leaving Cary to stand there, alone and helpless.

This couldn't be it. No. He refused to just shut up and accept defeat.

"Hey, wait!" He ran after the guy, who stopped and turned to face him again with a weary expression. "That's it? You roll over and let them take it?"

"What am I supposed to do? Run after the car and wrestle the bodyguards for it? You're confusing me with Superman."

"There must be something we can do," Cary said. That stubborn streak that had always landed him in trouble was rearing its head yet again, but if there ever was a time to be obnoxiously persistent, it was now.

"We?"

When Cary offered no answer, the other man sighed and shook his head. "Just go home. Chalk this one up to experience, suck it up, and lie low. Whoever that was, you probably don't want to mess with them."

"And you?"

"Ain't none of your business. Good night, Mr. Mars."

He headed to his car—a surprisingly flashy silver Chevy Cavalier convertible—and clicked the doors open. Cary watched in frustration and disbelief as he pulled out of the lot and sped toward the exit. The bastard at least could've offered him a ride home.

Cary was tired and wired at the same time. Not enough to run after the SUV like the guy had suggested, but he was itching to do something. The thought of giving up made him almost physically sick. But he wasn't ready to completely throw in the towel yet. And that sleight of hand remark wasn't entirely a joke.

He took out the plastic card he'd swiped out of the robber's jeans pocket and flipped it between his fingers.

The faded lettering read: Geary Lodge Motel.

Chapter Three

TY PULLED UP in front of a run-down apartment building. As usual, there were a number of homeless folk loitering on the dirty sidewalk. He got out and cast a discreet gesture spell, the invisible tattoos on his fingertips prickling with the surge of it. His car was way too ostentatious for this part of town, and this would prevent it from standing out like a sore thumb. Not invisible, exactly, but when protected with the spell, people's gazes tended to slide right past it and focus on something else. He'd used the same spell on himself on a number of occasions, but maintaining it on a moving person, as opposed to an immobile object, was a lot harder.

AJ, Ty's fence, lived on the second floor. Well, Ty had no idea if he actually lived there. Other than his "office," which took up most of the living room, the tiny space was crammed full of old junk Ty couldn't even begin to categorize. Most of it was packed in various crates and cardboard boxes, but some of it spilled onto shelves and the floor—clocks, books, vintage appliances, porcelain dolls, framed photos. The dolls with their dead, staring eyes creeped him out like nothing else. If there was a bed buried in there somewhere, he'd never seen it.

The short walk up the stairs left him more than a little dizzy. His head was throbbing, but that could wait to be taken care of later. There was no answer when he knocked, so he took out his set of picks and undid the lock. Opening the door, he found himself staring down the barrel of a gun.

This recent trend of being threatened with firearms was really getting old.

"Put that thing down before you hurt yourself," he told AJ irritably.

"I don't think so." AJ's hands shook a bit, but he kept pointing the gun at him. He was a short, middle-aged man with a receding hairline, but size didn't matter when one had a gun. His eyes darted behind Ty, as if he expected him to bring reinforcements. There was a sheen of sweat on his forehead, but that was probably due to the room being stiflingly warm. "You don't lockpick your way into a person's place to have some nice friendly tea."

"For fuck's sake, I texted you nearly twenty minutes ago to let you know what happened," Ty said. "You didn't think I'd come to have a chat?"

"Nearly gave me a heart attack, you did," AJ complained, finally lowering the gun and edging around the desk to shove it into a drawer. The sleek new laptop that was opened on the desktop looked startlingly out of place. "If I'd died, it would be on your conscience."

"Nice of you to think I have one." Ty freed one of the chairs that stood in front of the desk of the antique gilded globe that was occupying it, and sat down, stretching his legs. AJ was a hell of an actor, but he'd been genuinely panicked when Ty came through the door. "So what's the deal with selling me out, AJ? You set me up pretty bad tonight. I thought we had a healthy loving relationship here. Expecting you to show up to pick the merch and almost ending up dead tends to leave a sour taste in my mouth."

"We do have a loving relationship!" AJ said earnestly, not even bothering to deny the accusation. "Look, I had no choice. That creep barged in a couple of hours ago with all his goons, armed to the teeth, and made me spill the beans on the job. I had to tell him about the drop-off, or he threatened to shoot me right here. What was I supposed to do? Die, and then he'd find you anyway? Besides, I tried to warn you, didn't I? He told me not to—in no uncertain terms, mind you—but I couldn't leave you out to dry—"

"You sure took your sweet time about it," Ty said, cutting him off. "Your text came in too late. They took the damned necklace, so now you're out of your commission."

Losing a commission was hardly a fitting punishment for not having his back when the shit hit the fan, but Ty knew AJ all too well. The man didn't take to being threatened with physical violence. And he had tried to warn him, even if in the end it'd proven useless.

Ty had absolutely no illusions as to the depth of AJ's loyalty. Their partnership was based on profit, and profit alone. But he was a damn good fence, and his connections ran deep and wide. And that profit thing went both directions, so Ty couldn't be quick to let his indignation cloud his judgment, even if he was pissed off as hell.

"I was counting on your resilience and resourcefulness to get you through," AJ said gravely. "And I was right, wasn't I? Here you are, all handy-dandy, after you've lost my shitload-worth-of-money artifact, and I had to explain all this to my client. So hey, I'm the one with the problems here, go easy on me."

"Yeah, yeah, woe is you, AJ. Do accept my humble apologies for being coldcocked and losing your merchandise. Now, can you quit whining and find out who it was?"

"Oh, he didn't have to introduce himself. That's Tony Giordano, Nick Giordano's son." Seeing Ty's blank expression, he added: "That's right, you're not from around here. 'Old Nick' Giordano is a big-shot crime boss from North Beach. He likes to keep his business on the down-low, but Tony has always been more...brazen."

Ty frowned. "So now the mafia is interested in the occult? That's new."

Strictly speaking, the Italian mafia getting into the occult was new. The Chinese were into really hardcore magic shit, but they had their own network of supply and demand that Ty wisely stayed away from.

"Not the mafia," AJ corrected. He visibly relaxed as it became clear Ty wasn't about to throttle him. "I doubt Old Nick has any interest in this stuff. I bet it's all Tony's doing. He was always an ambitious sort of fellow, from what I've heard, and the Giordanos have been hard-pressed by the Chinese syndicates in the recent years. That might have something to do with him wanting the amulet, though how the hell he even knew about it, I have no idea."

Ty rubbed his temple tiredly. For anyone with any magic sense at all, Cary's performance was like flashing a neon sign that said Find Magic Item Here. And now with organized crime involved… He should have explained to Westfield how to handle these things properly, he thought, and then chided himself. He didn't have time to be so preoccupied with an amateur magician. There were some things Cary would have to learn the hard way, and besides, chances were he wouldn't see him again.

"And who was the woman?"

"What woman?"

"Never mind," Ty said. Apparently, Giordano hadn't risked offending the beautiful sorceress's sensibilities by bringing her into this dump, whoever she was.

"Anyway, everybody's all right, no harm done," AJ continued. "We'll just work out a plan to protect ourselves from similar shit in the future. 'Cause if the occult gains popularity with the crooks, its prices will go up, and not in the good way."

"I like how it's all 'we' all of sudden," Ty said. He might not be in any rush to drop AJ, but he wasn't about to let him off the hook so easily. "Who says I'm gonna be working with you after getting out from under that bus?"

"Oh, come on," AJ whined. "You can't seriously blame me for this. It was supposed to be a quick and easy job I'd managed to score for you. Take an artifact from a fucking common. How hard can it be?"

"Well, it damn well wasn't easy," Ty growled in annoyance.

A "common" was practitioners' slang for someone who lacked magical abilities, and Ty was dangerously close to being classified as one, since nearly all his skill came from studious practice rather than natural aptitude. But from what he could see, Cary was definitely not a common. Ty might not have the talent himself, but he recognized it in others. The depth of it remained to be seen, but there was no question it was there, beneath Cary's many layers of insecurity.

"That whole debacle was the result of a big misunderstanding," AJ said with fake conviction. "You know I wouldn't want anything bad to happen to you. In fact, I'll make it up to you. It just so happens we still have the chance to recover the fee."

"Oh? How's that?"

"I talked to the client right before you came calling," AJ said. He wiped his brow in a nervous gesture. That had probably been an interesting conversation. Ty wondered again who could have commissioned the job, and what they had to say about it being botched so badly. "And once I explained everything, they were very understanding of our predicament. And now, see, they still want you to retrieve it for them."

"The client wants me to steal it back from Giordano?"

"Yes! I talked you up," AJ said hurriedly, "and I made them see it wasn't your fault the merch was lost. And they're willing to pay an extra fifteen percent for the expenses." He seemed eager to get Ty hooked on the idea. "Which I am willing to pass on to you in full, as, um, moral compensation for my part. What do you say?"

"That's one hell of an operation you're talking about here," Ty said, stalling. He had to give it to AJ. He'd pulled quite a feat, convincing the client to give them a second chance. He certainly wouldn't entrust something so sensitive with a guy who'd already failed once. AJ was his own kind of magician, and it was part of the reason Ty was willing to continue working with him. "This isn't robbing some Harry Blackstone wannabe. These are some serious folks with some serious punch."

"And who better to handle them than you? Now that you know who to watch out for, it'll be a walk in the park for someone with your skill set."

"Flattery will get you nowhere," Ty muttered, but he didn't reject the idea outright. Yes, the ambush and the humiliation were fresh in his memory, but he was still alive and free to do what he wanted. "Okay, fine. I'll look into it. No promises."

"Sure, sure," AJ said, relaxing fractionally. "No pressure. You do your thing, scope the target, what have you. Just remember the client really wants that bauble, and our reputation is at stake here."

"Again with the 'ours,'" Ty said, though of course AJ was right on that point. Reputation was everything in their business, which relied on very limited clientele and word-of-mouth-only advertisement.

AJ just waved at him dismissively and moved to a nook that looked vaguely like some sort of a toy kitchen. "How about that tea?"

"I'll pass," Ty said, getting up. He'd gotten all the information he'd come for and didn't want to stay any longer than necessary. The cumulative energy of so many old and pre-owned objects piled on top of each other made his skin crawl unpleasantly. AJ didn't have a magical bone in his body, but while Ty wasn't a sorcerer by any means, he'd been trained over the years to sense these things more acutely. He'd also had to learn to tune them out—otherwise, he'd have gone completely bonkers at some point. "Oh, and AJ? You pull this kind of shit on me again, that gun won't help you."

AJ clutched his chest dramatically, but Ty wasn't staying for the rest of the performance. After he shut the door behind him, he could hear AJ move some stuff around, probably barricading it.

Ty paused in the dim hallway to light a cigarette, turning things over in his head. The idea of going after the amulet for an even larger fee sounded appealing on the face of it, but it was incredibly risky. Giordano already knew who he was and where to apply pressure if he suspected Ty was still somehow in the running after the prize. He didn't believe AJ would sell him out to Giordano when not faced with the possibility of torture or death. After all, they did have a good partnership going, despite the occasional glitches, and that was based on Ty making AJ a good amount of money. But as recent events had demonstrated, the fence wasn't one to stand his ground under duress, and no amount of potential earnings would prevent him from tattling on Ty if the mafioso had his gun to his head again, or if the mysterious sorceress decided to hold another *son et lumière*.

And another thing. AJ was usually good about keeping his clients' confidentiality, but this time he was being extra vague, and Ty had the distinct impression Giordano wasn't the only one the fence was afraid of. Unease stirred in his gut. Did he really want to get into all of this? Not that he hadn't already realized he was dealing with some dangerous people here, but he wasn't sure he should be messing with a crime boss, or the crime boss's son, as the case might be. Not to mention an actual sorceress, and this mysterious customer who was willing to go against the mafia to get what he wanted.

Ty was used to keeping to the shadows, sailing under the radar of both law enforcement and criminal elements, organized or otherwise. That part of his training had been deeply ingrained in him by Leland. There was nothing blatant about the way he got things done. In some aspects, he was not unlike a professional hit man, though he didn't usually have to kill anyone in his line of work. People in the business knew him well, of course, but he rarely got into altercations with any of them, except when it came to direct competition. Even then, it was almost never a life and death situation, which in this case it most certainly would be. Objectively, the fee for the amulet wasn't worth the risk, really, and he could always find some other useful magic trinket to replace his ring. The only thing that would suffer would be his pride.

But no. That wasn't how things worked. If all it took to discourage him was a little intimidation, soon no one would hire him, or worse, they'd make him do all the dirty work and then try to stiff him. AJ wasn't the only one who had a reputation to uphold. People came to Ty to obtain those rare, dangerous, hard-to-find and forgotten objects, and he was the best at it. He'd never turned down a job because it was too difficult, and he wasn't about to start now. It wasn't too late to remedy the situation before word spread about his blunder. Once he had a clear plan of action, the rest shouldn't be that hard, or that different from his usual contracts. Ty just had to make sure he didn't get caught.

He stomped on the butt of his cigarette and headed for his car.

TY WAS CURRENTLY staying at a cheap motel on Geary Street. The interior was dated and worn, and not in that vintage-y, quaint style. There were a few shady characters hanging out in the lobby even at this hour, but he paid them no mind and went straight up to his room on the second floor.

The first thing he saw when he reached the top of the stairs was the Incredible Mr. Mars huddling on the worn carpet next to the door to his room. From his posture, Ty assumed he was asleep, but the man looked up at his approach and flashed him the plastic room key.

"Looking for this?"

"God, you're a leech, aren't you," Ty said wearily. He was tired and aching, and all he wanted was to take a Tylenol, crawl into bed, and get some much-needed sleep to clear his head. But he couldn't help grudgingly admire Westfield's tenacity. "What do you want?"

Westfield scrambled to his feet, jutting his chin out defiantly. "I figure you owe me my amulet back."

"Do you now," Ty said levelly. "In case you failed to notice, I don't have it."

"But you can figure out how to get it back." Westfield was looking at him with those big doe eyes again, his eyelashes long and thick almost to the point of looking fake. An edge of desperation crept into his voice. "I mean, you probably do this stuff for a living, right? What if I hire you to steal it?"

Ty was certainly in high demand today. Was the kid even serious? It wasn't as if he could realistically afford his services, though he must not realize it. Still, there was something about him. Like the fact he'd managed to steal Ty's key card without him noticing (of course, he was dazed after a head injury at the time, but still) and had enough guts to follow him, despite the very real possibility of Ty shooting him on sight.

"Let's discuss it inside," he said.

Westfield hesitated for a moment, but finally nodded and unlocked the door with the card. It opened with a click that echoed too loudly in the empty hallway.

"After you," Ty gestured and then stepped after Westfield into the awaiting darkness.

Chapter Four

THE OTHER MAN moved past Cary to turn on the lights. The room was small and stuffy and smelled distinctly of mold and mothballs. A thick mustard-colored duvet on the king-sized bed matched the faded carpeting. Surprisingly, the room looked relatively clean and tidy enough to appear unlived-in. The bed was made, and there were no personal effects scattered around.

"So," Cary said, leaning against the TV dresser stand and crossing his arms on his chest. He was wrung out to the point of exhaustion and dying to shut his eyes and pass out, but now was not the time to let his guard down. "Thanks for the invite, um..."

"You can call me Ty." He removed his leather jacket, wincing, and sat down on one of the rickety chairs next to the small round table near the window. Cary suddenly thought that he must be just as tired as he was.

"Is it like, Tyson?"

"No, just Ty."

There was a small pause. "Do you know who that jerk in the parking lot was?" Cary asked.

The guy—Ty—nodded. "Tony Giordano, the eldest son of a mafia boss from North Beach."

"Great." Cary's heart sank a little. He'd had a feeling the suit was dangerous, just not *how* dangerous. He was way out of his depth. What could they possibly do against someone like that? This Ty (whoever and whatever he was) was no match for the mafia, as recent events had clearly demonstrated.

Ty was watching him intently. His eyes were a dark hazel color, sharp and intelligent. It was strange that Cary didn't feel intimidated by his presence. Of course, he wasn't waiving a gun at the moment, but even so, Cary instinctively didn't think of him as an immediate threat, as he had in his dressing room. It had been only hours ago, but it felt as if eons had passed. Sleepless, tense eons of running around the city to retrieve his property while trying not to get killed.

"Can you get it back?" Cary asked.

It was rather unlikely, but he had to give it one last try. There was no way he could do this on his own. He could ask around and get some feelers out with his past buddies, but the chances of anything surfacing were slim. If someone so high up the food chain was interested in this item, it probably wasn't going to end up in some pawnshop—especially considering its unusual nature. So if Ty was unable or unwilling to help, that would be it.

"Maybe," Ty said. He stretched his long legs, assuming a more relaxed posture.

"'Maybe'? What does that mean?"

"It means I haven't assessed what I'm up against yet. Theoretically speaking, yeah, I could probably steal it back, given the right circumstances."

"Okay," Cary said slowly. It was a better answer than he expected, but how much of it was sound judgment, and how much empty swagger? It had only taken one blow to bring Ty to his knees, after all, and he was damn lucky it wasn't a gunshot. "How much do you—"

"Look," Ty said. "I'm not gonna take your money, since you can't afford me anyway. But I tell you what. You want that amulet? You help me get it. Since you managed to follow me all this way, I'm guessing you can pull your own weight if you try hard enough."

"Gosh, you make it sound so flattering," Cary said.

He wasn't sure why Ty suddenly wanted his help. Frankly, the thought of going up against the mafioso in the expensive suit, his hired guns, and whoever that woman was, scared the shit out of him. But there was no way for him to find the amulet by himself, and he wasn't naive enough to believe Ty would just hand it back to him free of charge even if they did manage to find it. This was his best shot at getting anywhere near the amulet. Especially considering all the occult stuff he knew nothing about. He was, however, good at stealing things, or at least he used to be. "If you don't want me to pay you, what's in it for you?"

"If I get duped on a job, that means I'm out of my fee, and, more importantly, it hurts my rep with my clients. I can't be known as the guy that can't deliver. It's bad for business. Not to mention that they took my ring, and I want it back."

As far as explanations went, this was a good one, but Cary wasn't sure he believed it. Ty was talking calmly and looking him straight in the eye, but Cary couldn't shake the feeling he was being bullshitted somehow, and he tended to trust his instincts when it came to these things. He was pretty good at it. No illusion artist could hope for any kind of success if he couldn't correctly read his audience. The part about the ring was probably true—that was something Cary wouldn't mind having himself. And he'd seen it at work, when the mysterious woman couldn't bring Ty down while he was wearing it. But the rest... Cary would have to watch his step with this guy.

Ty was looking at him steadily with those sharp eyes, patiently waiting for him to come to a decision.

"Do you know who hired you to steal my amulet in the first place?" Cary asked, stalling.

Ty shrugged. "No idea. I get most of my jobs through my fence. He's the one dealing with the clients, and I get the info from him."

It probably didn't matter at this point, but Cary was still curious about who'd sent Ty after him. He bet lot of money had changed hands on this deal. Wouldn't that client be as frustrated as they were about losing something they wanted so badly?

"How do I know I can trust you?" Cary asked, though he already knew he was going to agree, despite all the reasons he shouldn't. At the very least, Ty could be his lead to the whereabouts of the amulet, and then... A lot could happen.

Ty offered a wry smile. "You don't, and I don't think I can say anything that would convince you. But hey, you came here looking for me, so who should be convincing who?"

"Well, excuse me for worrying about being robbed again."

"Remind me again what it was you've done time for?"

Cary huffed. "That was different. And how do you know I've done time?"

"Yeah, whatever. I do tend to research my marks."

"Okay, fine, Mr. Professional," Cary said pointedly. "We do it together. And just so you know, I was damn good at stealing people's wallets. I just wasn't good at taking the blame when my buddies decided it would be quicker to rob a convenience store than work a crowd of tourists on Fisherman's Wharf. And while we're on the subject of working the crowd, I must remind you that we had to leave my dressing room in a kind of a hurry, and I don't have anything on me, including my phone and wallet. And I'm so fucking tired I could pass out. Wearing that thing sure drains energy."

The night had become progressively more and more crazy, but now, when there was no immediate danger, the exhaustion came back with a vengeance. Cary really did have a hard time staying upright at this point, and the thought of having to walk all the way home or to the Garland filled him with dread. He could ask Ty for a lift, now that they were officially partners in crime, but the other man looked no less beat.

"That's because you were using it wrong, genius." Ty yawned widely, as if to illustrate Cary's thoughts. "I guess you could crash here for the night," he added, somewhat reluctantly.

"Hey, it didn't come with a manual," Cary retorted. It was reassuring that this Ty character seemed to know a thing or two about real magic, but right now, Cary was more interested in the en suite. He was sweaty, his clothes were filthy from crawling between parked cars, and he wanted to take a shower so badly he almost didn't mind doing it with an armed criminal in the adjacent room.

"Dibs on the bathroom," he announced, swooping inside, not bothering to wait for Ty's response. He shut the door behind him and locked it. After two years of prison showers, he valued his privacy.

The bathroom was shabby, but there was soap and a couple of towels, and that was all he cared about. As he let the hot water wash the grime off his skin, Cary thought about what he was going to do.

The one thing he knew with absolute certainty was that the amulet's magic had been real. His performances were always a massive success when he used it. Hell, he'd felt it working, as crazy as that sounded—a warm tingling all over his body, a rush he couldn't quite put a name on. Logic dictated this wasn't the only magical artifact out there, and that other people knew more about their existence than he did. How these people had found out about his amulet, he had no idea, but maybe Ty was right, and he'd been too flashy with it. Maybe. The question was—was he willing to risk messing with said people to get it back?

As potentially valuable as the thing was, he was loath to do anything that might get him in trouble with the law again. He'd been there, done that, done the time for it, and he was trying his best to clean the slate and start over. Chasing down the amulet would most likely entail doing things that weren't strictly (or at all) legal, and he could hardly afford being caught at it again. He couldn't trust Ty to have his back if whatever plan they came up with went south, so the probability of Cary ending up taking the fall for the both of them was pretty damn high.

And this was before he even considered how dangerous these guys were. Men with bodyguards and women with freaking superpowers were definitely out of his league. Whatever this Giordano character wanted the amulet for—he wasn't going to take well to the possibility of losing it again. And as opposed to Cary, he probably had more resources at his disposal to ensure against that.

Cary switched off the water and stepped out of the shower. He wiped the steam off the mirror and stared blearily into his red-rimmed eyes. His muscles ached as if he'd run a half-marathon, and he was ready to fall over. Any fateful decisions would have to wait until he'd had some sleep, though he suspected he was going to go through with it, regardless. Otherwise, he wouldn't have been sharing a motel room with a complete stranger. Okay, he *had* shared motel rooms with strangers, but that was for purely recreational purposes, and no guns or weird magic were involved. Only cheap thrills and cheap alcohol.

He actually wouldn't have minded spending the night with Ty under different circumstances. Whoever and whatever the man was, he was hot. Cary liked his sort of rugged good looks and easy attitude.

He emerged from the bathroom with a towel wrapped around his waist. Ty was still sitting in the chair, frowning at his cell phone. He glanced up, and from the look he gave him, Cary suddenly had the distinct impression he wasn't the only gay man in the room.

He cleared his throat, and Ty reverted his gaze to Cary's face.

"So what's our next move?"

Ty dropped the phone into his jacket pocket. "I'll find out more tomorrow. Tonight, I suggest we get some rest."

Well, that certainly curtailed the planning. Cary was kind of glad, since he didn't have the energy to stay sharp. However, there was another hurdle on the path to a much-needed rest. The room only had one bed.

Ty must have caught him staring at it longingly, because he suggested, "I can sleep on the floor."

"Really?" Cary asked. "On a motel carpet?"

Ty shrugged. The possibility didn't seem to fill him with the same disgust as it did Cary. "I've slept on worse."

Ty did owe him for putting him through a hell of a scare, so sleeping on the floor in the way of apology was only fitting. But Cary had never been a petty person, and it appeared as if neither of them would be shy or put off by sharing a bed with another man. Ty didn't behave like someone prone to outbursts of violence. In fact, ever since they'd entered the room, he'd been quietly subdued. He could be wrong about that, and all of it could be attributed to the aftermath of being hit over the head, but Cary had a feeling he wouldn't jump him in the middle of the night. He'd known some really brutal assholes in his life, and Ty didn't give off that kind of vibe.

Sharing a bed with a guy who had mugged him only a few hours ago would certainly be a fitting way to cap this bizarre day, wouldn't it?

Cary got into the bed and shed the towel from beneath the covers. "Nah. It's big enough for the both of us. As long as you don't poke me with that gun of yours."

Ty grinned. "It's a deal."

He got up and pulled a large black duffel bag from under the bed, which he took with him into the bathroom, also locking the door behind him. Cary briefly considered waiting to see him come out without any clothes on, but his eyelids suddenly seemed to have other plans and fell shut all by themselves.

Chapter Five

CARY WOKE UP suddenly, his mind clutching futilely onto the fragments of the nightmare. He couldn't remember what had scared him so much, but his heart was racing and his skin was clammy with cold sweat. He sat up, taking deep, steadying breaths. The stale air left a sour aftertaste in his mouth.

Next to him, Ty stirred and turned to face him, instantly awake. The room was dark, but the streetlights shone enough through the narrow gap in the curtains that Cary could make out his silhouette on the other side of the bed.

"Something wrong?" Ty asked, his voice husky from sleep.

Cary shook his head. It must have been all the excitement of the previous evening messing with his head or something. He touched his chest, where the amulet used to hang on its chain. Its absence felt like the phantom pain of a missing limb, and his lungs constricted as if he was suddenly out of air.

"Just a bad dream," he said, swallowing hard. "Sorry I woke you."

"S'okay," Ty said, relaxing again.

Cary lay back down, facing away from him, and tried to do the same, but this time sleep wouldn't come. He was still tired, but now he was too wound up. Having another person in bed right next to him, radiating tantalizing body heat, didn't help either. A mental picture of Ty's naked form under the blanket—completely imaginary but no less appealing for it—sprang unbidden to his mind and refused to go away, not matter how hard he tried to shake it off.

"It'll pass soon," Ty said suddenly, making Cary start guiltily.

"What?"

"It happens sometimes with strong magic. The withdrawal. Less intense than with drugs, but just as dangerous in the long run. That's why you need to be more careful when using it."

"What do you know," Cary muttered, staring at the wall. The shadows painted strange shapes on the plaster, all sharp edges and wrong angles, pulsing in time with his heart. He blinked, dispelling the fancy.

"Believe it or not, I know quite a lot. It's my job," Ty said.

Cary turned around to face him. Ty's eyes gleamed in the darkness, reflecting the faint light, their warm hazel color indistinguishable now in the darkness.

"What is your job, exactly?"

"People in the occult community pay me to get them the objects they want. Books, artifacts, ancient relics, you name it. If it's magic, I'll find it."

"'Occult community'? What is that, some kind of secret society where you meet up wearing robes and chant at each other under a full moon?"

"It's not a cult," Ty said. "There is no secret society that governs magic practitioners. Not the real ones, anyway. But there aren't many of them. They do tend to stick together, or at least know about each other. And there are some basic rules they adhere to, which are mostly based on simple common sense."

"Do these rules allow you to be a thief?" Cary asked, and then immediately regretted his tone as, strictly speaking, he was probably the last person who should have been giving anyone a hard time about thieving.

"When it's expedient," Ty said. "I'm can also be a businessman, or a mercenary, or a grave robber when I have to."

"If you're a part of this community, does that mean you can you do magic, like that lady did?"

"I'm a thief, like you said, not a sorcerer. I only get magical stuff for people who can do actual magic and use them. I don't...have the talent for it like most of them do."

"If you're not a sorcerer, or whatever, how come you know so much about it? How'd you get into this business in the first place? How does one find out about this secret underworld you got going there, anyway?"

Ty was silent for so long Cary thought he wasn't going to answer.

"I was lucky to be picked up by a sorcerer thief," he said finally. Cary felt the reluctance in Ty's voice, as if he wasn't sure admitting this was a good idea. Or maybe it just brought up some unpleasant memories Ty was hesitant to share with someone he barely knew. "His name was—is—Leland Bernard. I was young, basically living on the street. He took me in, taught me all he knew. Not just magic—the little I could take in, with my limited abilities—but the basics of his trade. How to do research, how to plan ahead, how to break in and get out without being caught on cameras, that sort of thing. He was my mentor for many years."

"Do you still work with him?"

"We parted ways some time ago," Ty said with a finality that made Cary swallow his next question.

There was a pause as each of them became lost in their thoughts.

"You could have offered me money for the amulet," Cary said accusingly, but with much less vehemence.

"Would you have accepted?"

Cary thought that over.

"No," he admitted reluctantly. "I wouldn't have. It really did belong to my grandfather, you know. He raised me all on his own."

"He did?"

"Yeah. I was too little to remember when my dad left, but my mom took it kinda hard. She died in a car crash when I was eleven. She was DUI. So my granddad took me in. He was a stage magician, had been since the seventies. He taught me all the tricks, but I wasn't into magic at all when I was a teenager. I gave him a lot of grief back then."

John Westfield hadn't been the perfect parent. He hadn't had the first clue about raising a grieving child. While he still had his health, he was too busy with his shows and appearances to pay much attention to Cary beyond dragging him along to hang out backstage, just on the edges of the limelight. He couldn't make sure Cary kept up with his schoolwork or monitor his questionable friends, but he had cared about him, in his own gruff but kind way, and tried to provide for him as best he could. He was the only family Cary had. It certainly wasn't his fault that Cary went out of his way to make life difficult for the both of them.

Cary didn't know why he was telling Ty all this. Most likely, he didn't care either way, but at least he was willing to listen. Even in the darkness, Cary could feel the intentness of his gaze.

It was almost embarrassing how much he missed his granddad, and it was the first time since he'd died that Cary was actually talking about him with someone else. And he never had the chance to say goodbye, or say he was sorry. His granddad died suddenly of a myocardial infarction last year, when Cary was still serving his sentence for grand larceny. Granddad's stage name and his collection of magic show paraphernalia, left in his rental apartment and storage unit, was all that was left of him. That was where Cary had found the amulet, just lying there in a pile of other trinkets and cheap jewelry. For some reason it had caught his eye, though it wasn't nearly as gaudy as the other stuff. It felt nice in his hand when he'd picked it up, almost warm, so he'd tucked it in his pocket without thinking. At the time he thought nothing of it. The whole magic act came much later, and then it proved invaluable, as mind-boggling as it was.

He was silent for another moment and then added bitterly: "That amulet... It was my only chance to make it. I've invested everything in this gig. I'd just begun breaking even. I don't know how this magic thing works, but it did, and it made everything work. And now..." He trailed off, unable to finish the sentence. He couldn't make it all work without the amulet. Ty was right—that thing could do real magic, and it wasn't just a trick of his imagination. When he was wearing it, anything he did on stage enthralled the audience; his illusions appeared to be real acts of wizardry. All he'd had to do was recreate his grandfather's old act from forty years ago, pepper it with some fake mind reading, jokes, and smooth talking, and the audience was ready to eat out of his hand. And now it was all going to slip away like smoke.

"Hey." Ty pushed himself up on one elbow. "Listen, if you're serious about this whole stage illusionist thing, you don't need the amulet to succeed. Sure, it helps a lot, but you can make it on your own, even if it means you'll have to work harder."

"Thanks for the input."

"I mean it. I've watched you perform. You're a natural. The crowd loves you. Your repertoire needs refreshing, but you've got the knack for the stage, and that's what's important."

Cary said nothing, mulling over this unexpected encouragement. He wasn't sure how to respond. He'd rarely had people express support for anything he did, and this brusque praise threw him off balance.

All of a sudden Ty's presence was too acute, as if his words had created a new link between them, filling the space with something more tangible than the darkness. Acting on pure instinct, Cary reached for him, closing the distance between them. Ty recoiled slightly at the movement and then held himself still as Cary ran his fingertips tentatively across his jaw.

"I thought you didn't want me poking you," Ty murmured.

"Maybe I'll do the poking," Cary replied and leaned in to kiss him.

Ty's skin was still sleep-warm, but he was definitely wide-awake now. His lips were a little chapped, but the kiss was sweet, slow at first, and then growing gradually more heated. It was good, and it was something simple and familiar, something Cary could lose himself in for a while and not think about all the weird shit going on around him. He pushed the other man flat onto his back and slid down, throwing off the covers. Ty's muscles bunched and relaxed under his touch, and he could feel the light dusting of hair on his chest, the long jagged line of scar tissue on his right side. Ty shifted under his touch, and Cary moved down again, sliding over the hard abs and settling between Ty's legs.

Ty was still wearing his briefs, but Cary helped him out of those, taking his time to run his hands over thighs and abs. He couldn't see much, but Ty definitely felt fit. Just like he'd imagined. Muscular, but not overly ripped. His cock matched his build perfectly, sporting a nice length. It hardened rapidly under Cary's hand, the velvety feel of it fueling his own need.

"I don't have anything on me," he said, regretting for the first time that he wasn't in the habit of keeping condoms and lube in the pocket of his costume trousers.

"Me neither," Ty said. He shifted, pulling slightly away, but Cary could feel the tension in his muscles, the restraint. The hell with it, he thought, there were other things they could do. No way this was going to end in them taking turns jerking off in the shower.

"I want to suck you," he suggested.

Ty barked a laugh. "Won't say no to that."

It was all the encouragement he needed. Cary dove in straight for the prize, taking it deep into his mouth, putting his lips and tongue to good use. Ty moaned and gripped his hair almost painfully, but eased the hold when Cary made a noise around his cock. That was okay. They were finding the right pace, the things they would both enjoy. Cary worked his mouth, and Ty made tiny thrusting motions, his hips barely lifting in an effort not to fuck his mouth, something Cary actually wouldn't have minded. Still, he appreciated the consideration. He was kind of surprised Ty wasn't more selfish in bed, all things considered, but it made him want to do that much better.

Cary paused for a moment, letting Ty's cock out of his mouth with a long lick, ignoring his groan of protest. He wet his fingers and pushed gently against the tiny hole even as he bore down again, sucking with renewed effort. Not all guys liked that, but Ty seemed to be entirely on board with the idea, as he swore softly under his breath and thrust harder, pushing up into Cary's mouth and then impaling himself on his finger.

If Cary wasn't so damned horny, he would have tried to prolong it. He liked the little sounds Ty made, the feel of hard muscle under flushed skin. But he was too on edge to draw it out. He was thrumming with nervous energy that clamored for release—so different from his earlier fatigue it seemed unnatural. Perhaps Ty was right about it being a side effect of withdrawal or something, but he didn't want to think about that right now. He sucked hard and twisted his finger viciously at the same time. Ty's fingers tightened in his hair, and he came with a restrained grunt.

Cary pulled away just in time to get spatter on his chest, but being covered in Ty's come did nothing to dim his arousal. He was so hard he was about to burst, and almost whimpered with impatience.

"C'mere," Ty whispered and pulled him upward. The traces of his release smeared between their bodies, mingling with sweat. Ty was still breathing heavily, his body now slack with satiation, his skin deliciously warm. But apparently, he was determined to make sure Cary had a turn, because he palmed his erection and gave it an encouraging tug. "What do you want?"

Cary didn't care how Ty was going to get him off, so long as he did. He ground against Ty's hand in lieu of a coherent answer, with tiny frantic thrusts, desperate for more friction that would send him right off that excruciating edge. Thankfully, Ty seemed to get the gist, because his grip tightened, one hand pumping Cary's cock and the other squeezing his ass. It was messy and graceless, with them moving out of sync, their bodies bumping awkwardly at first. But after a few frustrating moments they fell into a sort of a frenzied rhythm, a purposeful race to the finish. Cary buried his face in Ty's shoulder, the scent of him—damp earth mixed with musk and cigarette smoke—filling his nostrils. For a second, he imagined himself fucking Ty in earnest, pushing into that tight heat he'd only gotten to explore with his finger, and the thought sent him flying. Waves of pure rapture washed over him, drenching him in sweetness as he spurted all over Ty's hand and into the tight space between their bodies.

For a few moments, Cary lay there, his heartbeat in time with Ty's as it gradually slowed. He felt boneless, drained of whatever jittery mood that had overcome him. All he wanted was to draw the duvet over the both of them and sleep for a week in the comfortable warmth, but unfortunately, that wasn't how things worked. Cary rolled over to his side of the bed with a supreme effort. He really should get up and get cleaned, he thought, closing his eyes. At the very least he should make sure Ty had as much of a good time as he had. But he just couldn't summon the energy. The last thing he remembered was Ty shifting on the bed next to him, and the touch of a blanket on his bare skin.

Chapter Six

TY WOKE UP early, as usual. The room was dark, but the grayish light of dawn was beginning to dispel the lingering shadows. He could hear the noise of the traffic picking up volume outside, the sounds of a large city waking up. For a few moments, he lay there, listening. He wasn't keen on large cities in general, but they had their advantages when he needed to melt into the crowd.

He sat up quietly, wincing at the spike of pain behind his eyes. That was one experience he was hoping never to have again. Sure, it wasn't as bad as being stabbed or shot, but the risk of getting his skull crushed came pretty damn close. He checked the nightstand for his gun and then looked at Cary's prostrate form. He'd kicked off the covers at some point during the night, despite the air conditioner that labored noisily in the far corner, and was sporting some impressive morning wood. Ty briefly considered doing something about it, but they couldn't dawdle. Besides, sometimes what happened in the dark, in the heat of the moment, was less welcome in the light of day.

He got up and headed to the bathroom for a piss and a quick shower. This kind of felt like the morning after a one-night stand, but as fun as the little interlude had been, they had more important things to focus on right now.

"Hey," he said in a low voice after coming back and pulling his jeans on, nudging Cary's flank for emphasis. "Rise and shine, Houdini."

"Ngh," Cary said and opened his eyes. They looked a little on the puffy side, but other than that, he looked much better. He sat up and yawned, pulling up the sheet to cover his lap. The memories of last night were slowly returning to him, if his expression was anything to go by, because he glanced self-consciously at Ty and opened his mouth.

"We've got a lot to do," Ty said, cutting off whatever Cary was going to say. He really didn't want to hear any stumbling explanations about how it was all an unfortunate mistake or a onetime deal. They both knew how things went down. It was best to let them well enough alone.

"Wait," Cary said. "I still have to go back to the theater, to pick up my stuff. They're probably looking for me after all that racket. And it should be safe for me to go home now, right? I mean, they've already gotten what they wanted."

"I reckon so," Ty said, grabbing his leather jacket and the duffel bag. "Want me to give you a lift?"

It would be quite a detour, as he was planning on paying a visit to a buddy of his who was based right in the heart of the Tenderloin and had some useful connections in the San Francisco underworld, but somehow, Cary's grateful smile made it worth it. God, what was it with this guy? It was bad enough that he'd somehow gone into partnership with him, now he was going to run his errands, too? It hadn't been a date. He didn't even leave his phone number with most of his dates, preferring to keep things easy and uncomplicated. After all, his lifestyle didn't exactly facilitate having a long-term relationship. He must have had a concussion after all.

"Let's meet back at the motel later," he said once they were headed downstairs after Cary had had the chance to go through his own morning routine.

Ty doubted Cary would actually show up. Once he had time to stop and think about it, he might very well decide he'd rather lose the amulet than take the risk of trying to retrieve it paired with a complete stranger whom he had no reason to trust. And Ty preferred to work alone, even if sometimes that proved less convenient. People, in his opinion, were utterly unreliable creatures. Case in point—AJ, with whom he'd worked for years, and who apparently had few qualms about selling him out at the first sign of trouble.

Though, in all honesty, he probably wasn't being fair to AJ. Facing down Tony Giordano was probably more than Ty could ask of anyone, least of all AJ (who had his redeeming qualities, but had never been a brave soul).

The Garland Magic Theater looked deserted when they arrived, but it was still early in the day. Cary hopped out and waved at him before heading for the back door. He looked good even in yesterday's sweat-stained clothes, reminding Ty of a nimble but slightly battered alley cat.

His bizarre hunch about this guy had better pan out, Ty thought as he watched Cary go inside the theater. He couldn't afford much more bad luck. Not if he wanted to retrieve the amulet and complete the task set by AJ's mystery client. That was something he'd kept from Cary, of course. It wasn't like he could admit to wanting to get his fee for the amulet while promising to return it to Cary. The other reasons he'd stated for going after Giordano were all true, but there was no way Cary was getting it back like he'd made him think.

Was it wrong of him to use Cary like that while planning on conning him all along? Yeah, but that was the way of life. Cary wasn't some naive kid. He knew enough about how things worked in their line of business to watch out for himself. If he didn't, really, it was his own fault. For all Ty knew, he had to watch out that Cary didn't double-cross *him* in the process. Like Cary himself had said, there was no honor among thieves.

Ty kept repeating it to himself as he drove away, but for some reason it didn't make him feel better at all.

IT WAS ALREADY dark when Ty heard a knock on the motel room door. He was faintly surprised to see Cary through the peephole, but there he was, standing in the hallway with a large bag slung over his shoulder.

Ty opened the door, letting him in, and checked the dim hallway. It was deserted, with only muffled music coming from the floor below.

"Hey," Cary said, dropping his bag on the floor. He was wearing jeans, a gray T-shirt, and a worn dark denim jacket. All traces of his stage makeup and the gaudy costume were gone. It made him look less exotic and mysterious—just an ordinary guy in generic clothes—but also younger and more...vulnerable, even though there was nothing weak about him.

"Hey," Ty said.

"Those fuckers completely trashed my place," Cary said, bitterness lacing his voice. "They must have dropped by during the performance. They took all my props, my costumes, everything. With all that they broke, I'm gonna lose my deposit. What's up with that?"

"I guess they wanted to be thorough," Ty said. "I'm sorry."

"I can't sleep there. Both my mattress and my couch are torn to shreds. Can I crash here? We'll get an early start tomorrow."

From the haunted expression in Cary's eyes, Ty gathered the lack of a sleeping arrangement wasn't the only thing preventing Cary from staying in a home that had been broken into.

"Sure," he said. Staying together would be convenient while they were on the job, even if Ty wasn't exactly used to having a roommate. And the possibility of them hooking up again did cross Ty's mind, even though he wouldn't be the one proposing it. He couldn't deny the attraction, but perhaps it was better to keep things strictly professional.

"Thanks." Cary flashed him a dazzling smile, and Ty fought to suppress the sudden flash of arousal despite his virtuous intentions. "Any news?"

"Actually, yes. Come take a look."

Ty had moved the small round table to the center of the room, and now it was piled with papers, notes, and empty coffee cups. A small tablet PC was perched precariously on the edge. Ty pulled up a second chair for him, and Cary sat, giving the papers a cursory glance. He then looked up at Ty in surprise, his dark eyes going wide.

"Jesus. How did you get the blueprints for Giordano's house?"

Ty shrugged. He took one of the coffee cups, swirled the contents, frowned at them and downed them anyway, wincing at the stale taste.

"Once I had a name to go with the face, it was easy to find out other things. These are probably grossly out-of-date," he said, nodding at the blueprints, "but I only needed them to get a feel of the place. Cost me a nice chunk of change, but it was worth it. I also sneaked a peek at the house itself. Gotta give it to him, the guy does have top-notch security systems installed."

"Shocker," Cary said. He leaned back in the chair, crossing his arms over his chest. Ty couldn't help but let his gaze linger on the graceful lines of his limbs. "You can't be serious about breaking into this place. Look at the size of it. There would be more security personnel guarding it than the Federal Reserve."

"That would be inconvenient." Ty turned his attention back to the papers. "No, our best bet is to wait for him to be on the move. The amulet isn't something you keep locked away in a safe. That would defeat its purpose. He'd carry it with him, at least when he means to use it. The ring, too. He definitely knows about magic and what it can do, and he'd be a fool not to wear it at all times."

"So we just ambush him when he leaves the house?" Cary asked dubiously, probably recalling the number of bodyguards and the bulletproof van. Their chances of success there seemed equally slim.

"Too risky. Besides, he'd be prepared for something like that, and we're no match for him when it comes to brute force. Certainly no match in the magic department if that sorceress of his tags along. No, we need to be smart, striking when he doesn't expect it." Ty leafed through the papers and fished out a few written notes. "I've had some people look into his habits for me. It seems our friend Tony is somewhat dissatisfied with the family business. With the way things are going for them recently, I'm not surprised. He's looking to go into politics."

"Seems like the natural progression," Cary said. "He wouldn't be the first crook to rise to power in Washington, after all."

"It would explain why he'd want the amulet," Ty said. "You of all people should know how powerful charisma can be when combined with the power of suggestion. That would definitely tip the scales in his favor come election time."

It all made perfect sense, really. The effect the amulet's magic had on Cary's audiences had been mesmerizing, and the poor guy hadn't even been using it to its full potential. The thought of what it could do in the hands of someone bent on gaining popularity with the masses and guided by an experienced magic practitioner was more than a little disturbing.

"But I have the feeling he's going to use it much sooner," Ty continued, going through his notes. "Besides politics, Tony is heavily into gambling. High stakes poker. The amulet could be useful in something like that. Make people believe your bluff."

"You think he'd bring it to a game?"

"If it was important enough, sure," Ty said. "He frequently attends friendly games with his, shall we call them, business associates from all over the country. That would definitely give him a leg up on them, wouldn't it? Besides, it'd be a convenient way to test it without drawing too much attention. We know he has a sorceress helping him. There might be other practitioners he's involved with, so we should be careful of those going in."

"Practitioners?"

"A practitioner is anyone who uses magic. Even with only a basic knowledge, you can cast simple spells. Even I can do that, and I'm not very savvy, to be honest. Some people have a better natural aptitude for it than others, as with any talent. Now, a *sorcerer* is someone who has the inherent ability to handle magic, and more importantly, has spent a good deal of time learning their craft. You might have noticed it can be dangerous."

"What makes you think Giordano isn't a practitioner himself?" Cary asked. "He sure knew what he was after."

Ty shook his head. "I can sense magic ability in other people, and he had none. The woman, now, was another matter."

The sorceress was unfamiliar to Ty, and she was strong, there was no question about it. They'd have to factor that in when they went after the amulet.

"Are you a practitioner?" Cary asked.

Ty looked up from his notes. The question stung, like it always did, but Cary was looking at him with genuine curiosity, not derision.

"No. I don't have the talent. I only work for those who do, or think they do. There is lots of demand. Collectors, scholars, sorcerers, amateur magicians, cultists. And I don't deal with strictly magical stuff. People often hire me to find ancient or rare artifacts, books, jewels—that sort of thing. Stealing, if necessary," he added, interpreting Cary's expression correctly.

"What about magical...things?" Cary asked. "I'm not a sorcerer, or whatever, and the amulet did work for me."

Cary wasn't a sorcerer, but if Ty's instincts were anything to go by, he had the potential to eventually become one. A powerful one. Ty could see magic in objects and other people much better than even some sorcerers. Again, he considered telling Cary about his magic capabilities, but decided against it for the time being. Cary was still too green, too scared, too rough around the edges to grasp the full meaning of this revelation. There was a reason beginner practitioners usually found a mentor to instruct them. As scattered as their little community was, people dabbling in magic came to the attention of others fairly quickly, and letting a potential sorcerer run rampant in the world of commons wasn't something they were down with.

No, he'd have to lead him to accept the idea gradually. Ty had neither the ability nor the inclination to mentor anyone in the craft. When Cary was ready, he'd have to find himself a proper teacher.

"Most magical artifacts don't have any power by themselves," Ty said. "Pretty much anyone can handle them. They serve as a sort of focus for magical energy, designed to channel it for a specific purpose. You see, magical artifacts are basically just *things* in the beginning. But some people—and I'm talking about very powerful sorcerers—can imbue them with magical properties for whatever purpose they have in mind. Only then do they become magical."

"Okay," Cary said slowly. Ty couldn't fault him for being a little confused at this point. "So Giordano has a sorceress working for him to teach him how to handle magical energy, or whatever. What do we do?"

"Tomorrow," Ty said, getting up and turning off his tablet, "we go get ourselves a sorcerer too."

Chapter Seven

THE SORCERER LIVED in a basement.

It wasn't even a quaint, turn-of-the-century house basement. Dank and run-down, it was a subterranean apartment in a Mission District tenement, with a separate back entrance that opened to a narrow alley. Ty lead the way down the scuffed stone staircase and knocked on the door, while Cary braced himself against the smell of mold and wondered why the hell all these supposedly powerful people lived in such shoddy conditions.

On the third knock, the door opened, seemingly on its own accord, and Cary followed Ty into what appeared to be essentially a dark cave. Inside, there was a strong smell of perfumed smoke—most likely some kind of sweet wooden incense, but he wasn't sure. It made his nose itch, though the scent wasn't unpleasant.

It was a single room, its walls covered in tapestries and heavy velvet curtains. It created an illusion of shabby opulence, enhanced by a collection of antique furniture and silk-covered sofas, illuminated only by sparsely placed table lamps. If one looked closely, it became apparent that everything was in a state of mild disrepair. There were nicks and scratches on the wood, and the silk was threadbare in places. But the overall effect was still incongruous with the decrepit urban landscape directly above.

A man was lounging on one of the sofas, wearing a brocade dressing gown. Like everything else in the room, it had seen better days. He motioned for them to sit with a broad, imperious gesture. His skin was ivory-pale, his eyes an almost translucent blue. Long black hair and sharp red-lacquered nails completed the look, which was quite striking, overall. Cary had no idea what a sorcerer was supposed to look like, but in his opinion, this guy could pass for a leading man in a fringe theater production of Dracula. He looked around discreetly, but there were no overt magical or occult objects on display anywhere in the room. It looked like a down-on-its-luck antique furniture store more than anything.

"Hi, Bas," Ty said. He sat down on the other sofa, facing the sorcerer. After a moment's hesitation, Cary joined him, perching on the edge of the seat. There was a low coffee table between the sofas, covered with a dark red tablecloth. A pitcher and three glasses were arranged on a round etched brass tray, as if their host had been expecting guests.

"This is Sebastian Monroe," Ty continued, introducing their host, who was staring at Cary with unblinking eyes. "And this is Cary Westfield."

"Nice to meet you," Cary said. The intense scrutiny made him uncomfortable, and he couldn't stop himself from fidgeting.

Sebastian turned to Ty. "Nice to see you back in Frisco, darling. It's been too long. But I see it's not a social call. What do you want?"

Subconsciously Cary had expected some sort of an exotic accent, given the odd surroundings, but Sebastian's speech was no different from what he would hear anywhere around the city.

"I have a lucrative proposal for you," Ty said, settling more comfortably into the cushions.

"Is it anything like the last one?" Sebastian inquired.

Ty shook his head. "Nothing like that, no. It's all very conventionally proper this time."

"He had me crawling around catacombs under Kaposvár," Sebastian complained, turning his pale eyes to Cary. "Do you know what centuries-old, sealed catacombs smell like, darling? There's not enough perfume in the world to get rid of the stench."

Cary had no idea where Kaposvár was, but it had an Old World ring to it, and he wondered if traveling that far and wide was really in Ty's job description.

"There was no *crawling*," Ty said. "And smell aside, that sword you helped me uncover made us both a good deal of money, as I recall. Anyway, do you want to hear more, or not?"

"I'm listening."

Ty took his time answering. He took out a cigarette from the inner pocket of his jacket and lit it with a snap of his fingers, making Cary jump a little. He didn't ask permission, but the extra smoke would hardly make a difference with all the incense.

"This time, I have a heavily-staked, high-profile poker game I want you to win."

"Huh," Sebastian said. He sat up and poured an amber liquid from the pitcher into the three glasses.

Cary realized both men were stalling. But it was their game, and, not being sure of the rules, he stayed quiet. They seemed like friends, or at least longtime acquaintances, but he knew only too well that business and friendship didn't always mesh well. He took the proffered glass and tasted the contents gingerly. It was apple juice.

"How heavily staked?" Sebastian asked.

"One hundred thousand entry, five players, and the host is a notorious crime boss."

Ty had spent nearly all night and a good part of the morning gathering intel on Giordano's gaming habits. Cary had fallen asleep watching him chain smoke and consume countless cups of awful motel coffee as he talked on the phone—sometimes switching to other languages—and worked on his tablet. But by the time they'd had their bagel breakfast at the coffee shop across from the motel, he had nearly all the information they needed regarding Tony's monthly weekend Vegas trips, like the one he was planning this Friday. He'd drop in for an evening of poker in a private room with his long-term East Coast buddies, but sometimes they'd invite newcomers (usually wealthy businessmen or influential political figures) to join them for new cash inflow or making useful connections. That created a window of opportunity to insert an outsider into Giordano's immediate vicinity. The tricky part was getting Tony to select the right person, and making sure that person was up to the job.

The crucial bit would be up to Cary, though. Since Ty couldn't show his face anywhere Giordano could spot him, Cary would have to be the one to go undercover and extract the amulet—which meant he'd have to pick the man's pockets while he was sufficiently distracted during the game.

Sebastian stood up and started pacing the room, expertly avoiding the haphazardly arranged furniture. The long hem of his robe trailed behind him like a train.

"Where?"

"The Venetian."

"Classy."

Ty shrugged. "I have folks there who owe me a few favors. I can pull some strings to set things up."

Sebastian made a sound of approval and then gestured vaguely in his direction. "Be that as it may. You are one of my oldest and dearest friends, darling, and I do want to help since you ask so nicely. But what's in it for me?"

"You get to keep all the winnings."

The sorcerer halted and squinted at Ty suspiciously. "Now I gotta ask what's in it for you?"

"The game is just an opportunity. The crime boss in question stole a rare magical object we believe he plans to use during the game—an object that can captivate his companions. We want it back."

"Now it gets interesting," Sebastian drawled. "And the catch?"

"The mark might have a sorceress there to help him wield it. And maybe some other practitioner we don't know about. He also has a ring that makes him immune to external magic. Which he also stole, if I may add."

"Yes, I remember that one," Sebastian said. "So sad for you to lose it, darling. Very sad." He paused, as if in thought, and then looked from Ty to Cary, and back again.

"You two are fucking," he said suddenly, apropos of nothing.

Cary nearly choked on his juice. Ty drew on his cigarette and gave Cary a sidelong glance before looking back to Sebastian.

"Can you blame me?" he asked casually.

The offhand compliment was oddly satisfying, and Cary fought to suppress a grin. It wasn't entirely correct. They'd only done it once, and it wasn't *technically* fucking, but it was nice hearing Ty owning up to that. It made him recall the feel of Ty's solid body, the smoky scent of his skin, the little sounds of pleasure he'd made in the darkness. Cary shifted uncomfortably, hoping his body's involuntary reaction wasn't apparent.

"I'm not faulting your taste. I'm faulting his," Sebastian said, nodding to Cary. "Don't pretend he can't do better. But back to the matter at hand. This entire endeavor sounds sufficiently unfeasible. I'm in."

"Never doubted you for a second, Bas," Ty said, taking one last puff and putting the cigarette out on the brass tray.

"I accept your terms, then. Shall we seal the deal in blood and semen?" Sebastian looked expectantly at Cary.

"I...what?" Cary said, unsure if he'd heard correctly, and if he had, what exactly it had meant.

"Cut it out, Bas," Ty said. "Nobody's impressed with the traditional Fae shit. No touching, and definitely no bodily fluids."

Sebastian shrugged.

"Oh well, you can't blame a guy for trying," he said apologetically and winked at Cary.

"WHAT WAS HE on?" Cary asked as they emerged from the basement into the (comparatively) fresh air after giving Sebastian all the details of Tony Giordano's Vegas itinerary. The slight chill was welcome after the stifling perfumed warmth of the sorcerer's abode.

"Bas? He wasn't high; he's always like that," Ty said. He put his hands in his jacket pockets and walked briskly toward the parked car.

"What was all that talk about 'Fae shit'?" Cary asked, catching up.

Ty sighed. "There are other realities besides our own," he said. "Realities populated by other creatures. Fae, for example. As a matter of fact, my mentor was a bit of an expert on the Fae. From what I'd gathered, they're not a very benign folk. But they do place a whole lot of significance on oath keeping and bargaining rituals. Anyway, it was just a joke."

"Right," Cary said skeptically. He wasn't sure if he believed in the existence of magical fairies, but he supposed it was no stranger than some of the other stuff he'd already witnessed with Ty around. He shook his head and went back to the subject.

"How do you know him, exactly? Because I still don't see how he's gonna help us." Magic or not, there was no way this Bas fellow would weasel his way into a private high-roller event at a prestigious venue. He was too much of a weirdo, for one thing, and high stakes meant large amounts of cash. No one at that table would accept checks or antique furniture as collateral. Cary felt dizzy simply thinking about the threshold entry sum.

"Bas is a showman," Ty said. They got into the car, and Ty pulled into the busy Monday morning traffic. "I've known him for years, and I've worked with him before. He's a drama queen, and he likes to play. Not just gambling, but you know...toy with people's perceptions. He's a bit kooky sometimes, but he knows what he's doing."

"Can he pull a hundred grand out of thin air?"

Ty gave him a look. "Your problem is you're afraid to think big."

"That basement sure didn't look big to me, and you're not exactly staying at the Hilton," Cary pointed out peevishly. He was beginning to regret getting entangled in this mess. And he couldn't afford pouring any more money down the drain. Aside from a few hundred bucks in his cash account, he didn't have any more funds. Maybe he should rethink the whole cutting his losses thing before it was too late to back out. "Excuse me for worrying about insignificant little details like money."

"This is why I like working alone," Ty muttered.

"Well, it isn't exactly a picnic for me either! Why would you even want to work with me if you don't bother explaining what it is that we're working on?"

There was a pause as Ty visibly reined in his annoyance.

"Okay, fine," he said curtly. "Bas will take care of the money. Don't let appearances fool you. He's worth more than he lets on, and he's willing to shell out some cash if it means he'll get a chance to have some fun and a fat return on his investment. Besides money, he's there to create a distraction. Bas can get close to Tony, and if he uses the amulet, he will know. You and me, we're neither of us sorcerers, and we need some serious magic to tip the odds in our favor."

"You know, so far, all the sorcerers I've met have displayed strong criminal tendencies. It's almost as if having unlimited power makes you disregard the law or something," Cary said.

Ty shrugged. "Oh, you know. Things have a way of catching up with you," he said with a wry smile.

"No shit. Those things are usually called 'cops'."

Ty snorted. He glanced at Cary, and then reached over and opened the glove compartment. He shuffled around in there, eyes still on the road, and finally fished out a silver quarter, which he tossed to Cary.

"Here, try this," he said. "You're used to performing magic tricks, so this should be relatively easy for you."

The shiny coin caught the sunlight as Cary flipped it around his fingers. He knew enough parlor tricks, but those relied purely on dexterity. "Is this another magical artifact? What does it do?"

"It's a magic coin. It lands on the side of your choosing," Ty said, his attention on the surrounding traffic. "Now, remember—your mistake in handling the amulet was that you allowed it to draw energy from you. And that's very dangerous. A thing like that could easily tap you dry. You're not supposed to act as a source, but as a conduit. The energy is all around us. All you have to do is let it pass through you into the artifact. Even people with little to no magic talent can use them, but it's risky. A common can only serve as the source of the energy, with no ability to channel it from elsewhere. It's like using a sniper rifle—even a person who's never held a gun in their life can shoot it, but only a sniper can hit a mark from a thousand feet. Magic works better if you're attuned to it, and if you know what the object in your hand is supposed to do when used right. That thing," he nodded at the coin, "doesn't require a whole lot of energy to operate, unlike your medallion. Just focus on it, let the energy flow through you and don't overexert yourself."

Cary tossed the coin and caught it on the back of his hand. It landed on heads. It looked like any other quarter, and once again, he wondered if Ty was having a laugh at his expense. He could go on and on about magic, artifacts, and flowing energy, but Cary wasn't a magician, or a sorcerer, or whatever the right term was. Not a real one. He stuffed the coin in his jeans pocket and returned to staring out of the window.

"What got you so upset this morning? You've been on edge ever since we left the motel."

Cary wasn't sure he liked Ty being able to tell he was upset. He thought he did quite a good job at pretending he wasn't.

"I got a call from the theater while you were busy," he said. "They want to hold me to my contract. Five more shows, otherwise I'll have to pay a penalty."

"We got a few more days of preparations," Ty said. They stopped at a red light, and he looked at Cary. "You can still make it, and get on with the gig after we get back."

"Get real," Cary said. "I can't really do this without the amulet. I mean, I could, but nobody is gonna want to come see it."

All he could do was rehash the old illusions he'd learned from his granddad, since the magic that had attracted the crowds wasn't his own. As good as he might have been on stage, no one would come simply to watch him do card tricks and pull twenty-dollar bills out of oranges. It would take him years to work on his act and get to the same level of success, if he was lucky.

"We'll just have to get it back, won't we?" he said without much hope.

Ty said nothing, concentrating on his driving again. He glanced in the rearview mirror and frowned, and then took a random left turn.

"What's wrong?"

"I think that car is following us."

Cary twisted in his seat to get a better look. "Which one?"

"The white Honda."

The car in question didn't look at all suspicious to Cary's eyes. He couldn't make out the driver's face, as he was wearing sunglasses, but it was definitely a man in some sort of a dark blue parka. A few moments later, the car shifted lanes, indicating a right turn while they continued onward.

"I don't think it was anything," Cary said, turning back around.

The only one who'd potentially have any interest in their whereabouts was Tony Giordano, and Cary seriously doubted the mafioso would bother with a tail when he could simply order their legs to be broken if he considered them to be any kind of a threat.

Ty huffed noncommittally, but Cary could tell he wasn't convinced by the way he kept checking the mirror. They didn't see the white sedan again, and the rest of the way back to the motel was spent in silence, with both of them preoccupied with their own thoughts.

Chapter Eight

IT WAS JUST the two of them driving to Las Vegas. They'd decided Sebastian would arrive by plane. A limousine service had been arranged to pick him up at the terminal, true to his cover as a wealthy businessman coming to unwind and have a bit of fun at the poker tables.

Cary was quiet for most of the drive. Ty thought he'd have more questions, being plunged as he was into a world he hadn't known existed merely days ago. But Cary had said nothing. Maybe he was preoccupied with the dismal state of his finances, or worried about the potential outcome of their little adventure. Either way, his bad mood seemed to persist.

Usually, Ty would have been fine with the lack of meaningless chitchat, but he found the silence oppressing. Besides, he was kind of surprised to realize he actually wanted to know more about Cary, beyond the basic facts his recon research had yielded. He still didn't know any of the important stuff, like why Cary had decided to become a performer. Everything in his records indicated a deep rift between him and his magician grandfather (of whose existence Ty had been aware, even if Cary thought otherwise), so why would he choose to follow in his footsteps? If Ty had to venture a guess, he'd say it was Cary's inherent affinity to magic that was partially responsible. Cary, much like his late grandfather, couldn't help but be drawn to it, like a moth to a flame. A flame that, in this case, he couldn't even see, that he had no idea was even there.

But now that Cary knew more about the intricacies of magic practice, it was strange he hadn't inquired more about it. Ty was expecting him to at least suspect and be curious about his own magical potential, but apparently Cary chose instead to wallow in whatever self-inflicted misery that was troubling him.

There were a lot of other things Ty wanted to ask Cary—personal things. Every reluctant tidbit of information from him only served to fuel Ty's curiosity further. It was quite an unnatural fascination, really. There was absolutely no reason to be interested in anything other than the extent of Cary's pickpocketing skills, which were the only thing pertinent to their temporary alliance, and which Ty had yet to test. There was too much at stake to blindly take the guy's word for it. Ty had to make sure Cary was good enough before he let him anywhere near Giordano.

Ty chewed on his unlit cigarette thoughtfully. The wind was way too cold to lower the roof, and he didn't like smoking in a closed car.

"There's a truck stop coming," Cary said suddenly, snapping Ty out of his reflective mood. "We might as well grab something to eat."

"Sure."

Ty followed the sign and pulled into the parking lot by the side of the road. A small rundown diner called Molly's Place was huddled against the side of a one-pump gas station. Two semitrailer trucks, a California Highway Patrol car, and a number of pickups occupied the rest of the lot, making Ty's shiny silver Chevy look wildly foreign in comparison.

As it was the lunch hour, the diner was pretty full. They sat down in the only empty booth next to the window and took turns in the men's room before placing their orders with a harried middle-aged waitress.

"So why did you decide to become an illusionist?" Ty asked while they were waiting for their cheeseburgers to arrive. He wasn't looking forward to working alongside someone who was going to sulk the entire time. And, frankly, Cary's smile was much more attractive than his frown.

"I thought you'd done your research on me," Cary said, picking up a napkin and starting to fold it.

"Just the bare facts. There's still a lot I don't know, and I'm not actually psychic."

Cary sighed, pushed the napkin aside, and leaned back in his seat.

"I didn't want that at all when I was younger. My granddad's parents were carnie performers, and he was an illusion artist, so stage magic was kind of a family tradition. When I was a kid, I was...so angry all the time. With my dad for leaving. My mom for getting drunk and killing herself and leaving me with her father. My granddad for having no clue what he was doing raising a teenager. I wanted nothing to do with any of them, and I did some bad, stupid stuff to get as far away from them as I could. But when I was in prison... You know how they say prison changes people, and it sounds so damn corny and condescending? Well, it's true. At least it was for me. I had plenty of time to figure things out. And then my granddad died, and I didn't even have the chance to say goodbye. I was a shitty grandson, always had been, and he didn't deserve that. So I guess...I just wanted for my grandfather to be proud of me for once. Even if he's not around to see it."

The raw longing in his voice took Ty by surprise.

"Hey," he said. Cary's hand rested on the table next to the napkin dispenser, and Ty covered it with his own. There was only one thing he could say that would be both encouraging and true. "You're gonna be just as good as he was."

Cary looked at him, and the corners of his mouth tugged in a reluctant smile. As they looked at each other, the moment seemed to stretch, the clunking of the cutlery and the din of conversation fading. Cary's long lashes dipped, and he opened his mouth as if to say something.

"Damn faggots," someone growled loudly next to them.

Ty looked up, annoyed at himself for paying closer attention to the warmth of Cary's skin than to what was going on around them. It was a little slip, but he couldn't afford any more of those, not after allowing himself to be jumped in a parking lot like a schoolboy being mugged for lunch money.

His gaze met with that of an angry-looking bearded guy in faded jeans and a Red Bull baseball cap. A trucker, by the uneven tan on his face. Ty noted that despite the cool weather, there was a sheen of perspiration on the guy's forehead, and his pupils were slightly dilated.

"You got a problem there, buddy?" Ty asked, leaning back on the vinyl booth bench and taking his hand off Cary's as unhurriedly as he could. Cary glanced uneasily between him and the angry trucker but said nothing.

"Yeah, I got a problem." The trucker raised his voice, looming over their table like the embodiment of bigoted judgment. Several other customers looked up to see what the fuss was about, including the two state cops occupying the far corner booth. "I got a problem with you degenerates coming here and groping each other in public!"

Punching him seemed like a bad idea, given the police presence. Ty wasn't sure which side the cops would take, and seeing as they had yet to intervene in the impromptu farce, he couldn't rely on their understanding. Still, as much as he wanted to avoid drawing even more attention, there was only so much he was willing to let slide.

Ty started to rise from his seat, casually flipping the side of his leather jacket so that the holster he was wearing underneath was visible to the man in front of him, but it was then that the waitress, guided by some sort of clairvoyant intuition, moved in to diffuse the escalating tension.

"Now, Bill," she said, touching his arm. "Don't you go making a big stink. Why don't you sit down, and I'll bring you the usual. Extra cheese."

Bill threw her hand off roughly, glaring at Ty. He was a burly man, but Ty was taller by half a head and noticeably fitter. He didn't look like someone who'd be easily intimidated by a display of macho behavior. That seemed to give Bill pause as he sized Ty up, and the waitress swooped in again to calm things down.

"You two gentlemen enjoy your lunch," she offered with a tight smile at Cary. She took Bill by the arm again, and this time, he let her lead him toward the counter, where she poured him a cup of coffee, while chattering about the weather to no one in particular. Bill threw one last hateful look at Ty, who bared his teeth in response and sat down.

With the potential confrontation neutralized, the spectators, including the cops, got back to their food and conversations.

"Fucking asshole," Cary muttered.

"Screw him," Ty said, sitting back down. "Let's just eat and get the hell out of here."

They turned their attention back to the food, which was actually not half bad, but the companionable mood they'd shared earlier was ruined. They ate in silence and drank their refills of black coffee (which, unlike the cheeseburgers, was terrible).

"I'll hit the men's again before we go," Cary said. As he walked past the counter, which was nearly fully occupied, he bumped into Bill the trucker's chair. It was nothing more than a casual brush, and Cary apologized right away, but Bill muttered something unflattering about "those pansies" loudly enough to be heard by everyone at the counter.

Ty took out his wallet and threw a few bills on the table as he waited for Cary to come back from the bathroom. It was a larger tip than he'd originally intended to leave, but he had a feeling the poor waitress was going to need all the perks she could get today.

A few minutes later, Cary slid into the booth with a smug smile on his face.

"Nicely done," Ty observed.

"Yeah, I thought so," Cary said, pulling out a worn brown leather wallet with a chain attached to it. "William Hogen." He read the name off a faded Arizona ID.

Ty took the ID card, flipped it in his fingers, and then glanced at its owner, who was now arguing loudly with the guy sitting next to him about the new Interstate 11, completely oblivious of having been pickpocketed.

It was a small thing to go on, and could be nothing more than dumb luck. But Ty had had a hunch about Cary, and it was satisfying to see his instincts, at least, were still sharp. He couldn't deny he'd been apprehensive about taking on a complete stranger on such a delicate job, with so many unknowns thrown in the mix. But Cary hadn't lied about being a good thief. Perhaps the struggling magician really did have the skills to pull off the heist they were planning.

"You know what?" Ty said with a slow-spreading grin. "Let's see if we can't get Mr. Hogen here into some trouble."

THE SEMITRAILER WITH the Arizona plates was parked square in the middle of the lot, half-hidden from view from the diner by the other semi and the pickups. Ty and Cary circled to the driver's side, making sure no one was watching them. Ty took out a small set of lockpicks from his jacket pocket and got to work on the door while Cary kept a casual lookout. Once again, Ty was impressed with the way Cary fell naturally into his beat, picking up on his intent without asking and not batting an eye at Ty breaking into the vehicle. While that might have indicated deeply ingrained criminal inclinations, Ty was more concerned that so far they seemed to make a good team.

He muttered an unlocking spell as he worked, mostly out of habit. It couldn't undo a lock or a latch all on its own, certainly not when performed by Ty, but it helped ease things along—especially when more complicated mechanisms than picking a car were involved.

The lock clicked open, and Ty climbed into the driver's seat, keeping low. The interior looked and smelled pretty much like he'd imagined. There were empty Styrofoam cups and fast-food wrappers strewn all over the floor and the passenger seat, and a rabbit's foot charm was dangling from the rearview mirror. Ty could have told the owner that these kinds of things usually held no charms whatsoever, but that would be a waste of breath. People liked to cling to silly superstitions, since it gave them a semblance of control over events that were entirely out of their realm of understanding.

He rummaged through the glove compartment, but came up with only small change and used tissue paper. If Bill Hogen had anything interesting stashed in his truck (and Ty had a hunch he had), it wasn't in there.

"Hold on," he told Cary, who was still leaning against the side of the truck, his sharp dark eyes scanning the parking lot. "I'm gonna take a closer look."

The back of the roomy driver cabin smelled even worse. Ty threw the blankets off the sleeping pallet that was tucked there. Two empty beer bottles rolled around on the floor.

He finally found what he was looking for in a flat tin box tucked away behind a stack of tattered Playboy magazines. Ty unzipped the small plastic bag, tasted the white powder on the tip of his finger, and then spit it out.

"Our friend has expensive tastes," he told Cary as he climbed out of the truck and closed the door softly behind him. "Wouldn't figure one could afford a whole ounce of cocaine on that salary."

Ty checked the door was locked, and they walked away briskly.

"What did you do with it?" Cary asked in a low voice once they were safely out of the line of sight from the diner.

"Absolutely nothing," Ty said. He took a pack of cigarettes out of his pocket, lit one with a flick of his finger, and leaned on the hood of his Chevy, intent on the front of the diner. "And now I'm gonna watch. This should be good."

Cary looked dubious. He eyed the exit to the highway with longing, as if itching to get away from what was about to become a rather unpleasant scene. Ty couldn't blame him for having healthy instincts, but his work was rarely amusing, and he didn't want to miss out on the satisfaction of witnessing the jerk being brought down a couple of notches.

Ty took a drag on the cigarette and waited. It took about ten more minutes (by the end of which, Cary was fidgeting restlessly by his side) before a commotion in the diner caught their attention. They couldn't see inside from this vantage point, but in another minute their pal Bill burst through the door, accompanied by one of the state policemen. Unsurprisingly, he was pissed off and rather vocal about it.

"The fuck is wrong with this country?" he huffed while the officer followed him silently. "It's just a fucking wallet. I musta left it in the truck. What's the big deal? I ain't gonna split over a few bucks, for fuck's sake. They know me here, don't they?"

They approached the truck, and Bill unlocked the door.

"It must be here somewhere—" he began, and stopped short, looking at something on the driver's seat.

"What's that?" the policeman asked, pointing to the cocaine-filled plastic bag Ty had placed there.

"That ain't mine," the trucker said quickly.

"Sir, I must ask you to step away and place your hands on the side of the vehicle," the cop said in a whole different tone and then reached for his radio.

"Jack, request assistance here," he said, presumably talking to his partner who'd remained inside.

"That ain't mine!" Bill repeated. "I'm telling you, somebody stole my wallet and planted that thing in here!"

"This wallet?" the officer asked, picking up the leather wallet Ty had wiped clean and left lying on the floor next to the brakes. "Sir, hands on the vehicle."

"Okay, that's enough fun for today," Ty said. He got in the car and waited for Cary to slide into the passenger seat before taking the exit back to the highway. Bill's shouts of outrage dwindled into the distance as they sped away.

"I kinda feel sorry for the bastard," Cary said, checking the side mirror.

"Nah," said Ty. "He got what he deserved."

He couldn't help but glance at Cary as he said it. Unlike that bigoted jackass, Cary deserved so much more than he was going to get. If everything went according to plan, Ty was going to swindle him out of the little he had going for him. Somehow, being fed crumbs of information about the workings of magic Cary had no previous notion about in exchange for the only means Cary had to explore said magic didn't seem like a fair bargain.

"What about you?" Cary asked.

The question was so spot-on in echoing his thoughts that it gave Ty an unpleasant jolt.

"Sorry?"

"What made you go into this business of being a magic thief?"

"Magic thief," Ty huffed in amusement and relief. He briefly contemplated dismissing the question, but Cary had been open and honest with him earlier, about his family, so Ty felt he had to return the favor—to a certain extent. Besides, he'd already mentioned some of it to Cary.

"I learned the craft from my mentor," he said slowly, trying to gauge how much he should be divulging. "He was truly what you would call a magic thief. He was also a sorcerer and a scholar. He gave me shelter, education, taught me his trade. He was the only one who cared about me, the only family I ever had. I don't even remember what it was like before I met him. Maybe my birth parents or foster family had thrown me out. Maybe they'd been abusive, and I ran away from them. Either way, nobody ever came looking."

Ty realized that perhaps he was talking Leland up a bit too much, all things considered. Maybe it was some deeply ingrained loyalty that was refusing to let go, even after all these years.

Cary looked at him, his dark doe eyes intent and brimming with something Ty had a hard time identifying. Sadness? Concern? Empathy? It wasn't an emotion he was used to seeing, whatever it was.

"Do you still work with him?" Cary asked after a pause that seemed a little too long.

"We've had a falling out," Ty said, turning his attention back on the road. "I haven't seen him in years."

Perhaps his answer was a cop-out, but being thrown out by a man he'd looked up to, whom he'd thought of almost as a father, for no clear reason that he could see, had hurt him more deeply than he cared to admit even to himself. He wasn't ready to discuss it with Cary—to let him see just how damaged he was under the tough exterior. No matter how much he wanted to.

The road stretched on before them, the cracked asphalt peppered with dust and empty promises.

Chapter Nine

"WELCOME TO VEGAS," Ty said.

Cary sat up in the passenger seat, blinking sleepily. The Strip greeted him with a seemingly endless procession of winking lights that drove back the night with artificial brightness. Somehow, he'd managed never to have been to Vegas, and now he watched the neon-lit thoroughfare roll past with a sort of fascinated detachment. After the long, lonely stretches of road across Nevada, the sight was like a mirage, a perfectly crafted illusion.

They drove past a huge sign displaying scenes from Criss Angel's magic show at the Luxor. Even in the ad, it looked over the top, but Cary couldn't help but be jealous. How awesome would it be to perform in front of thousands of spectators, at one of the most famous venues in the world? And to think he could have had a chance to do that if he hadn't lost his damn magic pendant. With just a few years of hard work, he could have attracted enough interest to gain wider exposure.

Did the power of the amulet extend to TV audiences? Perhaps Giordano was counting on it to make potential voters enamored with him enough to overlook his shady business and criminal past. He could easily become a governor, a senator—hell, maybe even the next president. Using the amulet on stage might have been cheating, but at least it wasn't harming anyone. The country's political future wasn't hanging in the balance, only Cary's career as a magician—which was of little consequence in the grand scheme of things.

He had to get it back.

"Jesus," was all he said when they finally entered the lobby of the Venetian Hotel after availing themselves of the valet parking.

Ty, who was making for the registration desk, followed his gaze and looked upward at the beautiful frescoed ceiling.

"Want to take a selfie for your Facebook page?" he asked.

"Shut up," Cary told him, but couldn't stop staring at the painting and the golden spherical statue underneath. One of the mermaids (or whoever the women were supposed to be) that adorned it gazed serenely back at him as he approached to take a closer look. Her face reminded him of the Sphinx painted on his granddad's old magic cabinet, the one he'd used to hide in as a child during his mom's alcohol-induced bad moods.

"Coming?"

Ty came up to him, having concluded the check-in, and handed him his room card. Cary took it and followed Ty to the guest elevators. He caught a glimpse of the lavish expanse of the casino floor, but they weren't there to hit the slot machines.

"I could get used to this," Cary said as he plopped down on the sofa in the sunken living area of their suite. The contrast with the shabby San Francisco motel was staggering. The marble bathroom alone was large enough to fit most of his apartment. "This sure looks like people owe you a lot of favors."

Ty shrugged. He dropped his duffel bag by the king-sized bed and began to unpack. "It's not as expensive as it looks."

"God, I wish it was always like that. Shit not being as expensive as it looked, I mean." Cary sat up. The huge bed with its multitude of pillows looked cozy, and for a brief moment, he let himself indulge in a silly fantasy of staying in a swanky hotel on a vacation or a romantic getaway. He'd never been on a vacation—certainly not a romantic one. For one, these things cost money he didn't have, and for another, he had to actually be in a romantic relationship with someone, which had never happened.

It wasn't that he was opposed to having a romantic relationship, precisely. It just never worked out for him that way. Now, Ty... Robbery aside, he could really see himself falling for Ty, if he wasn't careful. He was damn hot, that was for sure. That lean physique, the beautiful eyes, the sensual curve of his lips... Oh, yeah. Even now, he couldn't help being slightly aroused just from looking at Ty's rear as he unpacked his bag.

But it was also so much more than that. Cary could appreciate professionalism, and Ty was definitely smart and competent. And, surprisingly, compassionate. It was ironic that the only man who really listened to Cary and offered some genuine encouragement was the one he had to watch his back around.

The thought was too depressing to dwell on, and he pushed it firmly out of his mind for the moment. "So, what do we do now?"

Tony Giordano and his entourage were arriving in Vegas the next day, which didn't leave them a lot of time. Cary still had only a vague notion of what was about to go down, and none of the details. He didn't like being left in the dark, and he didn't like feeling useless. Ty might know what he was doing, but Cary would have liked to share in that knowledge.

Ty grabbed a folder with his notes and joined Cary in the sitting area, taking the chair facing the sofa. He spread out large sheets of paper on the glass coffee table. They were hand-drawn charts of the casino floor.

"Sebastian will be here later today," he said. "He's basically our bait. His job is to pose as a high roller, rub shoulders with Giordano, and provide us with access to the little shindig of theirs."

He pointed to a small square near one of the corridors that led off the main floor.

"This is the private room. It's small, with only one poker table, but it has a bar, a lounge area, and an en suite bathroom. This is where you come in."

"In the bathroom?"

"At the bar. How are you at mixing drinks?"

"You want me to bartend?" Cary was reasonably sure he could pull it off—he'd tended bar briefly in a local nightclub before landing the gig at the Garland Theater—so he was familiar with the basics, at least. The men whom he'd be serving weren't likely to ask for anything overly exotic or trendy, after all. But when he said he wanted to take a more active role in the operation, this wasn't exactly what he meant.

Ty looked up at him. His dark hazel eyes were serious. "You have the most important task. Giordano will be wearing the ring, so neither Bas nor I can touch him with magic. You'll have to get close enough to him to swipe the amulet, and this is the only way to get you inside that room without causing suspicion."

"Are you sure they won't recognize me, though?" Cary asked.

"I don't think any of them would. Tony for sure has never seen you, and any of his goons that might happen to be there would remember the magician costume more than anything else, if they'd checked you out at all. Besides, there are ways to make oneself less noticeable. With the right spell, most of them would look right past you. The only one you'll have to worry about is Tony, and Bas is there to distract him."

He made it all sound so easy. And picking someone's pocket would normally be child's play for Cary. But the prospect of being alone in a closed room with crime bosses and their armed bodyguards filled him with a very real dread. Being caught stealing in such company wouldn't go down well, fancy hotel or not, and Sebastian didn't strike him as the type who'd have his back in a sticky situation.

Sensing Cary's hesitation, Ty said: "I'll be right there. Well, not really *there* there, but I'll be listening in."

"How? Can you hack the cameras?"

Were there even cameras in a private room like that? Cary imagined the casino would want some sort of record of the gambling, but these sorts of people rarely wanted anyone tracking their activities.

"Not really my area of expertise. But a microphone would be enough. You could easily wear one. It's not a drug bust; nobody's gonna strip-search a bartender."

Cary wasn't so sure about that, but he kept his mouth shut. Having Ty watching over him, even if it was only through a mic, was a lot more reassuring than being left on his own with no ability to call for backup.

"Once you have the amulet, get out of there as fast as you can, before Giordano notices it's missing," Ty continued. "You'll have to be quick. I'll be waiting for you here." He indicated a sketched in circle around a tiny symbol on the side of the chart. "The escalator to the second level, which leads to the parking garage. Then we haul ass."

"What about Monroe?"

"He can take care of himself. Trust me, he knows what he's doing." Ty looked at him. "So, what do you say? Are you up to it?"

"Do I have a choice?"

Truth be told, Cary wasn't thrilled about the plan. In fact, if he was being completely honest with himself, he was scared shitless. It depended entirely too much on other people—people he basically knew nothing about—and he'd had his fair share of making bad decisions when it came to falling in with the wrong crowd. He could almost hear his granddad berating his teenage self about his no-good friends, and this time, he was inclined to agree with him. Except now, it wasn't just taking the fall for an armed robbery. This could get him killed.

"Of course you have a choice," Ty said, with a hint of annoyance. "You came to *me*, remember? Nobody's holding a gun to your head. If you feel you can't do it, then don't. No harm, no foul. I'll manage on my own."

It was tempting to take the chance to bail out. He didn't belong here; he was in over his head with this caper. But that would also mean giving up on the amulet. On the only truly magical thing that connected him with his grandfather's memory. On any chance he had for success. Was it worth taking that much of a risk—of staking his life on the competence of complete strangers?

Probably not. But as his granddad had always complained to him, he was a helluva stubborn fellow, especially when he was being self-destructive. He was already losing a ton of money, with his shows being canceled. If he ever wanted to get out of debt, he'd have to plow on like he intended. It wasn't like he hadn't been aware of the dangers from the start. To quit now would be a coward's way out, and he wasn't ready to admit defeat just yet.

"Yeah, okay. I can do it."

"You sure?" Ty didn't look too convinced. Maybe he was also beginning to question Cary's capabilities, given his apparent lack of confidence. But if there was anything Cary was good at, it was sleight of hand. So yes, he was sure he could do it. The only concern was getting away alive after he did it.

He opened his mouth to say precisely that, but the suite door suddenly burst open without any warning. They both surged to their feet, and Ty moved a step forward, placing himself between the door and Cary, as if shielding him from the intruder. He reached under his jacket for the holstered gun.

"Surprise, darlings!" Sebastian announced, shutting the door with his heel. Dressed in an impeccably tailored suit, with his dark hair cut short and sleeked back, and a huge gold signet ring on his little finger—sans the nail polish—he looked every inch the flashy nouveau-riche businessman. It took Cary a moment to recognize him.

"For fuck's sake, Bas," Ty said, relaxing. He looked pissed off and relieved at the same time, and threw Cary a look that was almost embarrassed. "Could you not do that?"

"Where's the fun in knocking, sweetie?" Sebastian said, unfazed, as he joined them in the sunken sitting area. "Nothing interesting ever happens after you knock."

Cary sat back down, his heart hammering. They were jumpy, it seemed, even though they had no real cause for anxiety. Giordano wasn't going to arrive until tomorrow morning, so who would possibly be looking for them? That is, aside from a crazy sorcerer seemingly bent on giving them both a scare.

"How did you get in without a key card?" he demanded.

Sebastian sat down, sprawling in an elegant chaise longue, and gave Cary a look that suggested he was questioning his intellectual prowess. Sebastian's eyes, eerily translucent in his pale face, made Cary uncomfortable to meet them.

"He used an unlocking spell," Ty explained before Cary had the chance to get riled up.

"What's that?"

"Anything you wish it to be, darling," Sebastian said with a lazy drawl. "Anything at all."

It was all Cary could do not to grit his teeth. The guy's attitude was beyond frustrating, and it put Cary's nerves even more on edge.

Thankfully, Ty interjected again.

"He's right. The wording doesn't matter, only the intent behind it. The spell has no power in itself. It's only a tool to help you focus the magical energy and direct it to the specific purpose you have in mind. You can say 'Aperio', or 'Open, Sesame', or quote a Taylor Swift song—as long as you're channeling the energy into opening the lock. The same goes for every other spell. It's not what you say, or how you say it, or what language you're speaking. It's how you use the words in order to focus the magic inside you."

"Fine," Cary said, a bit testily. "Whatever. Although I'm a little disturbed by the idea of you being familiar with Taylor Swift's songs."

Sebastian huffed in amusement. He peered over at the table and cocked his head, examining the spread-out papers.

"Strategizing, I see?"

"We were just going over the details." Ty took his seat again. "You all settled?"

"Yes, in the Renaissance Suite. Can't beat that view. And the wet bar," Sebastian added after a moment's thought.

Cary still couldn't wrap his head around the fact that these people could afford staying at such a fancy place. Ty lived in a shady motel; Sebastian's home was no better than a slum. And now they were basking in luxury he'd ever only glimpsed in glossy ads. It seemed unreal, suspiciously like a scam of some sort, and it bothered him that he could neither unequivocally banish the doubts nor put his finger on the con. He'd have to be careful, and the mob boss wasn't the only one he had to watch out for.

"How exactly are you planning on crashing Giordano's poker party?" he asked, a little more sharply than he intended. "If that's such an exclusive bunch, why would they pick you, of all people?"

"Why, it's my irresistible charm, darling," Bas said with a lazy smile that made Cary bristle instinctively. "The crispy green kind, mostly."

"I'm sure you won't be the only one on the floor with money to burn. And whoever Giordano's poker buddies are, would they fall for your particular blend of crazy?"

Bas cocked an eyebrow and opened his mouth to say something, but Ty cut in.

"You're right. It's an exclusive bunch. In fact, let's go over these 'poker buddies'."

He produced a thin paper folder and took out several pages, with a photo attached to each, and laid them out on the coffee table.

"First, we have Tony." There was a picture of Giordano smiling that cold, reptilian smile. The page listed his basic game patterns and gambling habits—information that Ty must have obtained from the casino employees. The same points were covered for the rest of the players, four in number. Once again, Cary couldn't help but be impressed with the sheer amount of work Ty had managed to put in in such a relatively short time.

"Angelo Rossi, Tony's cousin and second-in-command," Ty said, going over the rest of the files. "Frank Biagi, a big shot in the Conti family from the East Coast and a real-estate entrepreneur; John Gladden, an independent consultant working for a growing arms-producing company; and Rodger Gordon, an investment banker from North Carolina."

"These are some odd choices," Cary said, looking over the pictures of rich men in expensive suits.

"Not really. Whatever Tony's relationship with Angelo, he's keeping him close for now. Biagi's an old pal of Tony's, and my guess is this Gladden fellow is there because Tony is actively seeking financial backing for his future political campaign from major companies that would support his agenda. Now, Gordon is the least remarkable one there and clearly invited as a cash cow." Ty tapped the photo of an elderly, pudgy gentleman with a bland face. "That's the one we need to eliminate so that Bas can take his place."

"Eliminate how?" Cary asked. He didn't think Ty would do anything extreme, but it never hurt to make sure he wasn't getting himself involved in something more sinister than he'd bargained for.

"Relax," Bas said. He leaned in to snatch Gordon's photo off the table and flipped it between his long fingers like a playing card. "Nobody's gonna whack him over the head and bury him out in the desert. I'll merely...distract him. It is Vegas, after all, the Sin City. Poker is hardly the only temptation to lure the not-so-innocent." The photo disappeared with a snap.

Cary wasn't exactly satisfied with the vagueness of this statement, but he had a feeling that was all he was going to get.

"Fine," he said. "So long as there's no whacking."

"Certainly not on my part, but I can't speak for the gentleman in question," Bas murmured with a beatific smile. "I suppose I should get on it, though."

He got up, straightening his jacket with a motion so gracefully casual it was as if he wore suits in his day-to-day life rather than threadbare silk robes. And who the hell knew, perhaps he did. Perhaps he was a bank teller, or an accountant, and that whole Gothic warlock getup was simply an act to fool gullible customers. Cary couldn't be sure of anything anymore.

"So long, darlings. Get back to whatever it was you were doing." Sebastian gathered the files to take with him and winked at them. He tucked the folder under his arm and squeezed Ty's shoulder, pausing.

"Oh, and Ty? Tell him," he added in a very audible whisper and then sauntered toward the door.

Chapter Ten

"TELL ME WHAT?" Cary asked suspiciously as the door closed behind Sebastian.

Ty grimaced. Bas was right, of course. He should tell Cary about his magical talent. He didn't feel right about withholding such crucial information. It was unfair, and it was downright dangerous in the long run. If Cary's powers should suddenly manifest, the result would be unpredictable. He needed someone to train him, to guide him, to teach him as much about concealment and discretion as about casting spells and channeling energy. Someone competent, who knew what he was doing.

It bugged him that Bas had picked up on all of that so fast—not only on Cary's untapped potential, but also that Ty had hidden that particular insight from him. But then, Bas had uncanny acumen when it came to human motivation.

"Nothing," he said.

He would tell Cary about the magic, just not now. They needed to keep their focus on the job at hand. He didn't have the time or the patience to answer all the questions a budding sorcerer would undoubtedly have. He could do it after they were done with the heist.

On second thought, perhaps he couldn't.

"Are you two...?" Cary paused meaningfully.

"What?" Ty looked at him in confusion, and then understanding dawned. He snorted and shook his head. "No. We're just business partners. On occasion. He's even more of a loner than I am. He just likes to tease. I think he was trying to make you jealous. I'm definitely not his type."

"Why would I be jealous?" Cary asked, a touch defensively.

Ty was a bit stung by that. Which was silly, because there was nothing going on between Cary and him. And he wasn't looking for a relationship, or even counting on a hook-up beyond what had happened that first night. And after all this was over, he wasn't going to see Cary ever again.

It bothered him even more that the thought made him a little sad.

Ty shrugged it all off and, without looking at Cary, busied himself with collecting his drawings. "No idea."

"And who's his type?" Cary asked.

"I'm not sure he even has a type. At least, I've never actually seen him with anyone, or heard him talk about them. And even if he did, I'm pretty certain he could do better than me."

"Don't say that. There's nothing wrong with you."

Ty raised an eyebrow at the dubious compliment.

"I mean, you're a cool guy. And, like, handsome," Cary hastened to explain. "I mean, you're definitely attractive." A faint blush tinged his cheeks.

"Thanks," Ty said, grinning at his chagrin. "You're definitely attractive too."

There was a charged pause as they continued to gaze at each other, Cary's dark eyes locked on his. Cary's lips parted slightly, and for a second, Ty thought he was going to issue an invitation, either explicit or unspoken. But Cary turned away and yawned rather exaggeratedly.

"I'm beat," he announced without looking at Ty. "If there's nothing more we should go over right now..."

The disappointment prickled, but perhaps it was for the best. They shouldn't get distracted, and Cary, with his close-to-perfect features and lithe body, was most definitely a distraction. They'd had their fun, once, and that was that.

"Sure," Ty said. "You go ahead and get some sleep. We'll do some actual recon tomorrow. I'll finish up here." He gestured to the papers.

Cary hesitated for a moment, but then nodded, took his bag, and headed toward the bed covered in white and purple pillows.

AN HOUR LATER, Ty looked up from his tablet to find Cary still awake. He was half sitting on the bed, with the bedside lamp turned off, tossing the silver quarter Ty had given him and slapping it on the back of his hand again and again.

"It's not working," Cary said. He was intent on the coin, but he must have felt Ty's gaze on him.

Ty pushed the tablet away and stretched. He gathered all the papers in a neat pile and then went up to the bed, where he sat down next to Cary. It was late anyway, and he needed to get some rest. But a couple of minutes of showing Cary the ropes wouldn't hurt. "Here, let me show you."

Cary scooted over, making room for him on the silk satin duvet. Even without touching him, Ty could feel the frustration rolling off of him. That was unproductive for anything, most of all the kind of fine-tuning that magic practice required. Cary's shoulders were set in a hard line, and Ty placed his hands on them, expertly finding the knots of tension.

"What are you doing?"

"Shh. Relax."

Cary stiffened reflexively and gradually relaxed as Ty kneaded his shoulders, even turning slightly to offer a better angle. Oddly, it felt more intimate than their hurried sex in the San Francisco motel. Ty enjoyed running his hands over Cary's smooth skin, feeling the muscles under his fingers. Perhaps a little too much. They were partners in crime, not fuck buddies. Not any kind of buddies, really.

"Now, close your eyes," Ty murmured, pushing the thought and tentative stirrings of arousal aside for the moment. "Breathe. Feel the air pass through you. Feel the warmth around you. Concentrate on the coin. Touch it with your pulse."

He could feel Cary's breathing even out beneath his hands. It slowed, became deeper. His chest rose and fell steadily.

"How do you want the coin to land?" Ty asked.

"Heads," Cary said quietly.

"Heads it is." Ty kept the pressure steady, drawing the tension out of his muscles. "Now just tell it to be heads."

Cary barked a laugh. "Seriously? I tell it? It's a fucking coin."

"I've told you, it's a magic coin. It wants to be what you tell it to be." Ty ran a thumb over the back of Cary's neck, and he let out a little sigh of pleasure that made Ty's cock perk up in interest. *Focus*, he told himself. "Feel the warmth flow into the coin from your fingertips. Now, flip it."

Cary tossed the coin with a flick of his thumb. It spun in the air, flashing in the low light, and landed in Cary's palm. It was heads.

"It could be just a coincidence," he quickly pointed out. "It could land on heads a hundred times now and still be a coincidence."

"Bullshit," Ty said, giving Cary's shoulders a final squeeze and letting his hands fall. "I could tell you felt it."

He'd lied to Cary, of course. The coin was just a regular quarter, about as magical as a brick. But if Cary believed the coin had special powers, he didn't have to come face to face with the fact it was his magic that made it work, and not some intrinsic mojo. It was a good exercise, though. Something simple yet visually compelling—something Ty could use later to prove his words when it was time to let Cary in on the secret.

Cary didn't answer. Ty started to rise, but Cary stopped him with a hand on his arm. "Come to bed. You've been driving for hours. You must be tired."

"I'm used to working nights. I just want to make sure we have all our bases covered."

"You're sure going to a lot of trouble. With all the money you must be spending on bribing the staff and paying for our stay."

Ty made a noncommittal sound. Cary was dangerously close to figuring out Ty was counting on taking off with the amulet—if he hadn't already. He'd be stupid not to be suspicious. It was just common sense.

"It's not necessarily money. I'm calling in a lot of favors on this one," Ty said. "Besides, Bas has connections here. He's no stranger to gambling, and he had pulled some local folks out of hot water when they were down on their luck."

"Look," he continued at Cary's dubious silence. "I know it's not gonna be easy, but you gotta trust me on this. I know what I'm doing. But if you're not on board with the whole thing, you can still back out. I'm telling you, you don't need the amulet to be a good stage magician." *Or a real magician, for that matter. A sorcerer.* If Cary told him right now he wanted out, Ty would tell him about his magic. He couldn't let Cary go without preparing him to deal with something like that.

"I'm in," Cary said stubbornly. "I just don't want to end up in prison again because I trusted the wrong people."

"Nobody's going to prison," Ty said. He meant it, too. Whatever happened, and regardless of the fate of their ultimate prize, he didn't want Cary to be left handling either Giordano or the authorities on his own. "We're partners in this. We watch each other's backs. Okay?"

Cary looked at him and nodded slowly. Despite the acquiescence, all the tension was back with a vengeance. Ty rose from the bed, hiding his disappointment.

"You're right—it's late. We can continue in the morning," he said. "I'm gonna hit the shower."

TY GRABBED SOME clean underwear out of his duffel bag and headed for the bathroom. It was all done in cream and white marble, with gold fixtures and an ample supply of soft, fluffy towels. There was even a TV fixed on the wall to be conveniently watched from the tub, and a vase with freshly cut white flowers on the vanity.

The shower was separate, though, and that was all Ty needed. He took off his clothes, grabbed a lavender-scented complimentary soap, and stepped inside the sparkling glass enclosure. The warm water felt good after the artificial chill inside the bedroom.

He was working the soap into heavy lather when the bathroom door creaked. Ty spun around, ducking for good measure, but it was only Cary. Ty opened the fogged glass door to see that he was wearing nothing but his briefs and holding two small foil packets between his fingers. Cary whistled appreciatively at the sight of Ty all wet and soaped up.

"Mind if I join you?" he asked, and walked up to the shower without waiting for an answer. He chucked his underwear, displaying a half-mast erection.

"No, I don't mind. I thought you weren't in the mood," Ty said, straightening and making room for Cary in the stall—not that it felt crowded, even with the both of them. He'd kept his tone neutral, though he couldn't deny his heart (as well as some other parts of his anatomy) leapt at the sight of the other man.

"I am now."

Cary stepped inside, closing the door behind him. He turned on the tap, and the water from the large rain showerhead splashed over his head and shoulders, instantly plastering his hair to his scalp. He placed the condom and the lube packet on the soap dish and ran a hand over Ty's chest, smearing the lather over the lightly tanned skin before the water washed all the traces of soap away. His eyes became a little glazed, his breathing shallow.

Ty was flattered that the sight of him naked could have that effect, and the truth was, Cary himself looked good enough to eat. Ty hadn't had a chance to get a good look at him the other night, when they'd fumbled in the dark, but he appreciated the view now—the lean frame, the deep golden-olive skin, the long, dark eyelashes. He was beautiful. Why he'd dismissed Cary as not being his type at first was beyond him. He cupped the side of Cary's face, and the other man leaned into the touch, allowing Ty to draw him in for a kiss.

Cary tasted of spearmint gum and something distinctly unique that reminded Ty of wild honey. The kiss was thorough, unhurried, their lips parting and locking again in a sweet enticing dance. When they finally drew apart, it was with palpable reluctance.

Cary's eyes dropped, and he traced a finger over a tattoo that spanned the length of Ty's left flank. Interwoven runic script created dense patterns that coalesced into the shape of a serpent, covering a long, jagged scar.

"An accident?"

"Something like that." Cary's touch was featherlight, and it sent pleasant shivers straight to Ty's groin.

"What does it say?"

"It's a healing hex. Keeps it from pulling."

"Looks pretty deep." Cary frowned as his fingers hovered over the scar tissue.

"It happened a while ago," Ty said reluctantly.

About ten years ago, to be more precise. He couldn't have been more than eighteen or nineteen at the time.

"My mentor, Leland, took me on a job. We were supposed to break into a mansion somewhere in northern Italy to score some Gaelic grimoire from a private library. A fucking beautiful place. Anyway, I climbed the outer wall and tried to undo the magic wards that sealed the windows, but the guarding spell was too strong for me to handle. The blowback flung me right onto the spiked ironwork fence below."

The memory made him wince, and he looked away from Cary's shocked eyes that mirrored his own pain.

"Leland was furious with me for failing to undo the spell and for botching the job. He made sure I wouldn't bleed to death, but was too angry and too busy getting us off the property before the owner had the chance to call in the local law enforcement to heal me properly. He always said the scar was a reminder that incompetence carried a price."

But later, Leland had tattooed the healing runes along Ty's mangled flank, just as he'd done with Ty's fingertips, so the scar didn't bother him that much anymore. Sometimes, he forgot it was even there, unless one of his quick lays made a face at it.

"Your mentor sounds like a real piece of work," Cary said, his voice tight. A dark emotion blazed in his eyes, sharp and unpleasant. Anger?

Ty had had plenty of people angry at him throughout his life, but never someone angry *for* him. The thought of Cary being upset on his behalf was like a shot of hard liquor, spreading sudden warmth through his veins.

"He wasn't that bad," he nevertheless insisted, almost automatically, and then shook his head. All this talk about Leland and the wounds of the past, open or otherwise, was draining his desire and making his erection flag. But he knew just the thing to remedy that.

Ty grabbed Cary, pinning him with his back against the wall before he could offer any insights, or worse, pity. He really didn't want to talk anymore. Instead, he went down to his knees, more than happy to return the overdue favor.

Cary made an impatient whimpering noise and bucked, his now fully erect cock pointing toward Ty's open mouth. But instead of taking him in, Ty dipped lower and lapped at his balls. Cary hissed and spread his legs wider, leaning back against the marble wall, giving him more access.

"Shit," he breathed. His fingers slid over Ty's wet hair, failing to get a good grip. His engorged cock nudged at Ty's face insistently, but he ignored it in favor of gently sucking on one ball, and another, and then licking the sensitive spot at the base, drawing a keening sound from Cary. Finally Ty wrapped his lips around the leaking head and sucked hard, reaching down to stroke his own erection. He shut his eyes against the streams of water and applied himself to the task, working himself with one hand while holding Cary's thigh with the other.

"Oh, god," Cary panted. He threw his head back, moving his hips. Ty could feel his muscles working, could taste the salty presage on his tongue. "Wait, I want you to fuck me."

The words and the breathless note in his voice nearly set Ty off. It was an exercise of will to pull away and let go of his own cock, but the temptation to have Cary under him, to fuck that nicely taut ass, was too great to pass up.

Cary regarded him through half-lidded eyes, his chest heaving. Drops of water clung to his lashes and ran in little rivulets down his flushed cheeks. Ty got up and splayed a hand on the marble wall next to his head.

"Turn around." He would have liked to fuck him like that, watching his face being transformed by pleasure, but in this setting, it wasn't really practical. They'd just have to do this again somewhere less slippery—if there was going to be another time.

Cary tensed, his eyes going dark for a second, but he complied, turning and resting his forehead in the crook of his arm against the wall. This presented Ty with a very nice view of his ass, and he took the opportunity to grope it, eliciting another hiss from Cary.

"Come on," he urged, and it was Ty's turn to obey. He ripped the lube packet Cary had so thoughtfully supplied and slicked his fingers before pushing them into Cary's tight entrance. Despite the roughness of the intrusion, Cary was pliant, offering himself up uninhibitedly. The tension was still evident in the line of his back, but he was bucking against Ty's fingers, silently begging for more.

"You're so fucking hot," Ty whispered in his ear and then twisted his fingers. Cary's huff turned into a moan, and Ty pushed harder.

"Jesus, Ty, just fuck me already," Cary panted in frustration, and the desperate edge in his voice shot right to Ty's cock.

As if he could get any more aroused than he already was. This would have to be enough; there was no way he was going to hold off any longer. Ty withdrew his fingers to the accompaniment of Cary's sigh, slid the condom on, and used the last of the lube on himself. He grabbed Cary's hip and guided himself in small, measured thrusts, until he was lodged all the way inside that maddeningly tight heat.

Cary shuddered and leaned further back against him. His hand dropped to his own cock, but Ty swatted it away, taking hold of him instead. It was his turn to take the stage, as it were, and he was going to make the most out of it.

He went slowly at first, careful despite the overwhelming need to claim that lithe body with everything he had. Christ, it had been a long time. Perhaps that was the problem. Perhaps this silly fascination with the wannabe magician was simply misdirected lust stemming from a too-long dry spell, and no more than that.

But the sounds Cary made—raw, needy, and bordering on obscene—were urging him on, and he drove deeper, harder, working his hand in time with his thrusts, while Cary pumped his hips, eager for everything Ty had to give to him. They were both burning so hot, he was surprised the water raining down and sliding between their bodies didn't evaporate right off their skin.

"God, yes, don't stop," Cary panted.

"I'm not stopping," Ty said, planting a half kiss, half bite on his shoulder. Not that he could stop even if he wanted to. Pleasure began to pool at the bottom of his spine, and Ty had to make a conscious effort to maintain the rhythm. But it was growing more and more difficult. Ty buried his face in the back of Cary's neck in a desperate attempt to hold on. He focused on their mingled breathing above the noise of the running water, on the sound of wet skin slapping against skin, on the velvety touch of Cary's cock sliding against his palm.

"Ty," Cary said brokenly. "I'm gonna—"

He didn't finish the sentence. Ty felt the muscles clamping down around him and Cary going rigid in his grip.

"Go on, baby," he urged, breathless, and then Cary was coming, shooting against the marble wall. Ty didn't have the chance to admire the mess because he was coming too, the searing sweetness of the orgasm lancing through his body, rocking him to the core, and leaving him breathless and wrung out, quivering with little aftershocks of pleasure.

Go on, baby? The hell was wrong with him?

Ty loosened his hold as he pulled put. Cary turned around and slumped against the wall with a lazy, satisfied smile that made Ty forget everything else.

"That was the best shower sex I've ever had."

Considering the probable scope and nature of Cary's past experiences, it probably wasn't much of a compliment, but in this case, Ty was inclined to agree. He grunted his assent and turned off the tap, resisting the urge to kiss away the water droplets from Cary's jaw.

"Come on. We have a long day tomorrow."

They tumbled out of the bathroom, barely pausing to towel off, and got into bed. The sheets, for all their luxury, smelled faintly of cheap detergent, and Ty tried to ignore the smell and the ghost feel of other bodies on the bedding. Thankfully, Cary snuggled close, his sweet scent pushing everything else out of Ty's mind, and closed his eyes with a contented sigh that lanced right through Ty's heart.

Ty drew the covers on top of them and sank back into the soft pillows. On the verge of sleep, he watched Cary breathe. The feel of Cary's skin against his, the sharp line of his jaw, the spill of his dark hair against the crisp linen—it all blended into an image of such precious beauty it made Ty ache. If he could have one wish, it would be to stay in this moment just a little bit longer, even if it meant yearning for something he could never really have.

Chapter Eleven

THE WAY CARY was staring, wide-eyed, at the pretentious lavishness as they strolled down the fake St. Mark's Square, made Ty a little sad. It was nothing but a gaudy tourist attraction, a sleek illusion to hide the undercurrents of greed that flowed beneath.

Cary wandered off to take a look at the gondolas, and Ty wished he could show him the real Venice. The shabby, old beauty of it and the wild history etched into the stones. Let him smell the stench of rot and stale water and feel the chill drifting off the canals at night. Venice had plenty of its own illusions to offer the naive traveler, but none of them as clean and sparkly as a Christmas ornament, like it was in Vegas.

But the prospect of that ever happening seemed very unlikely. Once Ty had the amulet safely in his hands, that was it. He'd leave, disappearing into the night—or whatever time of day it'd happen to be—never to see Cary again.

He tried to shake off his preoccupation and continued his walk, noting the position of the escalators and the security cameras. They weren't planning on reaching this area of the hotel, but he liked to establish all possible escape routes ahead of time. You never knew when you'd have to scramble for one in the thick of things.

His gaze kept slipping, though, trying to catch a glimpse of the other man among the throng of tourists and shoppers. It was distracting. That was all Cary was—a distraction.

There was no denying it was a pleasant distraction, at times. A small but sweet shiver ran down Ty's spine as he recalled the silky smoothness of Cary's skin, flushed with desire, and the little needy noises he'd made when Ty moved inside him. His brain helpfully conjured up half a dozen images of things they could be doing, given a chance, but Ty couldn't afford being invested in anything other than the task at hand. With an effort, he shifted his focus back to watching the flow of people and calculating the distance to the exits.

"How's the recon going?"

Cary's voice came through loud and clear. They were using this opportunity to test the audio equipment, with both of them wearing concealed mics. Of course, Cary couldn't chance wearing an earpiece during the poker game, but it came in handy for scoping out the main hotel levels. They didn't want any of Giordano's posse to spot them there together.

"Pretty good. I don't see any major deviations from the map," Ty said. "Think I got most of the camera positions figured out."

"Haven't you been here before?"

"I have, but it was some time ago. They do renovations—things change. It pays off to be thorough when possible."

"Were you here alone?" Cary asked with a peculiar inflection in his voice.

Ty glanced in his direction. Cary was standing right by the stairs leading to the dainty little bridge that spanned the faux canal. People were walking past him, chatting and snapping pictures with their phones.

"I rarely work with partners," Ty said very carefully. "And I don't do romantic partners at all."

Cary turned to lean on the rail, looking down at the green-blue water.

"Why not?"

Ty wasn't planning on having this conversation right now. He wasn't planning on having it at all, and now it had caught him off guard, and he didn't quite know what to say. Years of self-preservation had taught him to be cautious and mistrustful.

"It's just easier that way. No expectations, no complications. People will always bail on you when it's convenient, even those who say they're your friends, or that they love you."

"That's...jaded."

Ty barely stopped himself from shrugging. "It's realistic."

And yet some unexplored, visceral part of him whispered that Cary might be different. Ty liked him. Cary was funny, intelligent, and capable, even if at times he was prickly as a hedgehog. And Ty was edging precariously toward wishing there could be more to their relationship than mutual exploitation, which was something he was afraid to admit even to himself.

"We should continue," he said when Cary didn't respond.

They both started back toward the escalators, keeping their distance. For some reason, Ty couldn't shake the persistent feeling of being watched. Usually his instincts were pretty sharp about these things, but this time it was more of a nagging suspicion than a certainty. He cast about casually, but nothing stood out in any way. He couldn't pick up on the source of his discomfort—which had nothing to do with the awkward conversation they'd had earlier.

Perhaps it was just fancy, or nerves. Ty had never been the jumpy type, but he couldn't deny that the sheer number of people gathered in such a relatively confined space made him uncomfortable, despite the masterful imitation of open skies on the ceiling.

But despite his self-admonitions, the sensation of someone's gaze fixed on the back of his neck refused to go away. Ty recalled the white sedan that had briefly appeared to be tailing them in San Francisco after they'd left Bas's place. It had seemed like a false alarm at the time, but perhaps there was something more to all of this.

"Keep your eyes open," Ty said quietly as he descended after Cary to the main casino floor. Cary grunted in agreement.

Unlike the brightly lit square and canal promenade of the fake Venice above, the casino was set in a perpetually glittering duskiness that was just illuminated enough by flashing lights and huge chandeliers as to not be oppressing. The beeps and blares of the slot machines, the cheers of the spectators around the roulette tables, and the precise calls of the dealers blended into a background cacophony, as constant as the sound of waves crashing against a rocky shore. It also made blending in with the crowd that much easier, though Ty wasn't fooled about their ability to go unnoticed here—the floor was more tightly monitored by the casino security than some airports. The subtle magic that worked on people didn't fool surveillance cameras. But as long as they didn't stir up any trouble, the security folks didn't care who they were. Ty wasn't worried about being watched from this particular quarter. It was the other kind of attention he wished to avoid.

They made their way along the plush red carpet, keeping to opposite sides of the room.

"Check out the craps," Ty said, and Cary stopped to look at the table where a crowd of players and spectators had gathered for what was apparently a lively game in progress.

While he was pretty savvy about card games, Ty had only a vague notion of how craps was played. The swankier forms of table gambling, like craps or baccarat, just weren't his forte. From what he could gather, the game was dependent entirely on the shooter's luck, and it seemed like luck was on the current shooter's side. This wasn't at all surprising, given that the person throwing the dice in an elaborate flourish was, in fact, none other than Sebastian Monroe. A considerable amount of chips was stacked on the table's edge in front of him. Judging by the colors, there was about one hundred grand in that pile. Cary whistled softly in Ty's ear, no doubt having made the same calculation.

"Winner, seven," the stickman announced, and the people around the table cheered as Bas smiled his dazzling smile and kissed the hand of the beautiful tall blonde girl in a shimmering green dress who was practically draped around him. Apparently, a glamorous escort was as much a part of the "rich businessman on a romp" disguise as a tailored suit and an expensive haircut.

"That's impressive," Cary said in a low voice as the stickman deftly moved the chips on the table when the players placed their bets. Of course, as a sleight-of-hand artist himself, he was bound to recognize the telltale signs of manipulation that were too subtle for the dealers to notice, and which were enhanced by whatever spells Bas was currently reciting in his head.

"That's the idea," Ty said, keeping his attention on the folks jostling around Bas. He couldn't actually see magic at work, but after so many years of practice, he could feel its flow enveloping Sebastian, gently tugging at the people around him, making them stop and look. Even those who huddled around the far tables occasionally raised their heads and glanced in his direction.

"Well, he's certainly arousing interest," Cary said. He turned his head from side to side, assessing the situation. Ty could tell Cary was sensing it too—the pull of vaguely familiar power, even though he probably couldn't understand what it was he was feeling. "But isn't the point spending money rather than winning over the house by using magic?"

"Oh, don't worry. When he reaches a critical point, he'll lose quite spectacularly. Watch."

As they observed the game from afar, the crowd of spectators was growing steadily, as were the colorful piles of chips thrown on the green felt. Sebastian pushed a hefty-looking stack on the pass line to the applause of the onlookers and other players, who hastened to place new bets.

The numbers and words shouted by the players and the dealers seemed completely random to Ty, and he wished Bas had picked a different table to exhibit his ostensible gambling addiction, something simple and fast-paced, like blackjack or the roulette. Even though Ty had no stake in the game, he hated not being able to follow the moves. At least the reactions of the spectators made him aware that Bas was aiming for something rather entirely too straightforward for local tastes.

Ty saw Cary approach the table and followed him discreetly. Thanks to the larger crowd, they could risk drawing closer, if only for a minute. Cary's pull proved as impossible for him to resist as the tug of magic emanating from Bas was for the onlookers.

From his new position, Ty could spot the casino security folks in the wings, with their nondescript dark suits and earpieces, but for now, they stayed back, simply watching the proceedings around the table. If there were other "professional" observers, he didn't spot them. Bas continued to throw the dice, apparently on a winning streak with the bets growing bolder and the sums getting higher with each pass. Ty had given up on trying to follow the rules. It was high time for Bas to step down, anyway. They hadn't come to rob the casino, after all—just establish Bas as an ambitious but perhaps not very savvy high roller.

"Wow," Cary said in a hushed voice that echoed in Ty's earpiece as Bas bet a tall stack of thousand-dollar chips on a single roll. If Ty had to stake a guess, he'd say this was the one Bas intended to lose.

But Cary didn't know that, and as the dice flew over the table, Ty felt the magic surge within Cary, trickling down to his fingertips in an involuntary resistance to the possibility of Bas making the wrong move. Cary's instinct was to help Bas keep his money, and the magic responded to his unspoken, unformed command. Ty stepped up and grabbed his hand, willing him to stop before the power of his intent interfered with the throw. The runes in Ty's fingertips prickled, as if an electric current passed between them at the contact, but the magic receded as quickly as it had welled.

The dice hit the table wall and rolled onto the felt.

"Soft eight," the stickman said, which apparently was a bad outcome, since it elicited a collective sigh of disappointment from everyone around the table. Next to him, Cary inhaled sharply, and even Ty couldn't help wincing. Even though he knew the loss was premeditated, it was hard watching all that money disappear back into the house's pockets.

Sebastian stood up, smiled apologetically, and made his way to the roulette, escorted by the tall blond girl. Several spectators trailed after him, no doubt expecting to be treated to another show.

Ty and Cary hung to the back, behind a row of slot machines, as they surveyed the crowd. There were quite a number of people watching the game go down, but Ty couldn't pinpoint any of them as members of Tony's entourage. But the night—figuratively speaking, as it was only a Thursday afternoon—was still young, and Bas had a lot more money to burn and attention to garner. Ty was pretty confident about their plan working, especially since Bas had the means to tip the scales in their favor by making sure it was the right kind of attention he was attracting.

But there were other problems they were currently facing.

Cary's fingers flexed in Ty's grip, and he looked at him, as if noticing for the first time their hands were still touching. Cary must have misunderstood the intent behind the gesture, because his gaze, when he directed it at Ty, was a little bewildered. But he didn't remove his hand immediately, and his expression changed slightly, into something less guarded, less world-weary.

Their eyes locked, and Ty wouldn't have been surprised to feel the same sort of electricity in the air as had moments ago coursed through their clasped hands. Cary's eyes darkened with promise—just a fraction, but it was enough to set Ty's blood on fire. Heat crept up his cheeks, and he leaned infinitesimally toward Cary, the scent of his warm skin suddenly overwhelming the smell of stale air and expensive perfume, and Ty's resolve.

A slot machine jangled a few feet away, the loud noise shattering the strange, fragile moment. Cary blinked, and Ty took the opportunity to take a hasty step back, breaking both the visual and physical contact.

Risk of exposure aside, he couldn't let himself go down that path, especially after the whole "not doing romantic partners" talk. He had to get a grip before he let himself fall for a mark like some stupid sap from a sappy movie. They were only together until they relieved Giordano of the stolen amulet. After that, it was every man for himself.

"We should talk," he said, his voice sounding unexpectedly hoarse.

He didn't want to discuss the confusing things he was feeling. There was no future for Cary and him, no possibility that he could see of them ever exploring that tentative, surprising attraction that had somehow grown in a place he thought to be barren. And even if there was, Cary deserved so much better than Ty. It was safer, wiser, to save them both the heartache of disappointment.

But there was no doubt he should have a very frank and honest chat with Cary regarding his magical potential. The power was so ripe inside him that it brimmed just under the surface, threatening to erupt at the wrong moment, taking them all down if they weren't careful. He owed it to Cary to let him know.

"Sure," Cary said. Hurt flickered in his eyes before his expression closed off again.

Ty turned away. Something heavy was lodged in his chest, an unfamiliar emotion he did his best to ignore. *Soon,* he told himself as they split up again and continued their walk through the casino, trying very hard not to accidentally bump into each other. Soon he'd have his ring, Westfield's amulet, and his peace of mind back, free to return to his solitary existence, uncomplicated by all these ridiculous feelings toward a man who should have been nothing more than a mark, but who was so much more than that.

Soon.

For some reason, the thought wasn't as comforting as he wanted it to be.

Chapter Twelve

CARY TUGGED NERVOUSLY at the crisp white collar of his uniform shirt and glanced at himself in the mirror behind the corner bar. It's going to be all right, he told his reflection silently. It's just another performance. Just another feat of sleight of hand. Only this time, the audience was a murderous psychopath who had no idea he was square in the middle of a magic show.

He straightened his bow tie one last time and turned to face the room. As private gaming rooms went, this was as private as one could wish for. It was decorated extravagantly, like everything else, in red, cream, and gold, and there was only one poker table with six chairs around it. Aside from the wet bar, there was a large flat-screen TV on one of the walls, a lounge area, and an en suite bathroom—in short, everything needed for a few uninterrupted hours of high-stakes gambling.

Cary's job as a private-room bartender meant he had to be as unobtrusive as possible, and so far, that worked to his advantage. He'd spent all morning practicing mixing drinks and was reasonably confident he could handle the players' requests. So, as long as he stayed quiet and served the men promptly, he could watch them without anyone looking at him twice. That included the casino dealer, who must have known Cary wasn't an employee, but said nothing. Cary assumed money had changed hands there as well, but he could hardly ask the guy if he'd been bribed to let him slide.

Cary knew that no amount of money would convince a professional dealer to cheat in a camera-monitored, casino-endorsed game with such heavy rollers. The cheating was Sebastian Monroe's job, if such need arose.

To be perfectly honest, Cary'd had doubts that particular part of the plan would work. There was no shortage of people with money at the casino, and most of them were willing to lose said money just for the thrill of it. That Giordano would latch on to Bas, out of all these potential cash cows, was rather dubious, but Cary couldn't argue with results. Whether it was skill, natural charm, magic, or a strange combination of all of the above, Sebastian had gotten in.

Aside from the dealer, there were five more people in the room, seated around the table. Tony Giordano, with his slick hair and toothy smile, reminded him of a particularly handsome reptile. The chair on his right remained empty. Cary watched him closely at first, careful to avoid eye contact and looking away every time the man glanced in his general direction. But despite his apprehension, Tony didn't show any signs of recognizing him.

There was actually a greater chance of Angelo Rossi, Tony's right-hand man, recognizing Cary. Rossi was a medium-height, nondescript fellow with thick dark hair, sharp eyes, and a superficial resemblance to Giordano that spoke of a familial connection. According to Ty's briefing, he was the one who handled Tony's more questionable enterprises, so there was a better chance of him knowing Cary by sight. But he gave Cary no more than a cursory glance when calling for his whiskey, and after that, he ignored him altogether. Cary noticed he and Frank Biagi, Giordano's rival "pal" from New York, were eying each other like two male tigers suddenly forced to share a cage. Clearly no love was lost there, but Tony seemed unperturbed by the palpable animosity. Cary wondered what was going on there, but it was hardly important at the moment.

Gladden, the arms company consultant, wasn't unlike Tony in that he was attractive and slippery. But whereas Tony commanded the room with a genuine intensity, despite his relatively young age and well-groomed appearance, this guy was as fake as loaded dice. He chatted easily and fluidly, all the while wearing a big smile that showed rows of white teeth that looked a little too perfect.

It might seem that somebody like Sebastian would be the odd man out in this company. Perhaps he was, in the participants' minds, but it certainly didn't look like it from the outside. Sebastian was holding his cards with all the suave elegance of a bored modern-day aristocrat seeking expensive thrills, like he wasn't bothered by the proximity of all these dangerous people and their bodyguards waiting outside.

The news of Monroe being invited to Giordano's little shindig came in late last night. Cary and Ty had just returned to their room from their recon tour of the casino. Both of them were in a strangely dark mood, with Cary having no idea what it was Ty wanted to talk to him about (but judging by the grim set of his mouth, it was nothing good). Frankly, Cary didn't need any extraneous relationship talk, or whatever it was Ty had planned to set the record straight between them. They were partners—in crime, but with benefits, as it happened. He knew there was nothing more, even if the thought grated. Under different circumstances he would have liked to get to know Ty better, to have more than a glimpse of the complex layers beneath the tough-guy exterior, the unexpected gentleness mixed with often ruthless efficiency. Cary had never had that easy connection before, with anyone.

And it looked like he would never have it again. Because falling for someone who'd robbed you (and was most likely planning on doing it again) was too stupid to let happen more than once.

In any case, he didn't get to hear any pained explanations, because the second Ty opened his mouth, Sebastian came bursting into their suite, announcing his future engagement with a triumphant laugh, and then they were too busy setting up the audio equipment for tomorrow to have any meaningful conversation. Which had probably been for the best anyway.

As if sensing Cary's gaze on him, Bas looked up and winked at him conspiratorially before snapping his fingers. "A daiquiri, if you please."

Cary busied himself with preparing the drink. It probably wasn't going to be the best daiquiri in the world, but that was Sebastian's fault for not asking for something more straightforward—preferably something Cary could pour straight out of the bottle. Still, he was doing his best to appear as professional as possible, though no one was paying him any particular attention. The focus was all on the game. These were the early stages, when the players got a feel for each other's idiosyncrasies, so the bets were still relatively low. From watching on the sidelines, Cary could already tell Gladden was going to fold early on most rounds, while Rossi and Biagi would battle it out. Tony was more difficult to read, and he probably had very different goals in mind. For him, a much larger game was afoot. But for some reason, the sorceress Ty had been so worried about helping Tony was absent.

"How's that condominium going, Frank?" Giordano asked after taking a peek at his freshly dealt cards and throwing a couple of chips on the table.

Biagi stopped glaring at his opponent for a moment as he launched into an account of his newest investment in a large condominium being built somewhere on the east side of Manhattan, and the expected revenue. The other players listened politely.

"The excitement must keep you up at night," Rossi observed after Biagi mentioned two-year interest rates. Gladden laughed a bit too loudly, but Biagi didn't look amused. Sebastian said nothing, his light blue eyes flicking between the two men, and then focusing on the pot.

"Now, now, gentlemen, there's no need for that," Tony said in the indulgent tones of a parent chiding a naughty toddler, and just like that, the rising tension was gone. It wasn't even deference—it was as if the little display of mutual attitude had never happened. The men smiled at each other genially and raised the stakes by another ten thousand.

Cary blinked. If there ever had been doubts regarding the authenticity of the amulet Tony now had in his possession, that demonstration had effectively silenced them. Apparently, Ty had been correct about Cary not using the thing to its full potential. If its power was enough to turn a room full of gangsters into a church ladies' knitting circle, it could probably do anything.

As he brought Sebastian his drink with a polite but meaningless smile, Cary strained to catch a glimpse of the amulet, or at least get an indication of where Tony was keeping it. The thing was pretty conspicuous, and if he were wearing it around his neck, Cary would have quite a challenge ahead of him. But he couldn't see any sign of a chain. Most likely, Tony was keeping it in his breast pocket, where it would be close enough to touch, but wouldn't come into direct contact with his skin. It seemed even a mobster was smarter than Cary when it came to using magical artifacts.

As he looked over the card table, Cary noted the array of jewelry. None of these men were strangers to bling when it came to gold and diamond pinky rings and signets, but Tony was wearing only a simple gold band on his ring finger. Since he wasn't married, Cary assumed it was the ring Tony had also taken from Ty. It didn't look like much, but he already knew enough not to trust appearances. As Ty had predicted, Giordano was wearing it, and that meant Bas couldn't touch him with magic in any way. He and Cary were entirely on their own in their respective roles, aside from Ty listening in through the tiny mic Cary was wearing under his shirt. It felt a little like being part of a law enforcement undercover operation, except there was no chance in hell he'd ever be a part of a police sting. In any case, he hoped Ty could hear everything from his makeshift control center in their suite, because without an earpiece, there was no reverse communications channel.

"I fold," Gladden announced, not unsurprisingly. He was hardly betting his own money, but he wasn't one for daring moves. Certainly not when the pot held more than a hundred thousand dollars in chips.

"Looks like a good call," Tony said without batting an eyelash. He took a sip of his scotch and put the tumbler down on the raised table edge.

There was a pause as the other men let his words sink in. Even without looking at the cards, Cary could tell which of them had a good hand—Biagi and Sebastian. He wasn't a card shark by any means, but he could recognize the behavior of a confident opponent.

"I'm out," Rossi said readily and threw his cards on the table. A second later, Biagi followed suit. Sebastian was the last to fold. Cary hoped this was because he was playing along, and not because he too was affected by the amulet's magic, but it was difficult to tell. Giordano laid his cards on the table neatly, displaying a straight.

Even the dealer looked a little shocked by this development, and there was a long pause before he dealt the cards again, as if unsure whether he should proceed. However, none of the players seemed unhappy with the situation. In fact, they now hung on to Tony's every word and laughed at his witticisms as the evening progressed.

As far as Cary could tell, Giordano didn't influence the course of the game after that one incident, but his little experiments didn't stop at that. He let tensions run high, fueling Rossi's and Biagi's squabbling with casual remarks, and then quelling them with a smile, or a soothing word that in other circumstances might have infuriated the men even more. He was using the room as a test ground of sorts, and so far, it was all working. Cary recognized a con when he saw one, and this had all the classic signs of a mind trick, sans the actual trick. The magic was real, but the end result was the same. The men were eating out of his hand. An hour or so of this, and Tony could win the game by simply declaring himself the winner and having everyone agree.

So far, Cary could detect no foul play with the cards themselves. Something must have been going on, however, because gradually, the majority of the chips accumulated in front of Tony and Sebastian. And while Tony had the ability to take the participants' money all he wanted, none of them expected the slightly goofy rich newcomer to actually clean the table. Cary could see them growing more and more frustrated. He wished Bas would tone things down just a little, but the man was clearly in his element, and Ty had promised he could keep all his winnings. Cary could hardly blame him for wanting to make as big a score as he possibly could.

"That was some hand," Rossi remarked to Sebastian as the dealer once again swept the chips into the sorcerer's corner.

"Got lucky, I suppose," Monroe said.

"Yeah, for a fourth time in a row," the mafioso grumbled. Gladden, who sat on his right, shot him a quick look, but said nothing and called for another cocktail.

Cary quickly mixed a martini, poured it into one of the chilled glasses from the mini freezer tucked under the bar counter, and brought it over to Gladden while the dealer opened a new deck. As he collected the empty glasses, he noticed Tony rubbing the side of his chest absently, and wondered if he was feeling that slight familiar tingling.

Cary's heart beat faster, and he busied himself with unnecessarily wiping the edge of the game table with a paper napkin. The game could go on well into the night, but every passing minute brought him closer to the risk of exposure. Now was the time to make his move, to prove that, like Sebastian, he was there for a reason. He risked a quick glance at the sorcerer, silently willing him to make some sort of a move that would give Cary a much-needed window of opportunity.

Bas seemed to understand his silent plea, because he inclined his head ever so slightly before taking a peek at his cards. He couldn't do anything that would help Cary pick Tony's pocket while that magic ring was at play, but he could certainly divert attention.

But whatever Sebastian was going to do was doomed to remain a mystery, because at that moment the door opened, and the dark-haired woman—the same woman Cary remembered from the San Francisco parking lot—walked in, right past the two bodyguards stationed at the entrance.

Chapter Thirteen

"YOU MADE IT, Letti," Tony said with an expression closer to genuine pleasure than anything Cary had seen him display all evening. He got up and showed the woman to the empty seat next to him, and then turned to the other players. "For those of you who are unfamiliar, this is my sister, Leticia."

"Gentlemen," Leticia smiled with a general nod to everyone and sat down gracefully, while Cary picked up his tray and hastily retreated.

Sister. Cary could definitely see the resemblance. Leticia boasted the same striking good looks as her brother—with the added feminine twist—though the sense of danger that was so apparent in Tony was hidden deeper, under the flair of long dark hair, the stark white pantsuit, and the subtle makeup. But the edge was definitely there, and it was no less sharp. Cary sensed it instinctively, even without knowing anything else about her apart from her being a sorceress.

The other men murmured their greetings, although Cary could tell not all of them were happy to see her. Rossi was frowning, while Biagi had the bad taste to ogle her cleavage. Sebastian nodded curtly and promptly folded out of the round, to everyone's surprise. He sauntered over to the bar and leaned casually on the counter, grazing out of the Chex Mix and peanuts bowl while Cary got him a beer.

"She's a sorceress all right," Bas said in a barely audible whisper, taking the cold bottle from Cary's hand. "A damn strong one, too."

It was all Cary could do not to glance at Leticia. He wanted to ask how Sebastian could judge that from simply looking at her, but that would be wasting precious moments. If he said the woman was a strong sorceress, Cary had better believe him and focus on the implications.

"Can she tell you're a sorcerer, too?" Cary asked, keeping his voice down and going through the motions of wiping a cocktail glass.

"Depends on how suspicious she gets. If I try anything now, she'll definitely pick up on that. I can't risk her probing either of us too far," Bas said in the same low tone and took a swig off his beer.

Cary had no idea why the sorceress would probe *him*, but either way, they were in pretty deep shit. Ty had postulated Tony might have the sorceress close by to guide him, but not having encountered her so far, they'd believed they wouldn't have to deal with that particular challenge. Leticia's presence now rendered Sebastian's presence practically useless. And that meant he and Cary would have to rely purely on trickery to pull this thing off, because jumping ship at this point was out of the question.

"I'll distract them somehow," Sebastian said, pushing away the half-empty bottle. "Watch out."

Cary nodded. He hoped Ty had heard the exchange, although he realistically could do nothing to help them. It would give him a heads up if the situation went sour, but if it did, Cary wasn't sure he could count on Ty to help him out. Whatever feelings Cary was stupid enough to have developed toward him, he knew all too well when push came to shove, sentiment was a hindrance.

He flexed his fingers and took a deep breath. These thoughts weren't at all relevant to the task at hand. This was no different than fishing a wallet out of someone's breast pocket. He'd done it plenty of times. Magic or no magic, there was no reason to be nervous about it.

Cary repeated the lie to himself, but it did nothing to reassure him.

"Are you in town for business, Ms. Giordano?" Gladden asked with a smile no doubt meant to be charming. The previous round had ended with Biagi raking in the winnings, though he still didn't come close to beating Sebastian's current score.

"You might say that," Leticia said, somewhat enigmatically, and didn't elaborate further. Cary could only guess that the "business" was closely related to Tony's experimental application of the amulet. She didn't join in the game, he noted. It was unusual to have someone sitting at the table without participating, but no one had the bad sense to point that out.

"Leticia is a corporate lawyer," Tony said. "She's here to work out a legal strategy for our new joint venture."

"Don't tell me you're buying a hotel casino." Biagi laughed.

"Not with the market being what it is," Tony said lightly. "I have something else in mind, but it's too early to talk about it."

Rossi, who no doubt was in the know on Giordano's political aspirations, if not the magical component that would make them a reality, grunted in agreement. Gladden glanced between the siblings curiously; Cary could almost see the possibilities running through his head.

"May I have a champagne, please?" Leticia said, waiving imperiously at Cary.

"And a gin and tonic," Sebastian piped.

The guy was knocking down drinks like there was no tomorrow, but to be fair, they all were. Cary could hardly tell Bas to lay off the alcohol if he wanted to keep up with the rest. He mixed the gin and tonic and poured the champagne, and brought them over to the table.

"To the lovely lady," Sebastian declared after they'd been served. He stood up and raised his glass in a toast of typical gallant chauvinism, which Cary assumed to be some sort of move. Leticia gave a tight smile as she sipped her champagne with mild disgust.

Sebastian beamed at her drunkenly and brought the glass to his lips. The effort of coordinating his movements, however, must have been a little too much for him in his state, because he swayed unsteadily, almost toppling over. The full glass slipped from his hand and tumbled onto the beige felt, splattering liquid all over the tabletop, the cards, and the chips.

For a fraction of a second, everyone froze in place, and in that moment, Cary moved in, taking advantage of the unexpected diversion while the attention of the players was rooted on the table. He swooped past Tony, his fingers brushing ever so lightly against the side of the man's jacket and dipping into the breast pocket. He felt the familiar roughness of the amulet's embossed surface and nearly recoiled at the heat. Cary remembered how warm it had felt against his skin when he'd used it in the past, but it was practically burning, the metal so hot it almost seared his fingertips. Perhaps it was something to do with Tony's way of using it, with no magic of his own to feed to the thing.

In any case, Cary didn't stop to think about it. The amulet slipped into the pocket of his trousers unnoticed, and he started to reach for Tony's hand for the ring.

"How clumsy of me!" Sebastian exclaimed as he tried, even more clumsily, to straighten up the mess. Tony leaned over to push his chips away from the spillage, and Cary quickly snatched his hand away. There was no way he could take the ring off Tony's finger without him noticing.

Instead, he rushed to wipe the table with the tea towel draped over his arm. He hoped it was enough to cover for him moving so closely to Giordano. Cary's heart was pounding in his ears, but it was drowned out in the din of annoyed exclamations, the sound of chairs being pushed back, and Bas's fussy apologies.

Cary dabbed at the spreading stain with the towel. The amulet was so hot it felt like it was burning a hole in his pocket, but he'd done it. He'd gotten it back. Cary could hardly believe it had been that easy—a mere flick of his hand, and there it was, back where it belonged.

"THAT'S ENOUGH," ROSSI snapped at him, and Cary stepped away hurriedly.

"Well, that was great fun, but I'm afraid that was my cue, gentlemen," Sebastian said. He checked in with the dealer, tipped the guy a hundred-dollar chip, and gathered his winnings. "I really should call it a night. So sorry for the mess."

Cary could tell that did not sit well with the others. Rossi leaned back in his chair, watching Bas through narrowed eyelids. Biagi, who was even drunker than Sebastian was pretending to be, glared at him with open resentment. Even Gladden dropped his fake smile and was frowning, looking from one man to another. Enjoying a bit of a lucky streak—up to a point—was okay, but no one had counted on Sebastian actually winning and making it out with the money.

"That's too bad, Mr. Monroe," Tony said. Cary could tell he was far from pleased but making an effort at appearing congenial. "Accidents happen, but there's no reason to cut and run just yet. Why don't you stay a while longer, keep us company?"

"Sorry to disappoint," Sebastian said. He shrugged apologetically and made toward the door.

Leticia stirred in her seat and sat up sharply, looking at her brother with concern. "I can't feel it on you," she said.

The forced smile slipped from Giordano's face like an ill-fitting mask. There was no mistaking the moment when realization dawned that things weren't going as seamlessly as they had the entire evening. His hand went to his breast pocket, looking for the amulet.

"No one leaves," Tony said quietly.

The tone of his voice gave everyone pause. Even Bas halted, his hand on the doorknob. Sensing a change in his boss's mood, Rossi half rose from his chair, ready for action.

"Which one of you took it?" Tony said in the same deceptively calm voice, as Leticia stood abruptly and paced around the room. The plush cream carpet muted the fall of her stiletto heels, and Cary could have sworn she was sniffing the air.

"Took what?" Gladden asked, frowning in confusion. The dealer reached slowly under the table, no doubt to press the emergency security call button, but a warning look from Rossi stopped him in his tracks.

Giordano didn't answer. Instead, he let his gaze wander from face to face, until finally it came to rest on Cary, who was trying his damndest to blend into the background.

"It was you," Tony said slowly, his eyes locking with Cary's.

Cary's mind reeled, scrambling frantically to come up with some kind of a response that would take him off the hook, but he already knew it was futile. Giordano wasn't stupid—Cary had been the only one, save Leticia, to come anywhere near enough to fish the amulet out of his pocket.

He took a step back, shaking his head mutely and hoping fervently he'd pass for an innocent bystander. He didn't have to fake being terrified, because he really was scared shitless.

At the same moment, Leticia paused and turned to face Sebastian, like a bloodhound catching the scent of its prey.

"A sorcerer," she hissed, making some sort of weird gesture with her perfectly manicured fingers. Sebastian flinched, as though she had struck him. "I should have known."

"What are you talking about?" Biagi huffed. Like Gladden, he looked from one person to the next with a flabbergasted expression that would almost be comical if Cary was in any mood to laugh. "What the fuck is going on here?"

His question hung in the air, unanswered. Without waiting for Giordano's instructions, Rossi moved to counter the perceived threat, placing himself between Leticia and Monroe and reaching inside his jacket for a weapon that was no doubt hidden there. At the same time, Tony took a step in Cary's direction, extending his hand.

"Hand it over. Now," he said in a deceptively quiet voice. The gleam in his eyes was like light reflected off a steel blade.

Cary slowly took the amulet out of his pocket. Its embossed surface was still warm, but no longer searing hot. The chain he'd used to wear it on around his neck was gone. He glanced toward the door, where Sebastian was still poised mid-flight, but he was too far away to make it. Tony was crowding him, and there were too many people, too much heavy furniture, and too many guns in his way.

There was nothing for it. No matter what he did, he was screwed. He raised the amulet above his head, desperately hoping he was making the right move.

"You want it? Come and get it. Catch!" Cary swung his arm in a wide arc and threw the amulet across the room.

Tony's head jerked to follow the amulet, just in time to see Sebastian catching it. "Get him!" he shouted, but Bas was already pushing through the door, even as Rossi lunged after him. Cary ducked, taking advantage of the momentary disruption, and ran around the poker table, ignoring the dealer's shocked face and Biagi's swearing. He was sure he was about to hear gunshots from the hallway, but there was no time to worry about that. At least Sebastian would lead Rossi and the bodyguards stationed in the hallway away. He doubted Tony would actually shoot him with so many witnesses around. If he could only reach the door...

He almost made it. He was so close, only a few steps away. But then Leticia raised her hand again, and he went flying halfway across the room, as if thrown by a powerful blast. He hit the wall so hard the lamp on the side table next to him rattled with the impact.

Ty, get out, Cary thought, but never had the chance to say it out loud. Pain blossomed in the back on his head and darkness closed in.

Chapter Fourteen

TY RACED DOWN the hallway, internally cursing the maze-like architecture. He had the floor map memorized, but every split second counted when he had to round so many corners on the way and look for the right set of escalators to take him down to the casino level.

The extraction definitely hadn't gone according to plan. When he heard Tony's sister, Leticia, make her entrance, he had a feeling it wasn't going to turn out well, and he'd been right. It was time to split, but not before he got Bas and Cary out.

Ty ran across the carpeted expanse of the casino, dodging tourists and waiters carrying trays of cocktails and beers. He knew he'd draw the attention of the hotel security within moments, but he had no time for stealth. He made it to the private poker room hallway just as Bas burst from it into the open, the dregs of a paralyzing spell he'd probably used on the guards still clinging to his fingers. The sorcerer shook his hands comically, as if trying to air-dry them.

"I got the amulet," Bas breathed. He took the heavy metal medallion out of his pocket and pressed it into Ty's hand, making it nearly go numb with residual magic. "Let's get the fuck out of here!"

"Where's Cary?"

"He can damn well look after himself! We've got a sorceress and a couple of angry mobsters to worry about!" Bas grabbed Ty by the arm, giving him no choice but to follow as they ran toward the parking garage escalator.

Glancing back, Ty saw Tony and Angelo Rossi emerge out of the same hallway. They both looked beyond pissed, and Ty silently prayed to whatever gods he could think of that Cary had managed to get away in the confusion. He hadn't heard gunshots through his earpiece (which he'd had to discard with the rest of the audio equipment in their suite), but a lot could have happened over the course of the last few minutes. And with magic involved, firearms weren't always necessary to permanently incapacitate someone. Medallion or not, Ty didn't want Cary to get hurt, and he would make sure of that—after he and Bas got out of the hotel alive.

They weaved their way through the throng of people in the main casino space. It looked exactly the same at any time of day, but the influx of visitors indicated it was late evening, and it hindered their progress. They rounded the Bellini Bar and made straight for the escalators, with pursuit hot on their heels. Neither Giordano nor Rossi had shouted, but the sight of them chasing after Ty and Bas through the packed floor was enough to alert security. Ty saw two guys in dark gray suits going after them, maneuvering the crowd with the ease of experience and familiarity. Two more appeared ahead to block their escape route, effectively cutting them off from the escalators.

"Shit." Ty glanced around without breaking stride, trying to figure out a different way to get to the underground parking lot without having to tackle the security folks. A called-in SWAT team was the last thing they needed. The casino entrance leading to the Strip would probably be closed off as well.

His plan B was taking a sharp left turn into the hallway known as Restaurant Row and hauling ass to the Palazzo to use the escalators there, or creating some sort of distraction that would allow them to double back unnoticed. But just as

Ty was about to pull Bas with him in the direction of the restaurants, he caught sight of Cary, still wearing the borrowed bartender uniform, skulking behind a row of slot machines. Their eyes locked, and Cary waved frantically to him, inviting him to follow.

How the hell had Cary gotten all the way from the private room ahead of them?

For that precious split second, Ty paused in indecision, torn between the instinct that told him to stick to his tried-and-true way of doing things, and the urge to succumb to the new and unknown force that drew him to Cary. There was no doubt in his mind about which was the better course of action. He couldn't trust Cary to know what he was doing.

And yet, there he was, in the open, after somehow managing to extract himself from the poker debacle, make his way across the entire floor without anyone noticing, and come for them. Perhaps he really was as good and as basically decent as that. Maybe just this once, after so many years of deeply ingrained mistrust, Ty could finally place his faith in someone else's willingness to watch his back.

The thoughts blazed through his mind with the speed of a stray comet, and then it was time to make a decision.

"Come on!" He tugged forcefully at Bas's sleeve and veered sharply in the direction of the slots. Registering the maneuver, Cary nodded once and sprinted toward the escalators. But instead of running straight into the guards blocking the access, he headed to the elevators that were tucked in the far corner, right next to the sparkling gift shop.

"What are you doing?" Bas hissed, but there was no time to explain. The guards moved to intercept them when they neared the escalators. Ty plowed on, just as Bas made a sharp gesture with his hand, sending the security guys sprawling on the floor amid the startled gasps and cries of nearby guests. There were more guards on their heels, and somewhere behind them were Giordano and Rossi, who were even more disinclined to give up the chase. Ty glanced at the escalator going down, but Cary had ignored it, despite their original plan. So he did too. He just had to hope against hope that Cary knew what he was about.

Instead of taking the elevator, Cary pushed through the heavy metal door that led into the stairwell and ran up the stairs, his footsteps thudding in the confined space. Ty and Bas followed a few seconds later, the pursuit so close on their heels Ty could practically feel their breath on the back of his neck. He slammed the door shut with a loud bang and strained to hold it in place.

"Lock it!" he yelled to Bas, who splayed his palms against the metal surface and muttered a repetitive chant. The edges of the door glowed faintly silver, and the outside noise fell completely away, as if cut off with a knife.

"Hey, Cary!" *Where the hell did he think he was going?!* The stairway led to the guest suits on the upper floors. That was hardly a viable escape route, given that the car was waiting for them in the underground parking lot, right next to the escalator exit. And they could hardly get there without running into another security team along the way. He was beginning to regret his inexplicable urge to blindly follow Cary instead of trusting his own tactics. "Wait up!"

Cary didn't answer. Ty pounded after him, with Bas close on his heels, swearing under his breath in a lulling language that Ty assumed to be some dialect of Fae. It was all going spectacularly badly, and Ty had no one else to blame but himself for trusting a newbie with such a crazy job. There were no sounds of pursuit coming from downstairs just yet, but that meant nothing. Every inch of the hotel was canvassed with cameras, so it would take no time at all for the security guards to figure out where they were headed.

They didn't stop till they reached the roof exit. Cary finally halted in front of the locked door, waiting for them to catch up as he struggled to regain his breath.

"The fuck you think you're doing?" Bas barked as they gained the landing, echoing Ty's thoughts in more straightforward terms. "Unless you have a helicopter waiting for us on that roof, we're screwed!" He looked at Ty accusingly. "It's your fault for not being able to keep your head out of his ass!"

Ty couldn't very well argue with that. Cary looked from Ty to Bas and back, but said nothing. Something in the calculating quality of his expression felt off, but Ty didn't have time to dwell on it.

"Just open the door," he told Bas, gesturing toward the code lock and glancing down the stairwell to make sure it was still clear.

"Close the door, open the door," Bas grumbled as he ran his fingers over the keypad until they heard a loud click. "I'm a sorcerer, not your fucking picklock."

He pushed the red metal bar in the middle of the door, and it opened onto the windswept roof. It was long past midnight, but the world around them sparkled and glittered with a myriad of colorful lights—the blue-green glow of the pools and the artificial canal from below, the illumination of the gargantuan hotel complexes, the specks of traffic winding along the Strip.

Cary brushed past Bas, stepping into the open space and heading straight toward the edge. Ty slammed the door behind them and scanned the surroundings, looking for another exit or some sort of fire escape. They were right in the middle of the Y-shaped rooftop, which was empty save for some ventilation vents and half a dozen satellite dishes. Their best bet was climbing down onto the rooftop levels of either of the "arms," which were slightly lower than the one they were standing on, and figuring a way to disrupt or trick the cameras with some kind of an illusion spell while taking another set of stairs down. They couldn't stay where they were much longer, and there was no place to hide, but at least they could take two minutes to hammer out a more solid plan of action than simply running in random directions and tackling security guards as if they were bowling pins.

"Ty," Bas said quietly behind him.

The sudden change of inflection in his voice made Ty turn sharply and meet his eyes. Bas's face looked blank in the ambient lighting, which cast sickly shadows in the hollows. He nodded toward Cary, who stood a few feet away, watching them, silhouetted against the glowing darkness of the sky. The wind tousled his hair, and there was an odd gleam in his eyes.

The strange vibe Ty got off Cary earlier intensified. The hairs on the back of his neck rose. He took a few steps toward Cary, but stopped halfway when he felt Bas gathering magical energy behind him. Ty was near to useless at using it, but he sure as hell could feel it pouring in from the ether in quantities sufficient to blow up a building.

Something was terribly wrong—well, more wrong than it already was—and he was struggling to understand it. At least, until Cary calmly pulled a gun out of his jacket and pointed it at them.

"Stand down, Mr. Monroe," Cary said in a voice that was not his own. "Or your friend gets it before you have the chance to utter a spell, I promise you."

Ty's throat went dry. His hand itched to go to his own gun, but who was he kidding? It was Cary. He wasn't going to shoot him. Whatever was going on here, it suddenly became painfully clear he couldn't see Cary get hurt. Right from the moment he'd met him, when he'd made the choice to help rather than abandon him to whoever had come after him that night, he'd wanted to keep him safe.

And could he really blame Cary for turning against him when all the while he was planning to do the same? It had always been about getting back the damn amulet—for both of them. The fragile feeling that was beginning to unfurl somewhere deep inside Ty's chest, like a vine climbing over walls that had up until now been impregnable, had nothing to do with it. He should have known better than to let it grow.

"Cary—" Ty began, over the tight bitterness lodged at the back of his throat.

"That's not Cary," Bas said curtly.

"What?"

The loud bang of the metal door made them both duck instinctively.

"I should have guessed it was you," Tony Giordano said, stepping out onto the rooftop from a twin access door on the other side of the central roof area. He was holding a Beretta M9 semiautomatic trained on Bas. The narrow band of Ty's ring gleamed mockingly on his finger.

Angelo Rossi followed right on his heels, his weapon in hand. The hotel security were nowhere to be seen, no doubt by design, though how Giordano had managed to lose them was anyone's guess. Of course, Ty and Bas dashing to the roof had played right into their pursuers' hands, making it that much easier to isolate them.

"You just had to meddle in other people's business, didn't you?" Tony said to Ty. "Looks like I made a mistake by letting you off the hook that time. Thought you'd prove useful someday. Well, live and learn, I guess. Now, hand over the medallion."

Ty inched back, his hand hovering over his breast pocket.

"If you're thinking about trying to use it, I suggest you reconsider," Tony said. "It won't work on me or my sister, and your little friend here will pay for it."

At the snap of his fingers, one of his bodyguards dragged a man trough the doorway to stand beside them. His hands were bound in front of him with a zip tie, and he was wearing the casino uniform, but Ty recognized him even before he raised his head and glared at Tony in defiance. It was Cary.

Ty whirled around to the other Cary, the one who had led them to the roof and who was standing near the edge of it.

Bas had been right. That wasn't Cary, not any longer. Leticia stood there, wearing her true form and an elegant pantsuit, calmly pointing the gun at Ty's head.

Relief was the absolutely last thing Ty should have felt at that moment, but the sheer intensity of it left him dizzy. It looked like they were all about to die anyway, so it shouldn't have mattered that Cary hadn't betrayed him. But for some reason, it did. Somehow, it became the point of focus, a thought Ty held on to like a lifeline.

Tony grabbed Cary by the arm unceremoniously and shoved him down. Cary's knees hit the concrete hard, and he winced.

"Let me go, you fucktard," he demanded, but Ty could practically smell his fear. He was sure Tony could too. Cary had played a losing hand, and he knew it. And there was absolutely nothing he could do about it.

It was all Ty's fault, really. Had he found the time and the opportunity to tell Cary about his powers, he wouldn't be as defenseless as he was now. Naturally, a fledgling practitioner was no match against an experienced sorceress like Leticia, but at least he could have done something, anything, to perhaps avoid being captured.

"Cary," Ty said urgently.

The other man looked up. Their eyes met, but there was nothing in Cary's gaze but fear and despair. Cary didn't believe Ty would save him—perhaps with a good reason.

"I lied," Ty said, his voice sounding strangely distant in his ears. "The coin wasn't special. It was you."

It was all he dared to say in front of Tony and his sister, in hopes of Cary somehow getting the message. *It was you. Your magic. Your powers.*

Confusion flickered in Cary's eyes. He opened his mouth, but Tony kicked his leg, eliciting a low grunt from him.

"Enough bullshit. The medallion. Now." Giordano pressed the barrel of his gun to Cary's nape.

The moment stretched, with only the distant noise of honking cars and faint music from the hotel courtyard breaking the tense silence. As the seconds trickled by, Cary's expression shuttered, his earlier defiance replaced with grim resignation. He took a deep, shaky breath, no doubt bracing himself for the shot.

It could not come to this. Ty would not let it happen; he would not just let Cary die. There was so much still ahead of Cary, so much he could still accomplish, so much he could still become. There was so much Ty still had to say to him. And now all this potential, all this incredible life that bubbled inside Cary, would be gone in a puff of smoke.

Ty moved before he could think about what he was doing, leaping onto the raised concrete outer wall that ran along the edge of the roof. Before anyone had the chance to react, he took the amulet from his pocket, holding it in his hand above the 475-foot drop to the courtyard below.

"You want it? Come and get it," he echoed Cary's previous taunt to Tony.

Tony clutched Cary's shoulder to keep him in place and pointed his weapon at Ty, but hesitated. The impact of the bullet could push Ty over the edge, taking the amulet with him. For a split second, everyone froze in a mute tableau on the verge of violence.

Out of the corner of his eye, Ty saw Leticia throwing out her hand in his direction. The air thrummed with the force of released energy, but instead of hitting him, it exploded into a thousand tiny blazing fragments, like a storm wave hitting a rock. Ty ducked, shielding his eyes with his other hand, but not before he could glimpse Bas and Leticia locked in battle, both of them surrounded by an almost blinding glow, the energy surging between their outstretched hands like bolts of electricity. The air crackled around them with the promise of a thunderstorm.

They were pretty evenly matched. For a second there Ty wasn't sure who would emerge on top, but then Sebastian staggered and took a step back. Seeing her opponent crack under the pressure, Leticia stepped forward, and the glow around her intensified as she gathered force for a deadly blow.

Ty clutched the amulet tighter in his hand and whipped out the gun from its holster. The shot rang out across the roof, but the bullet had missed its target by a wide arc, its trajectory distorted by the force fields that engulfed the two sorcerers. He knew it wouldn't do any real damage. His intention was to distract rather than kill, to give Bas that much-needed moment to rally, but it would hardly matter to the would-be victim.

Leticia spun around to face him—a furious goddess of ancient times, her dark hair blowing in the wind, and her eyes smoldering with fiery rage. Ty didn't even have time to draw a last breath. The blast that had been intended for Bas hit him with the force of an avalanche. Suddenly, there was nothing beneath his feet, and he was falling, Cary's shrill "No!" ringing in his ears.

Chapter Fifteen

A BUMP IN the road jolted him awake. Cary jerked instinctively, hitting the side of his head painfully in the confines of the car trunk.

They've been driving for hours and hours, and eventually he'd dozed off in a fitful sleep, lulled by the motion of the car. At first, he'd tried to memorize the twists and turns of road, but soon gave up on that. All he could gather was that at some point the car had taken the highway, going straight and fast, but the direction was anyone's guess.

He'd tried to make as much noise as he could after Giordano's men had stuffed him into the trunk, but with his hands bound with a zip tie and his mouth taped shut, there was only so much he could do. His head and muscles throbbed dully, probably due to the awkward pose and the shortage of oxygen.

But Cary barely registered the discomfort. A deeper ache had settled somewhere beneath his breastbone, an ache that had little to do with his physical state. He felt hollow. The scene from the Venetian played over and over in his mind, and Cary kept seeing Ty's startled expression the second before he'd tumbled from the roof.

Shocked into numbness, he'd stared into the empty air as the afterglow of the magic dissipated. He saw Sebastian running toward the edge and peering down into the void, his hands outstretched almost comically in that "Superman swoops to rescue Lois midair" pose. But his movements had been far too slow to make any difference. There was no swooping down from that rooftop.

Somewhere in the distance far below, the police sirens had wailed, spurring his captors into action. Rossi had thrown open the roof exit door and ushered everyone to the stairs. Even Leticia abandoned her angry fury routine and hurried inside without further comment.

"Get him down," Tony had ordered brusquely, and Cary was hoisted, none too gently, by Rossi and one of the bodyguards, after a piece of duct tape was slapped over his mouth. Their little party made its way down the stairs and pressed on right past all the people on the main floor, but no one tried to stop them, not even the security guards that swarmed around like angered bumblebees. That must have been Leticia's magic at work again—something that didn't make them quite invisible, but difficult to notice. Ty had mentioned something like that was possible, hadn't he?

Cary didn't remember if he tried to struggle. He'd been so utterly dazed that chunks of time seemed to have passed without leaving an imprint on his brain. But he must have, because at one point he was shoved into the trunk of a car in an underground garage, with his hands still bound. He thought Giordano and his sister might have been in the same car, but he wasn't sure. All he could think about was that terrible moment, suspended in time.

Ty was dead. No one could survive such a fall—except by miraculously hanging on to a balcony railing or landing in a pool. But that shit only happened in movies, and Ty wasn't Batman. He was dead, and the amulet was gone with him, and Cary had done nothing to prevent it. It was his fault for being careless and stupid enough to have been caught in the first place, for being so fucking paralyzed by fear and helplessness that he couldn't prevent the man he'd come to care for from falling to his death.

A sob threatened to wrack him, and he blinked rapidly, holding back the angry tears. Cary didn't know for what purpose Giordano was dragging him along now, but it couldn't be anything good. Well, whatever these people wanted from him, they weren't about to get it easily. He was neither a sorcerer nor a fighter, but he'd do whatever he could to make them pay for what they'd done. For everything they'd taken from him.

Surprisingly, it wasn't the loss of the amulet he was regretting the most.

Cary sniffed and attempted to wiggle his hands out of the zip tie. His granddad hadn't been a proper escape artist, but he'd briefly dabbled in escapology sometime in the early '80s, and he'd taught Cary everything he knew about various knots and how to extricate himself from many types of bindings. After taking on his act, Cary had researched ways to escape more modern and pertinent types of restraints, such as paracord and zip ties. You could learn a lot of weird stuff online, if you knew how to look. But he hadn't had the chance to incorporate any of those into his performance. He was sorely out of practice, and his movements were limited by the confines of the trunk. Still, he kept trying right until the car took a sharp turn and entered what sounded like a gravel road. He bumped his shoulder painfully and groaned as he lost his grip on the plastic.

At length the car stopped, the engine going off. There came the sounds of doors being opened and shut and feet shuffling on gravel. The hood of the trunk popped open, making Cary squirm and squint at the morning light like some creature found under an overturned rock.

"Get up." A strong hand hauled him up. Cary tried to kick with his legs, but his limbs were too cramped for it to have any impact. Two large men grabbed him like a sack of potatoes between them and dragged him up the path to a large wooden house. They were surrounded by thick forest, and he glimpsed the brilliant blue surface of a lake glimmering between the trees before he was carried inside.

The house looked opulent, more like an alpine lodge than a cabin. It also appeared dishearteningly secluded. A quick look around showed no other rooftops peeking through the trees, and no sounds of either traffic or human voices reached the serene spot. He didn't have a chance to inspect the surroundings further, though, because he was taken to a side door that opened onto a dim flight of stairs leading down, no doubt to the basement. His captors didn't bother taking him all the way, and instead, shoved him unceremoniously down the last few steps into the gloom before retreating and slamming the door behind them.

Cary hit his knees on the concrete floor—again—and grunted in pain. He was once more plunged in darkness, but a little light filtered through a narrow sliver beneath the basement door. After letting his eyes adjust, he looked around.

The basement, if indeed it was one, was small and narrow and smelled of damp, though the concrete floor was dry. He was completely alone. There was nothing in the space, not even shelving. There were, however, faded stains on the floor and walls, the origin of which he refused to consider.

If not for the tape, Cary would have tried screaming and calling for help, though what good that would have done, he had no idea. *Must be nice having your own lake house with water access and private security,* he thought bitterly. One could get away with a lot of shit when one had a convenient spot to dispose of bodies, and people willing to look the other way.

Well, Cary would not be easily disposed of. They'd made a mistake in not blindfolding him. There was still a chance, a possibility of escape. There was no time to grieve or to make sense of the tangle of painful emotions that gripped his heart. He had to act fast, before Giordano and his buddies were done assigning blame and decided to take it out on him.

He rolled over and sat up, propping his back against the cold concrete wall. There was no telling how much time he had, so he'd have to act fast. His hands were bruised where he'd scraped them against the plastic ties while inside the trunk, and he flexed his fingers to get the blood flowing. The ties proved too tight to wiggle out of, but the tighter they were, the easier it was to actually break them. There was a trick to doing just that. All he had to do was stand, lift his bound hands up, and bring them down sharply while flaring out his elbows. It wasn't quite as easy as it sounded, but if he could just position the locking mechanism right between his wrists—

The basement door opened, flooding the space with unexpected light. Cary froze in place, absently thinking he must look like trussed game thrown into a cellar to cool. Apparently, the caucusing hadn't taken long. And why should it have, when it was painfully clear who the scapegoat was in this story.

Tony and Leticia descended into the basement, closely followed by Angelo Rossi. Leticia didn't look the least bit affected by a sleepless, action-filled night. Not a smudge of mascara marred her cheeks, not a crease ruined the perfection of her white blazer. Of course, this level of neatness was more easily achieved when one hadn't spent the night crammed into a car trunk.

On the other hand, Tony looked like shit. His eyes were sunken, his smooth skin almost gray and lackluster, and the sheen of perspiration covered his forehead. Cary guessed these to be symptoms of the draining effect of the magical energy from when Tony had used the amulet. Cary would have gloated if he had the leisure to focus on anything other than his imminent death.

Rossi came up to Cary and tore the duct tape off his mouth in one swift movement. Cary wisely bit back the expletives and merely licked his lips to ease the burn.

"Now, *Mr. Mars*," Tony said from where he stood at the bottom of the stairs. Despite the drawl and the slightly mocking tone, there was no mistaking he was seriously pissed. "We're gonna have a little chat."

Rossi kicked Cary in the stomach, the pain sharp and vicious, as he doubled over and wheezed. Rossi then crouched by his side and ripped open Cary's shirt. With complete disregard for Cary's snarl of outrage, he tore off the now useless mic wire taped to his chest. Cary winced at the burn.

"Where are your associates?" Tony asked.

"How the hell should I know?"

Angering Giordano any further was a bad idea, but Cary's inherent obstinacy reared its ugly head in the face of the pointlessness of the questioning. His granddad had always said he was stubborn as a mule and just as stupid. He might as well live up to that. For as long as he had left to live, anyway.

Rossi rose and kicked him again, harder this time, aiming for his kidneys. Cary moaned and shrank away, nausea rising in his throat.

"Cut it out! I don't know anything. I only met them a week ago. I just wanted to get my family heirloom back."

"This Monroe—the sorcerer. Where can we find him?"

"I don't know," Cary said. He hoped he sounded sincere enough, because he didn't want to find out what being tortured for information felt like. He certainly sounded panicked to his own ears. "We met him in Vegas. I have no idea where he is."

This earned him another blow. But it occurred to him through the pain that this insistence must mean that Giordano believed Monroe, who'd also had to haul ass from the rooftop, was still on the loose and somehow in possession of the amulet. Perhaps, with the police arriving and the commotion that would surround a man falling off the hotel roof, there'd been no time to search for the amulet, or worry about what Sebastian was up to.

Whatever Giordano's assumptions were and whatever he was trying to accomplish, one thing was clear. Cary was absolutely and completely screwed. He had to buy himself some more time, at least.

"Please," he begged, trying to sound as pitiful as possible. Frankly, it was no stretch at all. "Please, I don't know anything. I'm sorry I stole from you. Just let me go. I promise I'll keep quiet."

For a second, he thought Rossi was going to kick him in the guts again. But then, surprisingly, Leticia stepped closer and crouched beside him. Cary tried to move away, but she grabbed his jaw in a viselike grip, surprisingly strong for such a petite woman. A shiver ran down Cary's spine that had nothing to do with the coolness of the basement. Her fingers felt hot on his skin, almost burning, and he stilled, looking into her dark eyes, his fear spiking.

She could do anything to him. Granted, any of Tony's henchmen could beat the shit out of him and then shoot him in the head, but for some reason, the dark promise in this woman's eyes was much more terrifying. And he had nothing to defend against that kind of power. Ty had thrown some obscure hint just before all hell had broken loose, something to do with Cary's magic, but right now he felt about as magical as a gutted fish.

"Ah. I see it in you now. A touch of magic." Leticia chuckled, almost good-naturedly, as if in answer to his unspoken thoughts. "But it's not going to help you now. You poor little thing." Her grip tightened to the point of pain. "You shouldn't have let your friends get you into all this trouble. Now look at you. They got away, and you're left alone to deal with the consequences. Not much of a friendship, is it?"

Cary tried shaking his head, but she held him fast. Her eyes, glinting like fiery jewels in the faint light, seemed to bore into his mind.

"Perhaps not a friendship after all? This other fellow...Ty, is it? He seemed awfully concerned about your safety. Was willing to follow whom he believed to be you, no questions asked. Do you think he'd be willing to trade the amulet for your life? Or will he abandon you for a chance to make a quick buck?"

It he hadn't been lying on solid ground, Cary would have thought he was falling. His stomach lurched and his heart seemed to slow. She couldn't possibly mean what he thought she meant. Could she?

"He's dead," he managed through stressed teeth, afraid his voice would crack.

"Dead?" Leticia's musical laugh echoed in the tiny space. "Oh, no. He's very much alive, as it pains me to say it. He and his pet sorcerer, Monroe."

It's some kind of a trick, Cary told himself firmly. He saw Ty fall off that roof. There was no way anyone could have survived that unless they were some kind of superhero.

Or a magician, a voice whispered tauntingly in his head.

But Cary shook it off. He knew Ty was no magician. Leticia was simply toying with him, trying to elicit some sort of response, make him more vulnerable.

And yet, that part of his soul he forbade himself to look at too closely—the one that was gaping open like a jagged wound, leaking hope—trembled. If Ty was truly alive...maybe he could let himself breathe again without feeling like there was an iron band around his chest.

"Maybe he wants you to think he's dead," Leticia said, watching him closely. He couldn't fool himself into believing she hadn't picked up on his churning emotions, but right now, he couldn't help it. "But don't worry, sweetie. We'll find him for you."

Cary shuddered at her tone.

"If that bastard Ty has the amulet, I know how to make sure he gets the message," Tony said, addressing his sister. "Do you think he'll really be willing to negotiate for this pup?"

Leticia shrugged and got up gracefully, finally releasing him and wiping her fingers on her pants. Cary slumped back to the floor in relief.

"It's worth a try, but I wouldn't get my hopes up. The boy's cute, but I'm betting he didn't go to all this ridiculous trouble to get a bauble back for his boyfriend. Someone else must have paid him to retrieve it."

"Come on, then." Tony extended his hand to help her up the narrow stairs.

"Want me to rough him up, boss?" Rossi asked, eying Cary dispassionately.

"I believe he's earned it. Just remember we need him recognizable." With that, Tony and Leticia were gone, leaving Cary—as Leticia had so aptly put it—to deal with the consequences.

Chapter Sixteen

TY RUBBED HIS aching shoulders awkwardly and flexed his back. Hitting a wall of suddenly solidified air a second after tumbling off a roof was infinitely preferable to hitting the ground from thirty-six stories up, but it still hurt like a bitch.

He could see traces of panic in his eyes as he looked at himself in the bathroom mirror of the cheap motel room. The tattoos around the long scar on his side tingled as he ran his hand over the exposed skin. Bruises were beginning to form on his shoulders and on his chest, where Leticia's blow had hit him, but that was a small price to pay for being alive and kicking.

He sighed and splashed some cold water on his face to calm himself down. After turning off the tap, he pulled the amulet out of his jeans pocket. He didn't want to go back into the cramped bedroom where Bas had been pacing practically from the moment they'd arrived. If he were a cat, he'd be lashing his tail and hissing at Ty in a hyped state of annoyance and agitation. As it was, he was merely relegating his displeasure verbally, and rather explicitly.

Both of them were beyond exhausted and more than a little riled up. Ty was still unsteady on his feet, the aftershocks of him coming too close to being splattered amidst the decorative pools and walkways of the Venetian's courtyard coursing through his body. In one terrifying moment he'd plummeted, the air whooshing past him, and in the next, he'd been bounced back upward on an invisible trampoline. It was pure luck no one had chanced to see it, especially the part when Bas managed to grab him by the hand mid-flight as Ty was flung upwards, and the impact had sent them both rolling on the windswept rooftop.

After, they'd barely managed to get away before the police swarmed the casino and put the hotel on lockdown. And Bas had scarcely been able to cast a simple spell to lift the barrier gate and get the Chevy out of the underground parking lot.

Both of them were too wired to sleep. While it seemed no one had tailed them, they weren't completely out of danger.

Ty absently traced his thumb over the intricate design on the amulet's surface. His thoughts kept circling back to the events of the evening in an endless loop of helpless frustration. How could he have been so blindly stupid not to realize he was being duped? How could he not have seen it wasn't really Cary he was following? Guise magic required huge effort; to maintain the illusion so long and so well was testimony enough to Leticia's power. But he should have recognized the ruse for what it was. It was his fault Cary was currently being held captive by a mafioso and his sorceress sister. A very pissed off mafioso and sorceress. It was his fault for getting Cary involved in all of this in the first place, for agreeing to team up. For all he knew, Cary was already—

No. He refused to acknowledge that possibility. There was still hope, and he wouldn't just walk away. His old self would have, but he could no longer deny that he was changed. He wasn't the same person who had walked into the Incredible Mr. Mars' dressing room what felt like ages ago.

"We have to get Cary," he said, coming out of the bathroom and cutting off Bas's solo rant mid-sentence.

Sebastian, whose trajectory had just reached the entry door, turned to look at Ty as if he'd suddenly sprouted wings—with horns and hooves for good measure.

"Are you insane?" he demanded.

"We can't just leave him."

"You got what you wanted," Bas pointed out. "He's a sweet kid and all, but is he worth sticking your neck out for? Giordano doesn't give a crap about him, but he sure as hell won't let *you* go with a slap on the wrist."

Ty looked at the amulet clutched in his hand. The etching on its surface had left faint indentations in the skin. They'd fade in a few moments, without any trace of ever having been there. But other things weren't as easily dismissed. Things like betrayal. Rejection. Love. All the things he'd sworn not to be hurt by again. Their marks were permanent, and their scars cut too deep.

After the falling-out with Leland, he'd felt so lost. Leland Bernard had been his mentor for more than ten years, the only man who'd come close to being a father to him. He'd been the only one who had taken care of him, who had exhibited any sort of concern for his well-being. His casual dismissal, after Ty had believed there was a real attachment between them, had hurt more than anything.

The thought of Cary experiencing that same pain was more unbearable than the thought of Cary getting killed. Somehow the promise of a hefty fee and the satisfaction of rubbing Giordano's nose in his failure paled in comparison.

He opened his mouth, without any clear idea of how he was going to answer Bas, but was interrupted by his phone loudly vibrating on the nightstand. Ty snatched it up, having recognized the number.

"What do you want, AJ?"

"What, no 'hello,' no 'how's it going,' just straight up 'what do you want'?" AJ complained in a deliberately whiny tone of voice.

"I'm really not in the mood," Ty said curtly.

"Okay, fine, be like that. Oh, and by the way, next time you get yourself involved with organized crime, kindly leave me out of it. It's getting kinda old."

Ty sat down on the edge of the bed. "What do you mean?" he asked, although he already had a pretty good idea where this was going.

"I just got a call from your buddy Tony Giordano," AJ said, abandoning his simpering. "He made it clear in no uncertain terms that he wants to make an exchange. The "item" for your "associate" and your ring. Do I want to know what he's talking about?"

"Not really," Ty muttered. He glanced at Bas, who was listening in on the conversation, and made a face. Getting his ring back was what he'd wanted all along, but as valuable as it was, it wasn't enough of an incentive to risk open confrontation. But the promise of the ring coupled with the prospect of saving Cary... It seemed Giordano was aware of Ty's partiality toward Cary and was betting on capturing his attention this way. It rankled that his feelings must have been that transparent. Exposing his weaknesses was a bad idea. Having those weaknesses in the first place was a slippery slope that led to...well, precisely this kind of scrape. "When and where?"

There was some rustling, as if AJ was shuffling papers around his desk. "Tomorrow night. At a cabin he has on Lake Tahoe. Look, I don't know what you got yourself into, but I gotta remind you that my client is waiting for that amulet. If you have it—and I suspect you do—I suggest delivering it to him and getting the fuck out of Dodge."

"That's mighty daring of you," Ty said. "What makes you think Tony won't come looking for you if I don't show up?"

"Oh, don't worry about me. I've already set up an alternative base of operations, as it were. And I really should be billing you for the cost of moving all my stuff on a moment's notice," AJ complained. "You have no compassion for my poor nerves."

Bas snorted loudly, struggling to suppress his laughter. Ty waived at him to be quiet.

"Listen to me, AJ. I'm afraid your client is bound to be disappointed. And since you're already involved, I'm gonna need you to deliver a message back to Giordano. Ain't no way in hell I'm meeting him on his own turf. You tell him to meet me at ten PM tomorrow at a place of my choosing if he wants his precious 'item' so badly. I'll text you the coordinates."

He disconnected the call before AJ had a chance to respond and quickly typed a text. Once he was sure it went through, he took out the battery and threw it on the nightstand.

The sound of Bas clearing his throat was overwhelmingly loud in the sudden silence.

"That's...gutsy," he observed. "What makes you think Giordano would agree to any of it? Aren't you worried he'll just say 'screw it,' get rid of the kid, and take his sweet time hunting you down?"

Ty *was* worried. In fact, he was scared out of his mind. But if he wanted to have any sort of chance to see this thing through and keep both himself and Cary alive, he had to raise the stakes and make Tony come to him instead of the other way around.

"I have what he wants, so I have the upper hand here," Ty said with a conviction he wasn't feeling. "Besides, after the way I stole it right in front of his buddies, he'll do anything to get back at me. He's cocky enough to believe he'll be able to do it anywhere. He'll just make sure to pack enough firepower."

"Not to mention his sister," Bas said. "That one's more dangerous than a truckload of trained operatives with semiautomatics."

"Encouraging as always."

"No, really. You're not seriously considering going... wherever it is you think you're going, are you?" Bas sat down on one of the twin beds the room offered. His expensive suit was rumpled and covered in dust, and his hair was sticking out in a crazed imitation of a magpie's nest. "AJ may believe Giordano will honor a deal, but you and I know better. The real deal here is—'I'm gonna kill you, take your magical toys, and bury you under a pine tree'."

"I know," Ty said. He slipped the amulet back in his pocket and rubbed the bridge of his nose. Maybe it was the exhaustion forcing him into bad decisions. He needed to get at least a couple of hours of sleep to be able to think clearly.

"And not to put a damper on things, but your lover boy might be dead already," Bas pointed out, none too gently.

"I know," Ty repeated.

Bas looked him in the eye for a long moment and then sighed and shook his head. "You're going to do this anyway."

"Yep." He got up and took his jacket off.

"My, my, how the mighty have fallen," Bas said. He leaned back on his elbows on the bed, watching Ty with half-hooded eyes. "Never thought I'd see you succumb to foolish heroics and all that self-sacrificing for love nonsense."

"Shut up," Ty said halfheartedly. "Nobody's sacrificing anything. The goal is getting us both out alive."

He didn't like being put in a corner. Whatever he'd said, it was Giordano who had the advantage, with him holding a live hostage—and Cary was still alive. Ty refused to think otherwise.

"I'm sorry I can't drop you back at San Francisco," he said, turning and looking down at Bas. "I don't have time to make the round trip and set things up by tomorrow night. Giordano will most likely want to arrive at the rendezvous point ahead of time as well, to make his own arrangements. You got your winnings from the casino, right?"

Sebastian nodded. "What are you going to do?" he asked.

"I don't know. Get some rest, for starters." Ty sighed and kicked off his shoes before sprawling on the bed.

"That woman is going to fry you alive if you try going in there with any kind of magic." Bas was apparently unwilling to let the subject drop. "She's a damn strong one. And your dabbling is frankly no match—"

"I'm well aware of that," Ty snapped.

His relationship with magic had always been a fickle one. There was no question he got by with what he had, but it was never enough. It certainly hadn't been enough for Leland, who hadn't bothered hiding his disappointment with his student's progress. It was baffling to Ty why his mentor had bothered with him in the first place when it must have been apparent, even at an early age, that he wasn't destined to become a great mage. He'd never asked, and it'd seemed pointless after they parted ways.

So yes, Ty was very much aware of his shortcomings, and he didn't need Sebastian reminding him of them. He had to focus on his tactical advantages, few as they might be.

"I'm simply pointing out that going up against someone like that with no one to back you up is unwise, darling," Bas said. He sat up and began to unlace his shoes.

Ty closed his eyes for a moment as he digested that. He must have been too tired to think, because Bas couldn't possibly mean what he thought he meant.

"You're not suggesting going with me?" he asked incredulously.

"Why not?"

"Why not? Weren't you the one calling me crazy for wanting to rescue my—" he fumbled for the right word for a second and settled for "—friend."

"Friend," Bas repeated meaningfully and wiggled his eyebrows as he pulled his shoes off.

"Do you want me to spell out a fucking love letter? We all get what I mean. And it doesn't negate the point—which is you being suddenly willing to put your ass on the line after trying to talk me out of doing the same."

"God, you're cranky when you're tired." Bas rolled his eyes and took his suit jacket off before settling down on the comforter. "Okay, fine. While I do think it's a terrible idea, your chances of coming out of this alive would be much better if somebody were there to help you. And, I suppose, well, you *are* my friend. And by 'friend' I don't mean being besotted with your pretty face, mind you."

Ty let that last comment slide.

"I can't offer you anything in return, though," he said, still reluctant to agree. Him risking his own skin was one thing; putting Sebastian in harm's way was another matter entirely, even if he was volunteering of his own free will. Especially if he was volunteering. A deal was a deal. A favor wasn't something he knew how to accept.

"You've got that Fae bargaining streak ingrained too deeply," Bas observed enigmatically. He divested himself of the rest of his clothing before diving under the sheets. "I've got the money in casino chips. There's hardly anything else

I could ask for. But if it bothers you that much, how about you owing me a favor?”

“Can do.” Ty lowered his head on the pillow. His thoughts were too jumbled to form a more coherent solution anyway, and they had to make an early start tomorrow. He doubted he'd be able to sleep with so much worry gnawing at his heart, but he must have been more tired than he thought, because he was fast asleep moments after closing his eyes.

Chapter Seventeen

THE COMING TO was a lot more painful this time around, the various aches having nothing to do with a cramped trunk ride. The cool concrete was rough under his cheek, and his hands were numb in the tight bonds.

Cary moaned and rolled over onto his other side, wincing as sore muscles and scraped knuckles protested the exertion. He was once again plunged into darkness, with no idea of how much time had passed since Rossi had left him. He'd passed out at some point during the beating when his head accidentally hit the hard wall. The bump there was throbbing, but thankfully, he had a thick enough skull. Tony would have probably chewed Rossi's head off if he'd killed Cary, especially after his admonition to be careful. But that was poor consolation.

Not knowing how long he'd been out was quickly getting old. He didn't have much time to waste. Whether Tony succeeded in finding Ty (even if Cary was still boggled by the possibility of him being alive) or gave up on the idea of reaching him, Cary was better off hightailing it out of there. He didn't want to be a pawn in anyone's games—pawns being the most expendable pieces on the board. He had no illusions as to his chances of survival once Tony got what he wanted. Cary had already proved himself a pesky nuisance. Giordano wouldn't want a repetition of the Vegas fiasco, when it was so much simpler to make Cary Westfield disappear entirely after he got what he wanted from Ty.

There was, of course, another possibility, one that was far more probable. Ty could simply turn down Tony's offer, or fail to respond to it at all. If Ty was, in fact, alive and on the run, he'd most likely lie low somewhere till the shitstorm blew over.

As much as Cary wanted to believe his tentative connection with Ty had meant something more to the other man than a simple business partnership with side perks, he couldn't delude himself into thinking Ty would give up something so valuable—not to mention risk his life in the process—to rescue him.

Cary longed to see Ty again, to make sure with his own eyes that he was truly alive and well, but he didn't intend to wait on either his or Giordano's mercy. He had to escape, and he could only count on himself to do that.

With an effort, Cary rolled onto his back, groaning. Earlier, he'd considered screaming for help, but now he wanted to draw as little attention to himself as possible.

Other than the bump on his head and a bloodied lip, it didn't seem like he'd sustained any serious injuries. His ribs felt bruised, but he could breathe and move freely enough, and nothing felt broken. Now all he had to do was get the binds off his hands.

He got to his feet, swaying a little. His body was sore, and when he attempted to break the zip tie by swinging his arms down sharply and pulling sideways, like he'd intended to do before the Giordanos showed up, he couldn't quite gather enough strength needed to pull the plastic apart. After a few tries his hands hurt like crazy, and all he managed to show for his efforts was newly scraped skin.

Damn. This wasn't going to work—at least not until he had the chance to rest his hands a bit, and he couldn't waste any more time.

Cary sat down again. There was another option, a more cumbersome one. But fuck it, it wasn't like he could wait for a miraculous rescue.

He untied the laces of his dress shoes with both hands, tied the laces together, and then secured the resulting string around the right shoe toe with a bowline knot. The trickiest part was getting the loose end of the string inside the zip tie ring, between his wrists. There wasn't enough light to see what he was doing, and the bonds were almost too tight to accommodate even something as thin as a shoelace, but eventually he succeeded, using his fingers and teeth. He then tied the string around the toe of the other shoe much in the same fashion.

He moved his feet experimentally in a seesaw movement, testing the knots. The shoelace wasn't nearly as long as he'd have liked, encumbering the movement, but it still created a friction saw that tugged forcefully at the zip tie. With a renewed determination, Cary propped himself against the wall and moved his legs as hard and as fast as he could, holding them just above the floor.

When the zip tie snapped, it came almost as a surprise. Cary bit back a cry of triumph and paused, waiting out the tingling sensation as the blood flowed back into his fingertips. When he was sure he'd regained full control of his hands, he untied the string and laced up his shoes again, fumbling gracelessly in the darkness. He could hardly risk his footwear falling off at the wrong moment.

He got up slowly, using the wall as support. With the urgency to get his hands free gone, his head felt like it was going to explode, and his back ached as if he was an arthritic old man who'd lost his cane. Cary hoped he didn't have a concussion; running off into the night with his head spinning was hardly going to take him far. He hobbled in the general direction of the stairs. The light that had come under the door earlier was much fainter now, almost nonexistent. It must be nighttime. That would work in his favor, once he managed to extricate himself from his makeshift prison.

God, how crazy was it that only two weeks ago his biggest worry was whether his show had sold enough tickets for him to afford rent. It seemed Granddad had had a point—Cary did have a special knack for getting himself into trouble.

The basement door was locked, of course. But the lock on it was a simple one, and there was no latch on the outside, as far as he could recall. Picking it would be fairly simple, but the pockets of his Venetian uniform trousers were empty, save for that damn quarter Ty'd given him what seemed so long ago, and which he'd been carrying for good luck.

Cary took it out, its textured surface warm against his skin. Just a regular coin, Ty had said right before he was slammed off that roof. But why lie in the first place, telling Cary it was magical? And if it wasn't, where had the magic come from?

Could Ty and Leticia be right? Did he really have that talent, or was it just another ruse, a part of some elaborate deception? It hardly seemed likely that he could be a magician. A real one, too.

He flipped the coin idly, guided by some half-formed impulse.

"Heads," he whispered before it landed back in his palm, and crouched to look at it in the faint light.

It was heads.

Cary slipped the coin back in his pocket and stood up, a strange emotion tightening his chest. He could hardly compete with Sebastian or Leticia (or even Ty, for that matter) but maybe, just maybe, he had enough of a spark to help him out of a tight spot.

Well, there was only one way to test it.

He still needed something to trigger the lock from inside, and in lieu of anything else he could use the hard plastic tips of the zip tie. It was nowhere close to a pick, but when life gave you lemons, and all that.

His head pounded as he crouched opposite the door. He inserted one of the tips into the upper portion of the key slit and then pushed the other beneath it as far as it would go. He closed his eyes and concentrated, wiggling the lower tip in and out gently. What was it Ty and Sebastian had said about spells? The wording didn't matter as long as he was focused on what he was doing. So Cary relaxed as much as he could, keeping his eyes firmly closed, and just...let himself feel.

The air around him was cold and damp, and the silence weighed down heavily on his mind, an oppressive presence that was disturbed only by his breathing and the scraping of the plastic inside the lock. But there was also something else there. Perhaps his imagination was running wild, fueled by desperation, but he thought he could sense the faint stirrings of that energy Ty had always been rambling on about. The force that held everything together. Like in *Star Wars*. Where was R2-D2 when you needed him?

Stop being silly and focus. He exhaled softly and focused once again, this time reaching out to find those barely-there currents in the air around him, thrumming just below the threshold of his hearing. Cary didn't have a clear idea of exactly how he was supposed to utilize them, so he just pictured the invisible currents being redirected into the keyhole, adding some push to the edge of the zip tie.

"Open," he whispered, willing the energy to flow to tip the mechanism. He felt almost foolish doing it; he was just talking to a door handle. But then there was a soft click, and as he angled the plastic tip, the door opened.

Cary had to pause for a second, his heart hammering wildly. He hadn't really expected it to work. Not even after he'd witnessed true magic in play. That was for other people. He wasn't...a sorcerer. And yet, the lock had opened, and the coin had landed right.

He shook his head at himself. It could all be nothing more than coincidence. It was possible to pick a lock with a zip tie, after all. Though perhaps not with such ease—

No. He didn't have time to reflect on his newfound magical abilities or the lack thereof. Tony's goons could come for him any minute, and he wanted to be long gone before they did.

Cary peered out of the door to check no one was standing guard outside. While it was unlikely, he wasn't taking any chances. If there were any cameras, they'd probably be facing the perimeter. He had to be careful to avoid open spaces.

It was already fully dark, though it couldn't have been later than six or seven PM, and nearly freezing cold. Not enough for it to snow, but enough for him to wonder whether he'd make it through the woods with only a torn buttoned-down shirt to keep him warm. The only light was coming from the windows and the driveway, making the place look like a picture from a rental brochure. He waited a few minutes to be sure no patrol was going to walk by and then slipped quietly through the door, closing it softly behind him.

A thick pine forest surrounded the house and sloped down almost to the water's edge. Cary darted under the shadow of the nearest tree and huddled there, hiding behind the trunk and listening for any indication of an alarm going off. For all he knew, there was magical salt sprinkled around that basement, or some other such fuckery. But everything was quiet. No sounds came from the house despite the strong illumination, and there was only the rustling of the wind in the treetops, and the occasional hooting of an owl.

Cary had never been an outdoorsy person. He had no clue how to navigate his way through the forest without getting lost and freezing to death. He contemplated stealing a car from the garage, but the noise would hardly go unnoticed. No, he had to rely on his own two feet if he wanted to keep his absence secret for as long as possible. His best bet was following the winding dirt road that led away from the house, sticking to the shadows and undergrowth, and so he set off in that direction. He took a wide berth, creeping among the trees to avoid being picked up by cameras, and circled back to the dirt road beyond the reach of the driveway lamps.

As the fancy cabin gradually disappeared from view, hidden behind the rows of pines, the darkness became more tangible, like a living, breathing thing that lurked between the tree trunks, threatening to lunge at him the second he let his guard down. Cary kept looking over his shoulder as he trudged through the undergrowth by the side of the road. There were no signs of pursuit, but he couldn't shake the feeling of being watched.

It was just nerves, he told himself. His teeth were chattering from the cold, his head hurt, and his entire body was a tangle of sore limbs and bruises. He was hungry and thirsty, not having eaten or drunk anything since the day before. But he kept on, guided by a fickle rising moon that shone intermittently from behind the clouds. At least it wasn't raining, and the air was crisp and clear, filled with the overwhelming scent of pine and wet earth.

Cary tried to count his steps, but he was stumbling too much over roots and brambles to keep track, and he quickly gave up on that. He didn't dare making it easier by walking on the road itself. He would be too easy a target there. Keeping it just at the edge of sight was enough to maintain the correct course, even though he wished he could have been going much faster.

There were probably other cabins in these woods. Lakeside properties were very popular, after all, and even if Giordano had chosen a particularly secluded one, Cary's chances of coming up on another house or even a small community were still rather good. Most of these were probably summer residences, and he'd have to break in if he came upon a cabin that had been closed up for the winter. But that was all right—he only needed to find a place with a working landline to call Ty. He knew the number by heart, and if Ty was alive and in possession of his cell phone, Cary had to warn him not to fall into Giordano's trap.

The road went on and on for what felt like hours, though the position of the moon didn't change much at all. Occasionally, Cary heard rustles that scared the bejesus out of him, but they all turned out to be some small nocturnal animal or other, scurrying along on its business.

Maybe there was some sort of magic that could be useful in these kinds of situations. A spell of disappearance, for instance, or teleportation. It was one of those things he should have asked Ty or even Sebastian about. He'd had this incredible opportunity to learn so much about a world he knew nothing about, but instead of snatching it up, he'd chosen to be distant and skeptical. Served him right.

THE GLARE OF headlights somewhere up ahead took him by surprise. Apparently, with him being too caught up in his thoughts and trying to ignore the bone-chilling cold, Cary had missed the gentle curve of the dirt lane where it diverged from the main road that cut through the forest.

The car was approaching from the southeast, the rumbling of the engine crashing through the fragile silence. What were the chances someone would be traveling through this lonely portion of the forest at this exact moment? Even though there might be plenty of other luxury homes scattered along this stretch of the lakefront, it was hardly a heavily trafficked area.

Cary didn't stop to examine this stroke of luck too closely. He stepped onto the shoulder, taking care to be visible in the headlights but not go far enough to be run over, and waved his hands frantically.

The car passed him. Belatedly—the cold and the hunger were probably making his brain numb—he realized the chances of anyone stopping for some crazy guy jumping out of a thick forest were even lower than the ambient temperature. He was already trying to figure out which direction he would have to continue on when the car slowed down and stopped a few yards down the road.

The exhaust fumes curled up, mixing with the diaphanous night mist and glowing in the car's taillights. It was a white Honda Accord sedan. Something about it tugged at Cary's memory, but then the driver opened the door and stepped out, turning to face him. A man, roughly in his fifties, with salt-and-pepper hair and a neatly trimmed beard, dressed in a gray turtleneck sweater and black slacks. He definitely looked the part of a well-to-do local late for his solitary getaway weekend.

"Need a hand there?" he inquired. He moved with a noticeable limp and had to steady himself with a hand on the car door.

"Yeah." Cary threw another look at the empty dirt path that curved behind him. There was still no sign of anyone following him. Thinking quickly, he decided telling the truth wasn't the best strategy. Aside from his reluctance to give away too much to a stranger, he didn't want to take the chance of said stranger going to the authorities with an abduction story. "My buddies pulled a stupid prank on me and left me stranded in the middle of the road. I, um, got lost without my phone. Is there any chance of you maybe giving me a lift? I could really use some help."

There was a long pause as the driver seemed to take in Cary's disheveled appearance. Despite the surrounding darkness, there was no hiding that he'd been recently beaten.

"Sure, get in," the man said finally. He watched as Cary hurried to the car before getting back behind the wheel. "Lovely night, isn't it?"

Chapter Eighteen

TY'S SLEEP HADN'T been disturbed either by surprise assailants or bad dreams. Thankfully, he'd never been bothered by nightmares. Perhaps he had too limited an imagination, or lower brain activity, but either way, he was pretty happy about it. He had enough shit to deal with while he was awake.

After waking up that afternoon, he'd made a few trips to get everything they needed to go through with their plan, including a change of clothes for Bas. They'd left all their personal belongings, as well as some of Cary's things, in their respective rooms at the Venetian.

Ty had wanted to set out that evening and drive through the night, but Bas was still feeling weak after yesterday's exertions, so Ty reluctantly agreed to give him more time to recuperate, pushing their departure to the middle of the night. He was too agitated to rest any more himself and resorted to chain-smoking while staring out of the window instead.

He was taking a hell of a risk waiting for so long. Tony might not be as patient, and it was Cary who was bound to pay the price for Ty's overconfidence. But the board had already been set, and there was nothing more Ty could do, other than go through with his scheme and hope for the best. He had to, for Cary's sake.

After taking turns in the bathroom and another quick shower, Ty and Sebastian went down to the car. Ty flipped on the radio to catch the late local news, but even though there were jumbled reports of a disturbance at the Venetian hotel and casino the previous day, no particular details (like a description of persons of interest or their vehicle) had been issued. All they had to do was keep a low profile and avoid any run-ins with the cops—which was Ty's usual modus operandi.

"I need coffee," Bas grumbled as he slid into the passenger's seat.

"There's nothing around here you'd want to drink," Ty said, setting up the GPS. "There should be a gas station and a 7-Eleven a few miles down the road. We can get you something there."

"Wouldn't it be just the thing if it were my last day on Earth and all I had to drink was convenience-store coffee," Bas bemoaned, slumping dramatically in his seat.

"Who's cranky now?"

Bas huffed as Ty pulled the car out of the parking lot and headed for the highway. Ty couldn't help but think back to the drive to Las Vegas, with Cary beside him. It already felt like a lifetime ago, the memories painted with guilt and nostalgia.

The darkness made it seem as if the road was stretching into nothingness. The stillness made it easy to sink back into his troubled thoughts. There had been a lot of things to do before everything was ready. Ty was familiar with the location he'd picked for the drop-off, but it had been years since he'd last been there. A lot could have changed since then, and the least he could do was learn as much as he could about the surrounding area online. No amount of Internet research beat actual reconnaissance, but there might not be enough time to do that properly, given they still had at least eight hours of driving ahead of them.

They ended up getting that coffee, although Ty would've preferred to skip it and just keep going. But he needed to fill up with gas anyway, so at least it wasn't a complete waste of time. The coffee actually went a long way to calming him down, in lieu of a cigarette (Bas would flip on him if Ty tried smoking in the car). He'd been simmering ever since the phone call from AJ, and anger wasn't the right mindset for handling a rigged hostage swap.

And there was another thing that had been bothering him for some reason, like an annoying mosquito buzz he couldn't tune out even in the midst of the current shit storm.

"Hey, Bas?"

"Mmm?"

"What did you mean yesterday about me having an 'ingrained Fae bargaining streak'?"

There was a long pause.

"I just meant you put a lot of weight on everybody getting their due," Bas said finally, squirming a little in the passenger seat. He was examining his paper cup intently, avoiding meeting Ty's eyes.

"I can tell when you're shitting me," Ty said, glancing sideways at him. "That's not what you meant."

"Okay, fine." Bas put the nearly empty cup in the holder and looked at him. For once, his expression was serious, and Ty almost regretted starting the conversation in the first place, because he had a feeling he wasn't going to like the answer. "Just promise me you won't freak out."

"That's reassuring," Ty muttered. No, he was definitely not going to like it.

"I know why Leland took you in."

"What?" Ty looked at him sharply. When Leland found him, he tried his best to teach Ty the basics of magic practice and, what proved to be more important, how to steal without being caught. Leland hadn't been an easy man to get along with. He'd been a strict teacher, and compromise wasn't his strongest suit. But during those years, Ty had a sense of stability, and he'd learned so much that he didn't mind the occasional punishment. And Ty couldn't blame Leland for eventually turning him out for failing to live up to his standards. "He told me exactly why he took me in."

Bas sighed and rubbed the bridge of his nose. Somehow it looked a lot less dramatic than his usual theatrics. "Yes, yes, the 'spark of potential,' as he used to call it. But it wasn't just that. Lots of people have the spark, and in most cases, it doesn't amount to shit."

"No kidding," Ty muttered under his breath.

"The real reason he picked you up was because he saw you were Fae-touched."

"I was...what?"

"You were stolen by the Fae as a baby and returned to the human world when you were a little boy. Leland thought that made you special. Inherently magical, or some such nonsense—maybe even able to communicate with the Faerie world. You know how obsessed Leland is with everything Fae." Bas threw him a quick glance and shrugged, as if he couldn't fathom the fascination, even though Ty knew Bas was no less familiar with the subject. "In any case, he was wrong. You proved to be no different than any regular human child. That's why he was so disappointed. He said that must have been why they'd returned you to the human world—because you were so useless they hadn't even bothered raising you as a slave. His words, not mine."

Ty gripped the wheel so hard his knuckles turned white. He regretted starting this conversation in the car, because the white noise currently filling his ears was hardly conducive to safely driving at seventy miles per hour.

"How do you know that?" he asked. His mouth felt dry, and it wasn't because of the over-roasted coffee he'd had earlier.

"Leland had come to me for help a few times," Bas said. He shifted uncomfortably in his seat. "We used to be closer. You know, before he treated you like a dick. Anyway, he told me about it all one day, and—"

"Why didn't you tell me before?" Ty cut him off. He wasn't quite sure he believed what he was hearing—the part about him being abducted by faeries. It wasn't as if it hadn't been known to happen. He'd heard enough stories about changelings and people being carried off to the other realm. But he didn't remember any of that. Wouldn't he have retained some recollection of such a fantastic place?

"It's kind of a big thing to spring on someone, you know?" Sebastian said, a touch plaintively. "It just never came up."

Ty bit off a caustic response. Getting mad at Bas wasn't going to change anything. He didn't even know who he was truly angry with—Bas, for keeping this secret from him for so long; Leland, for treating him as either a curiosity or a means to an end and discarding him like a pair of old socks while deeming him unworthy of the truth; or some unknown Fae he still wasn't convinced even existed, for depriving him of the family he'd always yearned for.

"Look, I'm sorry," Bas said, turning to look at him. "Maybe I shouldn't have said anything."

"Did he say anything else?"

Who were my real parents? he wanted to ask. *Where was I born, and when?* Time flowed differently in Faerie. Even different parts of the realm weren't synchronized with each other, much less with the human world. If he'd indeed spent his early years there, there was no telling when exactly he'd been born. It could have been decades and decades ago. It could be that none of his biological relatives were still alive.

Bas shook his head. "No. I'm not sure how much he knew about it, really, and he isn't the man to confide in anybody even if he did possess more information."

Ty took a deep breath, willing himself to keep his eyes on the road and his mind focused on the task at hand. A million questions buzzed around in his head, blurring his vision. But now wasn't the time to try to make sense of it all. Whatever the truth was, it had lain dormant for years. It could wait a bit longer—unlike Cary, whose life expectancy could be measured in hours. Ty would have a chance to grill Sebastian (and maybe even Leland, if he could find him) further when it was all over—assuming he'd make it out alive.

"I swear to God, you can be such an asshole sometimes," Ty muttered. *Just breathe and let it go*, he reminded himself. They had a long drive ahead of them, and they should be using it to come up with a plan that wouldn't backfire as spectacularly as their last one.

"But you love me anyway, darling," Bas said, reclining back in his seat.

"THIS IS THE place?" Sebastian asked as he got out of the car and looked around.

The dirt road they'd driven up ran around a hill overlooking a tiny pond. A farmhouse stood on the top of the hill, its roof slightly askew and its wide wraparound porch sagging in places. It had been abandoned for quite some time; the fields around it were nothing but overgrown wilderness, bordering on a natural forest. A tractor and a stripped-down farm truck were rusting away on the slope of the hill, and pieces of machinery were strewn around them, nearly invisible in the tall grass. The red paint on the barn behind the house had turned brown with the years, and the entire structure looked ready to collapse at any moment. The sun had already risen, washing everything in a pink glow that made the overall shabbiness look slightly more picturesque.

There wasn't another dwelling around for miles, as far as Ty recalled. The quiet, broken only by the chirping of birds and the rustle of wind in the grass, had a weird, hushed quality about it, but perhaps it only felt that way after the familiar urban bustle. Bas took a few steps toward the rickety house and stopped, eying the porch suspiciously.

"Why did you pick it?"

Ty slammed the car door, the loud sound spooking the handful of water birds that occupied the puddle-like pond.

"It's remote," he said, coming to stand beside Bas.

"Very convenient for hiding the bodies. You're doing Giordano a service."

"He'd never go for anything more public." Ty started for the house, and after a reluctant pause, Bas followed him. "This works to both our advantage. Besides, I know this place. It was my first solo gig after splitting with Leland."

"Here?"

"Yes." Ty went up the stairs that led to the porch, running his hand along the wooden rail. His skin prickled with the anguish and screams soaked into the old, sun-bleached wood. It always seemed strange to him that for all his magic, Sebastian could never sense objects like he did, could never read the imprints left in them by past owners and events. It was a gift of sorts, he supposed. Or maybe this was what being Fae-touched felt like, now that he thought about it. "It was one of the spots where Mason Shear held his gatherings."

"The cultist?" Bas asked. He ascended the stairs gingerly. Perhaps he couldn't sense past impressions as well as Ty, but he was uncomfortable, and Ty bet it wasn't just worry over the possibility of the decrepit house collapsing on them.

"Yes. It was after he was killed in the police raid. I was hired by the relatives of one of his victims to search for her personal belongings that had been used in his rituals."

"That must have been fun."

"Considering none of his victims were found in one piece, it really wasn't."

Ty pushed open the front door, which creaked on its hinges. The interior welcomed them with the dank smell of rotting wood and mold. A thick layer of dust covered the floor and what was left of the broken furniture, and shards of glass were still piled under smashed windows. Aside from the advanced state of disrepair, nothing set the farmhouse apart from any other abandoned homestead in the area. At least, what it would appear like to any outsider.

"What now?" Bas asked, looking around with such distaste it was easy to forget he'd been living in a basement for the better portion of the last decade.

"Now we have some setting up to do," Ty said. "Let's see if we can arrange a warm welcome for Giordano and his posse."

Chapter Nineteen

FLOATING BACK TO consciousness this time around was less painful, but a whole lot more disorienting. Cary blinked owlishly, trying to expel the grogginess. His mouth was parched; it felt as though something had crawled inside while he slept, and died there. He was thirsty, and he desperately needed to use the bathroom.

Then there was a sense of movement. He was sitting in a car that was speeding down a darkened highway. More accurately, he was slumped on the back seat, his hands tied once again, but this time, behind his back.

Cary jerked upright, or at least he tried too. His limbs felt heavy and unwieldy, as if he'd been drugged, and his vision swam. The last thing he remembered was getting in the car with the salt-and-pepper-haired stranger in the middle of a deserted forest road, and then...it all went blank.

Panic laced through him. What the hell was happening? Had Giordano found him again? From what he could see, it was dark outside. Was it still night? Was it the next night? Where was he?

"What's going on?" was what he intended to ask, but all that came out of his mouth was: "Ughaa naah..."

The men occupying the front seats turned to look at him at the same time. The driver was definitely the same older guy who'd picked Cary up, but now he was wearing a beige knit sweater instead of the turtleneck. So, it was probably already Sunday night. No wonder he felt so groggy—he'd been unconscious for nearly twenty-four hours.

The man in the passenger seat was younger, perhaps in his mid-thirties, with pale blond hair, a slightly weak chin, and a dour expression. He was wearing a dark blue parka.

"Look who's up," the driver commented. His voice was deep and pleasant, almost soothing, like that of a TV news anchor. Or those voice actors who played the parts of fathers in old cartoons. "Did you have a good nap?"

"Maybe you should knock him out again," the blond guy said to the driver, who meanwhile had turned his attention back to the road.

"Don't tell me you're afraid of some wannabe illusionist, Vincent," the older man said dismissively. "He's practically a child. A lost, clueless child."

Vincent? Who the fuck was Vincent? For that matter, who was this man who spoke of him so condescendingly? A lost child?! Like he knew shit about Cary's life. Wait, how *did* he know what Cary did for a living, and what did he want with him?

The indignation and fear sharpened his focus. He breathed deeply, struggling to expel the dregs of whatever it was that was addling his brain. He worked his mouth before managing to push out:

"I need to take a piss."

His voice was raw, as if he hadn't spoken aloud in weeks. The various aches from the beating Angelo Rossi had so generously bestowed upon him were beginning to come back in force now that the drugs, or whatever it was, were slowly wearing off. There had been one or two instances in his life when he'd felt more wretched, but this was coming up pretty damn close on the shittiness scale.

"Shut up," Vincent told him menacingly.

"I don't want to smell his urine for the rest of the drive if he wets himself," the older man said. Judging by his authoritative tone, he was definitely the one in charge. Without further debate, he swerved and brought the car to a stop by the roadside. "Take him outside." Vincent didn't look particularly happy, but he got out and hauled Cary out as well.

The sudden onslaught of nearly freezing fresh air overwhelmed Cary. He stumbled on unsteady feet like a newborn colt, his awkwardly bound arms making him wobble even more, and fought to keep from vomiting. When his head finally stopped spinning, he risked raising it to have a look around.

It was utterly dark and silent, save for the soft purring of the running engine and the long beams of the headlights. It was hard to discern the landscape, but it looked like they were on a country road of some sort. Distant hills were black shadows against a vast starry sky, and lonely fields stretched out on both sides of the road behind low wooden fences. Cary had absolutely no inkling as to where they were, but it was clear they were a long way from the lake.

"You either untie my hands or unzip my pants," he told Vincent when the man made no move to help him. "Your choice."

Vincent scoffed at him, but undid the piece of rope that was wrapped around his wrists. After the cutting plastic zip ties, the rope felt almost old-fashioned.

Cary flexed his fingers as he briefly considered making a run for it across the fields. But he was still too dazed, and his body was a mess of aches that would surely hamper his escape. Not to mention he'd caught a glimpse of a gun tucked under Vincent's jacket. He couldn't outrun a bullet in the best of times, and he certainly couldn't do it in his current state. That didn't mean he wouldn't look for a more convenient chance to escape, of course. Whoever these folks were, Cary doubted he was safe in their company.

He relieved himself unhurriedly, turning away both from Vincent and the car. The nausea and the sensation of vertigo gradually subsided, and he felt much more alert and in control of his faculties when the other man tied his hands in front of him and shoved him back onto the back seat. The headache and bruises went nowhere, as did the thirst and the hunger, but at least he was fully awake now.

The driver turned back to the road, and Cary tugged his hands experimentally to test the binding, but he doubted he'd be able to wiggle out of them, given his condition—certainly not without the two men noticing.

A few minutes passed in complete silence as the car sped down the deserted road.

"So who the hell are you?" Cary asked when it became clear no further conversation was forthcoming.

"Oh, I'm sorry," the driver said, glancing at Cary in the rearview mirror. "We haven't been properly introduced, have we? I'm Leland Bernard, and this is my associate, Vincent Graves."

Leland's name sounded vaguely familiar. Usually Cary was good with both names and faces, but now, perhaps thanks to his persistent headache, he was drawing a blank.

"Did you have to give our names?" Vincent complained.

"I don't see the harm in it." The airy way he said it sent chills down Cary's spine. No one threw their name around in front of their kidnapping victim if they intended to let them live.

"Frankly, I'm surprised Ty never mentioned me to you," Leland continued. "I'm rather disappointed. But then, he always was an ungrateful little brat."

It took all of Cary's self-control to keep a straight face and not let his shock show. Of course, it was Ty's old mentor. How could he have forgotten the name? Now he wished Ty'd been a little more open about his past, because all he knew about this man was that he was some sort of sorcerer, a career thief, and that Ty had had a falling out with him years back. This Vincent fellow hadn't featured in his stories at all.

That meant his kidnapping hadn't been random. Leland had sought him out, and he'd known exactly where Cary would be at the right moment. Had he been tailing him and Ty, and then Giordano? Ty had mentioned a white sedan following them in San Francisco, but back then, Cary had thought the idea absurd.

Despite the fear, there was also a spark of hope. If this Leland knew where to find Cary, perhaps he had more solid information regarding Ty's fate. If he really was alive, or—

No. Ty had to be alive. Even Tony and Leticia believed it to be so. Of course Ty being alive didn't mean he was in the clear and out of danger. Cary just hoped he had enough sense (and selfishness) to refuse whatever proposal Giordano had made. And Cary would much prefer Ty walking away from it all than coming to his rescue only to be killed.

The realization hit him like a runaway car coming out of a left field. He cared for Ty enough to consciously admit that he wanted him to stay safe more than he wanted to save himself. Had he actually fallen in love with the man over the course of these past days? God, if this was what being in love was like, he was definitely screwed beyond repair.

"What do you want with me?" he asked. Leland wasn't averse to talking, and Cary's best bet was to keep pressing him for more information. Until he knew at least where they were going, he couldn't form a decent plan of action.

"Well, it had come to my attention that for whatever reason, Ty finds you, shall we say, appealing," Leland said. "So you, my little friend, are going to be my leverage. Thank you for sparing me the hassle of having to extract you from that lake house, by the way. That was rather impressive on your part."

"Don't mention it," Cary said. He risked a quick look at Vincent's profile. He definitely didn't look pleased, but perhaps it was a perpetual scowl. Cary hardly cared. He didn't even mind being called "leverage." All he could think about was that Leland's words confirmed Ty was really alive.

"What do you want from him?" Cary asked, mainly to keep the conversation going. He imagined he had a pretty good idea of what a sorcerer like Leland might be looking for, but every little bit he could glean might prove important later.

"All I asked was for him to get me that amulet," Leland said. Vincent shot him another troubled look, but Leland seemed unconcerned by his partner's apprehension. "And I went through all the proper channels, mind you. Paid that scumbag of a fence in advance, too. Sort of a last act of goodwill on my part—to allow the boy to profit from everything I'd taught him. But of course, he proved as incompetent as I thought. Couldn't even steal a bauble from a common without getting himself in trouble. Ridiculous! And now, I'm forced to track down where he and that criminal Giordano have set up a meeting. All this traveling has been quite a nuisance."

Cary kept quiet during the rant, but the wheels in his head were turning rapidly. So Leland was the mystery client who had hired Ty's services in the first place, the one neither Ty nor his fence AJ knew anything about.

He wanted to defend Ty to Leland, to say that he was hardly incompetent, and that he couldn't have predicted that an actual crime lord would be going for the same prize. But it was painfully clear that nothing he could say on Ty's behalf would sway Leland's opinion.

Besides, wouldn't it be weird for him to stand up for his robber? It was his heirloom, after all, and he didn't want it to fall into the hands of either of these vultures. Leland, who'd apparently tailed them this entire time with the skill and efficiency of an FBI agent, knew enough of their relationship to try to use Cary as bait. But Cary wasn't about to supply him with any more ammunition if he could help it.

"Why do you want the amulet?" he asked instead. "You're supposed to be this great sorcerer, right? What's the matter, you can't cast a spell without some magical Viagra to give you a boost?"

Vincent turned around in his seat in a manner that was decidedly unsafe, given their current speed, and backhanded Cary across the face with surprising force.

"Ow!" Cary licked his split lip and glared at the guy.

"No more sass, or you're going to spend the rest of the way in the trunk," Vincent warned.

I've been beat up by worse than you, Cary wanted to tell him, but the prospect of being cramped in a confined space yet again kept him from being unnecessarily snippy.

"Ignorant commons," Leland said as if nothing had happened. "You had such unique power in your hands, and all you could think of was using it to get folks to see your pathetic magic show."

Could he use magic to get himself out of this mess? Surely, if he'd succeeded in picking a lock with magic, he could open a car door. But he wasn't yet confident enough in his abilities to try anything in front of a sorcerer. Leland would certainly pick up on him gathering magical energy. He didn't know where Vincent's talents lay, but it was safe to assume he was some sort of practitioner as well. No, Cary would have to wait for an opportunity when he was alone or their attention was directed elsewhere.

"That upstart mobster is no better," Leland continued. "Politics! Who gives a damn about that. Any moron with a dirty campaign can weasel his way into government. And his sister is as obtuse as he is. Worse, for being a sorceress."

Vincent was looking out of the window, his slightly exasperated expression reflected in the glass. It would seem this wasn't the first time Leland had gone on this particular tangent.

"Do you know what that thing really does?" Leland glanced briefly at Cary. "It opens a portal between worlds. Just imagine being able to summon a force greater than anything you've ever known, witnessing magic that we can only dream of in our reality. Pure, wild, untainted magic, wielded by beings of terrible power—and it's all yours to control if you're strong enough to bend it to your will."

"You're going to summon...demons?" Cary asked, because it sounded more like the ramblings of a madman or the premise of a cheesy horror flick than something a sane person would do, power-thirsty though he might be. He looked at Vincent again, to check whether he was as taken aback by the demented scenario, but Vincent's face showed no sign of surprise.

"Not demons." Vincent had caught him looking, apparently, because he was the one to answer, his voice gruff. "We're going to open the door to Faerie."

"That's right, my boy," Leland said into Cary's stunned silence. "And you're going to play a star role in the show."

Chapter Twenty

TY HAD TO award the Giordanos extra points for preparedness. As he watched from his vantage point at the barn entrance, he could see the approaching light of no less than three SUVs coming toward the house. It was a clear night, the air crisp and carrying the promise of a cold winter to come. The moon shone brightly over the hill, its pox-covered face so much sharper than in an urban environment.

As the cars approached, all other noises hushed, the nightlife spooked by the unfamiliar rumble of the engines. Ty leaned on the scratched door frame, the cigarette in his hand trailing smoke that mingled with his breath, coming out in small puffs, momentarily white against the backdrop of surrounding darkness. He didn't stir even as the SUVs stopped at the end of the driveway, just behind his shiny convertible, and about a dozen men armed with heavy semiautomatics poured out, spreading around the house and the barn.

Unlike the vain and dapper cinematic villains, Tony and Leticia had traded their designer suits for more casual attire. Neither of them was any less impressive in jeans and biker jackets as they climbed out of their vehicle. Leticia, with her hair in a low ponytail and a determined look on her face, looked especially ready for combat. Tony, on the other hand, appeared much more relaxed. But then again, he was used to relying on other people to fight for him—like Angelo

Rossi, who followed the dynamic duo with his gun already drawn, surveying the surroundings. Cary was nowhere to be seen, and the darkened windows made it impossible to peer into the SUVs.

Tony's mouth pressed into a hard line when he saw Ty lounging against the barn door. He definitely wasn't pleased at not having arrived first. He picked his way along the gravel toward the barn, giving the house a wide berth. Perhaps by now he was familiar enough with the history of this place to let his distaste show, much like Sebastian had. Rossi shadowed his approach, while his sister remained close to the vehicles.

Ty stubbed out the cigarette on the wooden door and stepped forward to meet them.

"Where's your roller friend?" Rossi's weapon was trained on Ty, but his attention was divided between him and the potential threats lurking around them in the shadows.

"He ain't here. This is just between us," Ty said. "Isn't that right, Giordano?"

"Cut the crap," the mobster said curtly. "Where's my amulet?"

"Where's my ring?" Ty countered. It was safer to let Giordano think he cared more about it than he did about Cary. It was never a good idea to let your enemy—or even your so-called friends, for that matter—know exactly where your soft spots were. Even if it was rather late in the game to worry about subterfuge of that sort.

Tony lifted his left hand, and the narrow band on his index finger glinted in the moonlight.

"Sweet," Ty said, though it didn't look like Tony was planning on taking it off any time soon. "And my partner?"

Tony shook his head, almost apologetically. "I want to see the amulet first."

It wasn't at all hard to guess that Ty was going to get shot the moment he took out the goddamn pendant. No one was going to resort to half measures this time around. He crossed his arms over his chest.

"I don't have it."

The game they were playing wasn't unlike poker. Everyone was bluffing in some way or other, and only those who kept their cool had any hope of winning. Unfazed, Tony raised an eyebrow.

"That puts us at an impasse. So what are we doing here, exactly?"

It was beginning to bother him that he couldn't see Cary anywhere. Had Bas been right? Had Ty dallied too long, taking his sweet time arranging the drop-off? Had Tony decided to dispose of any potential nuisances, and was Cary already dead? Had he miscalculated once more, with Cary yet again being the distraction that wreaked havoc on all his plans?

To hell with the plans, he just wanted the distraction.

"The deal was the ring and my partner for your little trinket, and I ain't seeing him anywhere," Ty said. Out of the corner of his eye he could see Leticia making her way toward them, flanked by two burly guys.

"I'm getting tired of this shit," Tony announced. "I was willing to let you off the hook because apparently you're a useful man to know in the business. But you know what, I'm not buying that anymore. There are plenty of other burglars to go around, magic or no magic. If you don't hand me the amulet in the next thirty seconds, we'll see if you're as lucky with bullets as you are with heights."

"If you shoot me, you won't know where it's at."

"I'll take the chance," Tony said. "It'll be easier to search for it with you out of the way. So, what'll it be?"

To emphasize his words, Rossi raised his gun and took aim at Ty's head.

Ty shrugged. He was walking a fine line with Giordano's patience, but so far this was playing out exactly as he'd predicted. Aside from the ambiguity regarding Cary's fate, that is. The scheme he'd devised with Bas hinged on Cary being there—as a hostage, perhaps even wounded or hurt, but present. There was hardly any point, otherwise.

He let the silence stretch for a few more seconds, considering his course of action while making it look as if he was letting his defeat sink in. But at this point, his best bet was proceeding as he'd originally planned. If Cary was here, he'd find him. Finally, he nodded toward the barn entrance.

"It's in there."

Tony, looking more impatient than smug, turned to Rossi and gestured for him to go in. "Check it out. You," he said to Ty, "stay where you are."

Ty made sure to throw Rossi a dirty look as the man shoved past him through the door and disappeared inside. A subtle glare cut through the darkness as Rossi turned on a flashlight and moved around.

"So what about that ring?" Ty asked, hoping to cover any noises that might come from the barn.

"I bet you could've used it on that rooftop," Leticia said as she came to stand by her brother's side. "Then again, your little sorcerer buddy wouldn't have been able to save your neck with his magic. Either way, you're very hard to get rid of."

"Like a cockroach," Tony muttered without taking his eyes off the doorway. "What's taking so long?"

"Boss, I think you should come see this." Rossi's muffled voice came from somewhere deep inside. Tony and Leticia exchanged a look.

"Stay here and secure the premises," Tony ordered the guards that had accompanied his sister. "And search him."

One of them nodded and proceeded to quickly pat Ty down while the other one held him at gunpoint. Ty scowled, but held still with his arms stretched out until the search was over.

"He's clear," the guard said, stepping back.

"Good. Now get inside," Tony told Ty, probably judging it safer to keep him in his sight.

He didn't have to pull out his own weapon to force Ty into doing it. They both knew Leticia's presence was just as effective as a loaded gun in terms of intimidation. So Ty stepped inside, with Tony and Leticia following closely on his heels. The sorceress snapped her fingers, and a soft fluorescent-like light flooded the barn interior.

At first, it looked like the interior of any other barn on any other farm aside from the signs of advanced disrepair. Rotting hay was stacked along the walls, from which also hung pieces of tack. In the corner, an old plow was slowly rusting away and various remnants of farm equipment were piled haphazardly all over the floor. But there was something else. A huge block of gray granite—a perfectly smooth rectangular cuboid rock—stood near the far wall. There were wooden steps leading up to it on each side, and chains hung from the rafters right above it. If one were to look closely, narrow drain slits could be seen at the corners of the stone block.

It was clearly some sort of altar. An elaborate sigil was painted on the wall behind it, the brownish paint beginning to peel off in places. The pattern was marred by smears of soot, but the entwined runes making up geometric shapes were still clearly visible. The ghostly stench of blood and death was so strong it almost made Ty gag. He knew the others couldn't sense it, especially over the smell of damp straw and decay, and he pushed down the wave of nausea that rose up in his throat. Whoever had died on this altar was long gone. He had to keep his shit together and focus on the living.

Angelo Rossi stood to the side of the altar, his weapon lowered in his slackened hand. Sebastian Monroe, half-hidden behind the massive stone monolith, grinned and waved at Ty. The etched disk of the amulet dangled from his hand on a new chain, a pendulum gone haywire.

"You," Leticia sneered as her attention locked on Bas. "I should have known I'd see you again. Haven't you had enough?"

"What can I say? I can't resist the lure of a beautiful woman," Bas said with a smirk.

"Rossi, shoot him," Tony ordered, but his right-hand man remained motionless, his eyes riveted on the amulet swinging to and fro in Sebastian's hand.

"He's under his spell," Leticia said, somewhat unnecessarily.

Tony swore and turned on his heel to call on his security backup, but at the same moment, a cold blue fire erupted along the entrance to the barn. The suddenness of it made them all recoil and shield their eyes against the glare.

Leticia was the first to recover. She hissed and threw some sort of spell against the newly erected barrier of flames, but they held. By now they would have spread all around the barn, effectively cutting off all access and outside noise like an impenetrable cocoon. Bas had spent hours drawing the runic script on the ground all around the barn with barely minutes to spare before show time, but the prep had been worth it. The runes were drawing energy directly from the earth, feeding the spell and keeping it alive.

In the momentary stunned silence, Ty dove for cover behind the altar a split second before Tony had a chance to gather his wits and draw his weapon on him. It wasn't lost on anyone that Ty—non-magical, unarmed and unprotected—was the most vulnerable guy in the room. A bullet whizzed past him, chipping the corner of the stone block and ricocheting off the wall. Had Cary been there, he'd have grabbed him. But as things stood, Ty had to get himself and Bas away while the others remained locked in the barn with no chance of immediate escape.

"You're not going to get away with this!" Tony informed him.

"The hell I ain't," Ty muttered.

At least Ty didn't have to worry about Cary getting caught in the crossfire. *Please, let him be somewhere safe*, he prayed silently to whatever deity would deign to listen.

Another blast hit the edge of the altar, this time coming from the left. Bas ducked behind it too, evading Leticia's charge, which sent an explosion of green sparks flying into the air as it hit the stone near him. It barely missed Rossi's head, and he dropped to the ground with a curse as the power that held him spellbound snapped. He grunted and grabbed the gun that'd fallen out of his hand. Tony remained quite unaffected, the magic blasts dissolving around him as if an invisible shield protected him.

Damn, Ty needed that ring back so bad.

"You're up!" Bas shouted.

Ty hardly needed the reminder. The air sizzled and crackled above his head as volleys of Leticia's deadly energy broke against Bas's impromptu blocking spells, but it couldn't go on for much longer. They were literally seconds away from being shot by the two mobsters while their focus was on handling the sorceress.

Ty reached into the space between the wooden steps that surrounded the altar, scraping his knuckles raw, and pulled out the SIG he'd stashed there. But the weapon wasn't his ultimate goal. He reached deeper into the recess and fumbled around for the lever to the hidden mechanism. The original design required that whoever was conducting the ritual had only to activate the lever by foot, but he had to apply all his weight to push it down by hand.

Something under the floorboards creaked, but otherwise nothing happened.

"Ty, *now*, for fuck's sake!"

Another bullet hit the wall behind him, right at the edge of the sigil, and Ty flattened himself on the floor. Rossi was advancing on them from the left, under the cover of Leticia's charges, and there was only so much Bas could do to hold all of them back.

Ty pushed the lever again, grunting with the effort, but the mechanism that was supposed to open a trap door that led to a secret passageway beneath the altar wouldn't budge. It had either been deactivated or was too rusted with disuse.

Shit. This was going nowhere. He and Bas were now trapped as effectively as he'd planned on the Giordanos being at this point. Ty bitterly regretted not testing the mechanism beforehand, but he could hardly have done so without its moving parts disturbing the dust and debris covering the floor, causing suspicion. He remembered it working perfectly a few years ago, and that was why he'd relied on it coming through today. Apparently, his luck had run dry.

Ceasing his futile efforts, he grabbed the gun and fired a few rounds at Rossi without stopping to see if he'd hit his mark. Bas scrambled to get out of the line of fire, and another blast of angry energy scorched the floor and steps behind him. Bas cried out in pain and rolled on the ground, clutching at his leg where the fabric of his trousers now hung in burnt tatters around seared flesh.

"Fuck."

Ty sprang to his feet and leaned over the altar, both hands on the gun in a steady hold. If they were going to die here, at least he could take out the serpent's head. Hot green sparks whirled around his head like fireworks, but he paid them no mind as he took aim. He just hoped that if he managed to take Tony out, it would give Cary some chance of making it out alive, wherever he was.

But he didn't have the opportunity to take a shot as the sound of an explosion tore through the barn. The ramshackle structure shook, and dust rained down from the rafters. The blue flames that had been blocking the entrance went out as if someone had pulled a switch, and sounds of screams and moans drifted in from the outside on the sudden blast of cold wind.

"The hell—" Tony began, taking a step toward the door. But he stopped as a dark figure appeared on the threshold and stepped inside, into the soft light of the magical illumination that still engulfed the barn. The newcomer looked around, taking in the scene with sharp eyes.

"Lovely evening, isn't it?" Leland said.

Chapter Twenty-One

TONY GIORDANO WAS the first to break the silence.

"Who the fuck are you?"

"I'm hearing this question quite a lot today. But let us skip the introductions for now. I'm only here to take back what should have been mine in the first place."

Ty couldn't take his eyes off Leland as he strode the length of the barn toward the stone altar with a pronounced limp in his right leg. He was dimly aware of Rossi pointing his gun at him, and of Bas huddling on the floor at his feet, but all he could focus on was the man walking toward him, casually oblivious to the drawn weapons and the magic floating around the cavernous space. Ty's thoughts seemed to scatter like a flock of birds spooked by the crack of a shotgun. *How? Why? What was Leland doing here?*

But for all his shock, Ty couldn't fool himself into believing Leland had come with any sort of benevolent purpose. He straightened, pulling himself together mentally and physically. Facing his former mentor hadn't been easy at the best of times, and he had a feeling this was when it would all come to a head between them.

Instinctively sensing the threat from the older man, the Giordano siblings moved to stand shoulder to shoulder in front of the altar. Tony raised his gun, while Leticia's fingertips glowed bright green with unreleased energy.

"Hold it right there, old man—" Leticia began.

"You know what, I don't think so."

A wave of unseen force, like an aftershock of a tremendous explosion, rolled through the barn. It shook again, the old wood creaking pitifully. One of the supporting posts snapped with a loud crack. The blast threw everyone to the ground, with only Leland and Tony left standing. Ty's gun went flying out of his hand, landing somewhere behind a stack of moldy hay.

As Ty hauled himself upright, he saw Tony, unaffected as he was by this show of strength, rush to help his sister get back on her feet. But she ignored him. Undaunted, she flung out her hand, her elegant fingers curved like claws. Fire sprang around Leland, bright yellow-green flames engulfing him and nearly obscuring his form.

But the fire died as suddenly as it had appeared. Tendrils of smoke rose from the scorched floorboards beneath his feet, and a strong smell of burnt sulfur wafted through the air, but as Leland stepped out of the blackened circle, not a single mark marred his clothes and skin. Ty heard Rossi's sharp intake of breath, but he didn't turn to look at the man.

"Amateurs," Leland said with utter contempt, and Leticia's dark clothes caught on fire, the flames seeming to descend on her out of thin air.

"What did you do?! Stop it!" She shrieked in pain and outrage, instinctively swatting at the flames in a desperate attempt to put them out.

"That's how it's done, child," Leland said as he watched Tony and Rossi scrambling to divest Leticia of her burning jacket. The fire shied from Tony's hands as if it were liquid flowing in the wrong direction, but otherwise defied all their efforts to extinguish it.

"Bas, can you do something?" Ty shouted over the sorceress's anguished screams and the men's angry yelling. She had been about to kill the both of them, but even he couldn't watch a woman burn to death and do nothing about it. Enemy or not, she'd had the courage to stand up to Leland while Ty had frozen at the mere sight of him.

Bas pushed himself up on one elbow with a moan and peered around the corner of the stone block. But before he could say or do anything, Rossi sprang to his feet from where he'd been kneeling by Leticia and fired three shots, one after the other, in Leland's direction.

There was no doubt in Ty's mind Rossi was a good shot. Giordano seemed like a man who surrounded himself with competent people, especially when his personal security was at stake. And yet, none of those bullets reached their target— instead changing their trajectory midair, ever so slightly, a split second before impact. Leland was still standing there, safe and sound, watching them all with a derisive smirk.

Ty could have told Rossi it was pointless. Leland was by far the most powerful sorcerer among them—stronger than Sebastian, and infinitely superior to a self-taught practitioner like Leticia, talented as she might be. Their weapons and tricks were useless against someone like him. The gun in Rossi's hand grew red-hot, and he let it drop with a cry. Even as the weapon clattered to the ground, an invisible hand seemed to pick Rossi up and fling him against the closest post. There was a sickening sound of breaking bone, and he crumpled to the floor in an ungainly heap, his neck twisted at an impossible angle.

Tony barely spared him a glance. He was too busy trying (futilely) to beat out the flames on Leticia with his jacket.

"Make it stop!" he yelled at Leland in desperate outrage. "Put the fire out!"

"Or what?" Leland cocked his head, looking at them with much the same expression as an adult would look at misbehaving children that aren't his own.

"Leland, for fuck's sake," Ty said, taking a step forward. He could take no more of this. "What do you want?"

Leland turned to him, shifting his attention away from Giordano and his sister for a moment. Out of the corner of his eye, Ty could see Sebastian inching toward them, but what the sorcerer was planning to do in his current condition was a mystery.

"You still can't guess?" Leland asked and then tsked. "I'm disappointed. I'd hoped you'd have figured it all out by now."

Ty gritted his teeth, but there was simply no time to let Leland get under his skin. He just needed to divert his attention from the others.

"I want Westfield's amulet," Leland said, as if it was the most obvious thing in the world.

Sudden realization dawned. It was as if a flash of lightening banished the shadows that lingered in Ty's mind, blurring his insight.

"It was you," he said. It wasn't a question. "*You* are the mystery client."

"Correct. And you managed to botch the easiest job in the world. Not to mention getting Monroe mixed up in this disaster. He's the only one I'm sorry to see here today, but we all choose to make our own mistakes, don't we?"

There was nothing Ty could say to that, because it was all too true. He had failed quite spectacularly, and every attempt to rectify his failure only resulted in him getting into deeper and deeper shit, dragging his friends along with him. Bas was going to pay for Ty's screwups, and Cary...Cary already could have, for all he knew, and it was no one's fault but Ty's.

"Fuck!"

They both turned sharply at the exclamation. Sebastian was half kneeling, half lying beside Leticia, but as he'd reached toward the flames to try to draw them out, the fire had seared his fingertips rather than respond to his spell. He held the injured hand to his chest and rolled onto his back, whimpering. Ty hurried to kneel by his side as Sebastian clutched his hand, panting heavily, his eyes scrunched shut. Something warm and round pressed into Ty's palm, and he struggled to keep a straight face as he discreetly swiped the metal disk from Sebastian's hand into his pocket.

Next to them, Leticia lay thrashing, the skin on her face and hands already starting to blister. The smell of burnt flesh mixed with the lingering odor of sulfur.

"You can't put it out like that," Leland said. "It's ancient Fae magic that can't be countered by your feeble tricks. Only those who can call on the true name of fire can control its energy. But I will help her if you give me that pretty ring." He extended his hand to Tony imperiously, fully expecting immediate compliance.

Giordano's face worked. It was clear he wasn't used to being bossed around so casually, nor would he want to give up the only protection that prevented him ending up like Rossi or those poor souls whose screams they'd heard coming from the outside. But his sister's life was on the line. It was him against the sorcerer—and while his magic couldn't touch Tony, other things could. Being killed by a falling rafter was as effective as being incinerated by a blast of energy drawn out of thin air.

Finally, he pulled the ring off his finger and threw it at Leland, who snatched it mid-flight and put it on his own hand. Then he whispered something, a word Ty couldn't quite catch, and the flames winked and went out. For a split second, there was only deafening silence, and then Leticia began sobbing uncontrollably. Red blisters covered her skin, but they were quickly fading, her damaged skin healing itself. She was still shaking so badly her feet rattled on the floor.

Ty had seen burn victims, and he could tell that, surprisingly, Leticia wasn't hurt very badly. Apparently, Leland had controlled the fire, just as he'd said, to cause pain rather than serious injury. With her own magic (already apparently at work) and proper medical care, Leticia would probably only need a few days to recover. Given, of course, they ever got out of the damn barn alive.

"You son of a bitch—" Tony began in a voice that was a touch shaky.

"Don't," Ty said curtly. He still hunched over Sebastian, holding his hand and trying not to look at the burnt mess that was his right leg.

"Yes, yes, off with you," Leland said airily, waving Tony away like a chastised schoolboy.

Tony shot him a baleful look. He scooped Leticia into his arms and made for the door, glancing at Rossi's body but not stopping to check on him. It was clear there was nothing to be done there.

"You'll pay for this, old man," Leticia spat as they made their way out. Her trembling voice was laced with pain, but the intensity of hate she directed at Leland was unmistakable. "All of you will pay for this."

"Now, for the matter at hand," Leland said, ignoring Letitia's outburst. "The amulet."

"Go to hell," Ty said. By this point, Leland would have to pry the pendant out of his cold dead hands, which was probably what was going to happen anyway. His only regret—apart from providing his former mentor with so many reasons to gloat—was that he wouldn't see Cary one last time. He'd failed to save him despite his best efforts. It figured that the moment he realized how important Cary had become to him, he'd lost him forever.

"I hate to be cutting in line," Leland said. He lifted his hand, and a low-pitched sound, like the tolling of a distant bell, reverberated through the barn. Bas moaned at the annoying vibration, and Ty tensed, steeling himself for whatever was coming.

But nothing happened. That is, not until a shadow fell across the doorway, and someone else stepped in.

Ty didn't know the man. He was about his age or a little older, dressed in plain jeans and a parka, his pale dishwater hair slightly disheveled. But Ty couldn't care less about his appearance, because he was dragging Cary by the arm while pointing a gun to his face.

Ty's breath caught, and he froze, his heart threatening to burst out of his chest. Cary's hands were tied in front of him with a piece of rope, and he sported a spectacular black eye and an assortment of bruises. His shirt was hanging around his body in tatters, but he was most definitely alive, glaring defiantly at his captor.

"You fucking shit," Ty breathed. He wasn't even sure whom he meant—Tony, for pulling a trick-and-draw on him with a prize he didn't have; Leland, for jumping on the "let's use Westfield as a hostage" bandwagon; or Cary, for making his knees weak with relief at the mere sight of him.

Even though it was no more than a whisper, Cary turned in his direction, and their eyes met. Cary inhaled sharply, taking in the scene, but otherwise stayed silent.

"Move it," the man with the gun said and shoved Cary forward.

"I don't think there's a need for any further games, is there?" Leland said to Ty. "You have spunk, my boy, I'll give you that. But there's nothing more you can do here."

"Let Westfield and Monroe go," Ty said, his voice sounding foreign to his own ears. He rose from his kneeling position on the floor and took a step forward. "They're no threat to you anymore. If you want to gloat over me, fine. I'll give you the fucking amulet, just let them go."

Leland clapped his hands with a mocking grin.

"How touching. But you overestimate your importance. I'm not here because of you, and your pleas mean nothing. You're in no position to bargain. Now, the amulet, Ty, or we'll see how long it takes for that pretty boy of yours to die."

"Fuck him," Cary growled. "Don't do it, Ty. He's a complete psycho. He'll—"

The guy holding Cary momentarily loosened his grip to hit him across the face while still holding him at gunpoint, and Cary grunted as blood welled up from a split lip.

Slowly, Ty took the amulet out of his pocket. It dangled on its long chain, the elaborate raised pattern on its surface catching light in odd angles. He balked at the idea of giving up, of simply yielding, but just like Giordano, he had no choice. He didn't believe for one second that Leland would simply let them go their merry way once he had the amulet, but if parting with it meant buying a few more precious seconds for Cary, he'd do it.

But he'd lingered a moment too long. Seeing his hesitation, Leland walked up to Cary—his limp almost incongruous in the aftermath of the little showdown—and grabbed Cary by the scruff of his neck, forcing him down on his knees. Cary huffed in pain as he hit the floor with a loud thud. He struggled against his bonds, but Leland held him in a vise-like grip. Ty knew only too well Leland was much stronger and more agile than he looked, both physically and magically.

"The amulet," Leland repeated, his voice now devoid of any trace of amusement.

"Fine," Ty said quickly. "You win. I'll give it to you. But you must let Monroe go. He only got involved in all of this because he was doing me a favor. He has no stakes in this game."

Leland seemed to consider that, his gaze flicking to where Sebastian sat, grimacing with the pain and whispering healing spells through pressed teeth. The angry welts of burnt skin on his leg had lost their reddish vibrancy and had visibly shrunk, but the spent energy, coupled with shock, was taking its toll on Sebastian, and the healing was slow, excruciating, and incomplete. He posed no threat to Leland in his current condition, and Ty only hoped he'd be able to walk.

"I'm feeling quite generous, it seems," Leland remarked. "An auspicious day—night—like this should be marked by an act of munificence. Very well. He can go."

Sebastian raised his head to look at Ty. His pale blue eyes were dark with pain and emotion, and he shook his head ever so slightly in negation.

Ty could hardly expect such loyalty. He didn't deserve it, neither coming from Bas not from Cary. But he could at least try to protect them now. Whatever it took, he had to make sure Bas and Cary made it out alive, even if it cost him everything he had.

"Bas, go," he ordered gruffly. "There's nothing more you can do here. Take my car and get the hell out."

Sebastian stared at him for one more second and then hauled himself up. He swayed dangerously but somehow managed to stay on his feet and hobble toward the exit, like Giordano had done minutes before.

As he stepped out of the barn, Ty proffered the amulet, holding it by the chain.

"It's yours," he said but made no move to hand it over.

Instead of coming to him, Leland nodded to his partner. "Vincent."

The other man approached Ty cautiously, his gun at the ready. Ty briefly considered tackling him and wrestling away his weapon, but Cary's position was too precarious. He could barely breathe, being caught as he was in Leland's iron grip, and the sorcerer could snap his neck in a second if he wanted to. So Ty just stood there as Vincent snatched the amulet from his hand.

"Excellent," Leland said as Vincent brought it to him. He held it up in his free hand, admiring it like a collector would an exquisite *objet d'art*. "How beautiful. They just don't make things as fine anymore."

In a swift motion, he hauled Cary to his feet and pushed him roughly, ignoring Ty's cry of protest.

"Now, let's see what it can really do."

Chapter Twenty-Two

CARY STUMBLED, PAIN flaring in his bent arms and receding as the sorcerer released his hold. He didn't have a chance to do anything about it, though—Vincent pressed the barrel of the gun against his back and prodded him forward.

"The hell, man!"

"Up you go," Vincent said, unmoved by his outburst. There was a dangerous, almost maniacal look in his eyes now, and for the first time, Cary thought perhaps he'd been underestimating the depth of Vincent's motivation.

"Where?"

Vincent nodded toward the thing that looked suspiciously similar to a sacrificial altar from a cult-inspired episode of *Criminal Minds*. It didn't look like a TV set, however. The setup, despite the overall shabbiness, made Cary's hackles rise. The mere thought of going anywhere near that massive chunk of granite filled him with almost primeval panic. And that was before he stopped to consider *why* they wanted him anywhere near it.

"No fucking way," he said, bracing himself for the incoming blow.

"Leland, stop this." Ty intervened before Vincent could punish him again for being too mouthy for his own good.

Ty's voice thrummed with tension, and Cary spared him a quick glance. Ty's face was smeared with dirt, and dust covered his clothes, but Cary had never been so happy and freaked out to see someone. Ty was here, which meant he'd agreed to Giordano's ransom demand, that he'd cared enough for Cary to risk his own life by coming to his rescue. The sight of him facing off Leland was almost too much; the feeling was so intense it threatened to overwhelm him and reduce him to a sniveling, bawling mess of inexpedient joy.

But there was no time to come undone. Whatever had made Ty come to his aid had also made him vulnerable. It was clear they were at a dire disadvantage. Sebastian was gone, and the Giordanos hadn't been any help. Spotting Rossi's broken, unmoving body, half-covered in dust and debris, made Cary even more anxious. All the carnage only made him realize that Leland was not only batshit crazy, but downright dangerous.

Stay out of it, he begged Ty soundlessly, willing him to shut up, but Ty's eyes were focused on Leland. His fists were clenched, his mouth set in a hard line.

"By the way, I must thank you for choosing this specific venue for your little shindig," Leland said in a conversational tone, totally ignoring Ty's plea. "Despite the inconvenience of getting here, the setting fits my needs perfectly."

Vincent shoved Cary forward again, and he had no choice but to shuffle along. Ty made a step forward as if to stop them, but halted at a warning sign Leland made in his direction. He didn't say anything, but the look he gave the older sorcerer sent shivers down Cary's spine. It was clear that despite the threat, Ty wasn't going to take any of this lying down, and it scared him. He didn't want to die and he didn't want Ty to die trying to help him. Their only chance was by somehow rallying together. Because if he made it to that altar like Leland and Vincent wanted, it was over.

Without giving himself any more time to think about it, Cary dropped to the ground like dead weight and rolled under Vincent's feet, aiming to knock him off balance.

Vincent yelped, and a shot rang out as he'd lost his footing and involuntarily pulled the trigger. Cary didn't pause to see if the stray bullet had done any damage. He scrambled, struggling to maintain balance with his hands still bound, and managed to come to his feet. At the same moment, Ty, fast and silent, lunged at Vincent and tackled him to the ground, using the moment of confusion. Both men went down as they grappled for the gun, hitting the floor hard as they missed Cary by mere inches. He ducked instinctively and looked around just in time to see Leland take a step toward them, his expression that of utter exasperation.

Before Leland could raise his hand or say something that would make them all explode from the inside or something equally as pleasant, Cary threw himself at him. He was younger, fitter, and Leland was already unsteady on his feet. If he managed to knock him out even for a minute, it would give Ty and him a chance for escape.

But he didn't have the opportunity to throw a punch. As he slammed into the sorcerer, Leland sidestepped, so instead of tackling the man, Cary merely brushed against him. He grabbed Leland's hand with both of his so as not to go down with the force of his momentum, but Leland twisted his arm out of Cary's grip with a much greater ease than Cary expected. Cary skidded to a stop and then wheeled around, already knowing he'd lost despite the adrenaline pumping in his veins.

Leland stopped, facing him with a sneer that twisted his features. He didn't appear to have done anything, but all of a sudden Cary was jerked back. It was as if an unseen tidal wave of solid air picked him up and crashed him against the floor, knocking the wind and consciousness out of him. There was a fraction of a second of pure panic, too short for any coherent thought, and then there was only blackness.

CARY OPENED HIS eyes slowly, staring into the dimness that lurked high above, between the ancient wooden beams. Rusted chains swayed gently above him. He blinked, watching specks of dust as large as mothballs drift serenely through the air for what felt like eternity. They blurred at times, as the throbbing pain in his temples made it difficult to focus his eyes, or to think about anything but the invisible currents that made the dust spin.

He blinked again, fighting against the sluggishness. This was just like regaining consciousness in the car on the way here, after Leland had dosed him with magic. God, he was sick and tired of waking up like this. He wasn't sure he could take any more of this skull-splitting headache.

As seconds crept by, he took stock of himself. He was lying on his back on something cold and solid, his arms free and stretched by his sides. He tried to move, but that only made him nauseous. When he turned his head to the side, very carefully, his vision swam, a kaleidoscope of muted colors. But after a few moments of disorientation, he was able to take in his surroundings.

Of course—the barn. He was lying on top of the weird altar Leland and Vincent had been so eager to haul him onto. Well, it seemed like they'd gotten their wish. Cary wasn't tied, but he could barely move. His fingers twitched as he remembered what was hidden in the pocket of his trousers, but he willed himself to keep still for now.

Cary swept his gaze across the barn and immediately spotted Ty, as if drawn to him by some sort of magnet. This time, however, it wasn't a welcome sight. Ty stood near one of the posts, his hands held up by a chain hitched over a beam. In fact, he was almost hanging by the damned chain, his shoulders slackened and his head lolling on his shoulder. His chest rose and fell almost imperceptibly. Dried blood crusted around a deep gash on his forehead, and Cary winced even as a tightness that was clutching his heart eased. Ty must have put up quite a fight to land himself in that position, but at least he was alive. Cary could only guess at why Leland had decided to incapacitate him instead of killing him outright. Whatever the reason, Cary was grateful for it, because while they were both breathing, there was still hope—even if it was as feeble and stupid as he felt.

Vincent was standing near Ty, holding the gun at his hip. He was looking at Cary, or rather, at something or someone behind him, on the other side of the altar. Cary gradually became aware of a low chanting, barely a murmur at first, then growing stronger and louder. He couldn't make out the words, but he wasn't sure if that was because it was in some foreign language he didn't understand, or because his brain was still addled in fog. He risked lifting his head just a little, to see where it was coming from.

The first thing that caught his attention was the gleam of metal on his chest. The amulet rested on top of his stained and torn white shirt, the chain secured around his neck. The gleam was so bright it hurt his eyes a little, and Cary squinted, trying to make sense of what was going on. The silver disk was growing warm, too, and as familiar as the feeling was, it was making him decidedly nervous.

Cary shifted uneasily, but jumping off the altar and tearing that thing off his neck was out of the question. Even trying to use the damn thing, to influence Vincent, for example, was impossible in his current condition. His limbs felt as if they were full of lead; just moving his head took enormous effort. All he could do was wait for the daze to wear off and hope he regained control of his body before it was too late.

The chanting became louder, and he recognized Leland's voice. A shiver ran down his spine, which had nothing to do with the coldness of the stone, but rather the way the amulet seemed to respond to the incantation. It was almost vibrating, gathering energy that even Cary could feel. The energy was flowing through him, all around him, moving through air, stone, bone, and wood, circling and converging into a single point. The amulet was acting like a magnifying glass, concentrating scattered light into a single powerful beam. But where this beam of energy was directed, Cary had no idea. It scared the shit out of him, being right there, at the eye of the vortex. Leland's words about Cary playing "the star role in the show" suddenly resonated with a whole new meaning. Considering the amulet was apparently supposed to open some sort of portal, he really, really didn't want to be there when that happened.

His fingers fluttered above his right trouser pocket. If only he could slip his hand inside without drawing Leland's attention. The solution was right there, literally at his fingertips. But then Leland stepped into view, and Cary let his hand fall. He was definitely not strong enough to fight the sorcerer off if he noticed Cary was up to something.

If Leland saw Cary was awake, he gave no sign. He made some weird gestures with his hands above Cary's body, never interrupting his chant. Cary guessed the hand waving was meant to direct the currents of energy, which were now so strong as to be almost visible to the naked eye. His heart raced as he watched Leland warily.

Wisps of purple and silver smoke began to rise from the center of the amulet, thin and insubstantial at first, like fogging breath on a cold winter's morning. It was kind of beautiful, in a terrifying way. But it had never done that before. The silver disk was so hot Cary was afraid it would burn a hole through the fabric and fuse with his skin, but that particular worry took a back seat for the moment. He flexed his feet, just a little, and had to suppress a thrill when he felt them move.

The chanting, repetitive and monotonous, was wearing on Cary's nerves—like the buzzing of a mosquito he couldn't swat away. The purplish smoke was becoming thicker, and it billowed around the altar and spilled down the wooden stairs like steaming liquid. It filled his mouth and nostrils, and Cary coughed, choking on the unfamiliar, almost sour taste at the back of his throat.

Every breath made him dizzy. The smoke rushed through his lungs, and he suddenly imagined it rushing through his blood in a foul tide and retreating as he exhaled, leaving him weak and confused. The smoke he huffed out was darker, closer to the shade of dried blood, streaked with silver, and it coalesced into a vortex that swirled above him, faster with each exhalation.

The amulet was draining him. The sudden realization was utterly clear. Living energy was more readily obtained than whatever could be sapped from the ether, as he well knew from his own meager experience. He was being used as a battery, providing power for the amulet to do its thing. Every breath he took, every mouthful of that smoke, was killing him. He was going to die on that altar as surely as a victim of a bloody ritual, sacrificed to Leland's madness and ambition.

He looked to the side again, and his breath hitched. Ty had regained consciousness and lifted his head ever so slightly. A soft groan escaped his lips, so quiet Cary couldn't be certain he'd heard it at all. There was a dazed look in his eyes, but he was blinking rapidly and shaking his head as he looked around.

Their eyes met above the wreckage, and Ty jolted against the chain that held him suspended. He whispered something inaudible, and Cary thought he saw Ty's lips forming his name—whether in disbelief or in silent plea, he couldn't tell.

Cary's heart clenched. He wanted to say he was sorry. He was the one who'd insisted on this crazy adventure. If it weren't for him, none of them would have been in this situation. And there were other things he wanted to say to Ty before the end. Things he'd never said before to anyone, things he'd never thought would be true for him, things he had to say even if Ty had made it clear he didn't want to listen.

But maybe Ty could help after all. If he could only distract Leland for a second, make him look away from Cary... Just one moment would be enough. As much as Cary hated the idea of shifting Leland's attention to Ty in the middle of his grand scheme, he was desperate. It was the only chance to maybe save them both.

He looked at Ty again, mouthing the word "talk." He didn't dare do more, for fear of attracting Vincent's attention. Luckily, the other man's gaze was riveted on the vortex forming above the altar, his sour expression replaced by something close to rapture.

Ty's gaze sharpened and shifted momentarily between Cary and Leland. He nodded in response to Cary's unspoken request, almost imperceptibly.

The smoke swirled, the silver streaks joining together, creating an almost solid reflective surface in the middle of the vortex. It looked like someone had placed a mirror inside a mini galaxy, and Cary thought he could almost discern a picture in that mirror—not his own dirty, terrified visage, but the hints of a foreign landscape. Jagged spires loomed on a hill behind a thick forest, and the air shimmered in the rays of the noonday sun.

Cary took a ragged breath, inhaling a reluctant mouthful of purple smoke just to smother an involuntary whimper. His vision swam, mercifully obscuring the glimpse of the window to another world opening up right above him.

"You have no idea what you're doing, Leland." Ty's hoarse voice cut through the chanting. "If you think you can deal with the Fae on equal terms, you're a damn fool. They're not ones to share their magic willingly."

Leland paused, but it seemed the amulet no longer needed his words to be activated. The smoke swirled faster and faster, and the silver mirror—the portal—grew in size and sharpness.

"Be quiet, child," Leland said gravely.

At his sign, Vincent turned and took a step toward to Ty, raising his hand to hit him, and that was when Cary took his cue. His shoved his hand inside his pants pocket and felt for the thin gold band that was hidden there—Ty's ring, which he'd shucked off Leland's finger when he'd grabbed the sorcerer's arm. He held his breath and slipped it on.

Chapter Twenty-Three

THE CHANGE WAS instantaneous. It was as if the world around him suddenly came back into focus, and Cary's body was all at once his own to command. The fog that had bogged his thoughts was gone; he could breathe, and he could see and hear with absolute clarity. Neither Leland's nor the amulet's magic could touch him.

The tendril of smoke that flowed from his mouth to the spinning vortex vanished, as if severed by an invisible hand. The window was still there, but it grew dimmer, and the edges of the silver surface wavered. A tremor ran through the stone, down into the ground, shaking the walls.

Cary heard Leland's gasp of surprise and outrage. He only had a second's worth of opportunity, so he threw himself off the altar, instinctively putting out his left arm to shield his head. He hit the wooden steps (so hard stars danced in front of his eyes), and rolled down to the floor, hoping the sickening cracking sound had come from the rotting wood and not his ribs. He wasn't sure his body could take any more abuse.

Pain flared in his arm, dashing his hopes at a clean escape. It definitely felt as if the bone cracked. Apparently, he'd misjudged the height of the stone block and how cramped his muscles were, and he was too weakened by the life-draining magic to have made a graceful landing.

A bullet whizzed past his head, sending splinters flying as it hit the floorboards. Cary hissed and flailed with the agility of a newborn kitten, trying to push himself up to get out of the line of fire. The amulet was burning against his chest, but he ignored it in favor of more pressing concerns.

"Don't kill him, Vince!" Leland shouted. His regal features distorted, and his outstretched hands shook as he fought to maintain control of the magical whirlpool that swerved in the air. Another tremor shook the long-suffering barn. "We need him alive to hold the portal open!"

But Vincent had no chance to respond. Ty grabbed at the chain that bound his wrists and swung himself in a violent arc, using the momentum to kick Vincent in the back and sending him sprawling. The gun cluttered out of his hand and skidded on the floor, two or three feet off to Cary's side.

Cary heaved himself up on all fours and lunged for the gun, though perhaps "lunged" was too big a word for his awkward scuttling. He never knew two fucking feet could be such a huge distance to cover. He reached with his good hand, but it was just a split second too late. Vincent, who wasn't encumbered by a broken arm and bruising, grabbed the gun, swatting away Cary's extended hand, and rose to his feet, pure rage coloring his face in shades of purple. Cary cowered, waiting for the shot, but apparently Leland's admonition had some effect, because Vincent hesitated, weapon in hand.

"What are you waiting for?" the sorcerer cried, his voice strained. "Bring him back here, now!"

Behind Vincent, Ty swore. The wound on his forehead had opened again, and a thin trickle of blood oozed down his cheek and neck behind the collar of his jacket. The chain rattled as he tugged at it in frustration.

"Cary!"

This was it, Cary thought. No more second chances. He could feel the magic flowing inside him, but now it was his, not something poured on him, drowning him. He could control it. He'd done it before, hadn't he? It had worked when he wanted to get out of Giordano's lake house basement. This was no different—he'd just have to amp it up, draw the energy and direct it with razor-sharp precision. And after all, there was no shortage of magical energy in the barn at the moment.

He took a shaky breath just as Vincent bent down to haul him to his feet, and whispered an opening spell, imagining the invisible currents streaming through the air like a river flood.

The metal bands around Ty's wrists snapped open, and he tumbled to the floor as he lost his balance. Not having a chance to steady himself, he rolled with the fall, and yanked the chain off the high beam. Holding it in both hands, he launched at Vincent from behind, using the chain to crush the man's windpipe.

Vincent made a gurgling sound and let go of the gun to clutch at the chain at his throat. Cary crawled to the gun again, cussing at every inch of ground he had to cover. Agonizing pain radiated from his left forearm into the rest of his body with every jolt. *Don't pass out. Bad shit happens when you pass out. Suck it up and deal with it later.*

His fingers closed on the gun handle just as he heard the wooden stairs by the altar creak under Leland's steps. He was coming down, presumably to drag both Cary and the amulet back on the altar himself, despite the limp that was hampering his movement. The clouds of purple smoke thinned, and the window was getting smaller now that there was no living creature to feed it. Leland's magic wasn't enough to power it without an external source.

Leland raised his hand, and Cary could almost imagine something vibrating in the air around him, dissipating before it could hit him. The ring he was wearing had neutralized whatever spell Leland had directed at him.

The sorcerer's expression changed. He glanced at his own hand and then back at Cary.

"You thieving little shit," he hissed.

Cary didn't bother telling him it was quite a compliment, especially coming from him. His right hand shook as he raised the gun, pointing it at Leland. The weapon seemed to weight a hundred pounds. Guns were never his forte, and Cary had the vaguest idea of what he was doing.

"Stop right there, or I'll shoot," he said.

His voice was trembling as badly as his hand, so it was no wonder Leland didn't seem to take him seriously. But instead of coming at Cary, he turned and walked to where Ty was strangling Vincent.

The chain burst, the individual links flying and scattering across the floor. Ty staggered and took a step back. Vincent sagged to his knees, coughing. His face was now a deep shade of red, and an angry welt ran across his throat.

Ty's gaze flickered between Leland and Cary, and Cary couldn't discern his expression. There was grim acceptance, and sorrow, and something almost tender as their eyes met, and that single look knocked Cary's breath away as effectively as any magic spell.

Leland extended his hand in Ty's direction.

"I wanted to give you a chance," he said, fake regret underlying his words. "A chance to walk away, for old times' sake. But you're just too stubborn, Ty. You always have been. And as much as it pains me—"

Cary had no idea what Leland was about to do, but he had no intention of waiting till the end of his self-indulgent tirade to find out. He took a deep breath, closed his eyes, and squeezed the trigger.

A shot rang out, deafening despite the noise of the rushing wind, the creaking wood, and Vincent's coughing.

Cary opened his eyes. For a moment, he was sure the shot had gone astray, or worse, hit the wrong target. Then Leland sank to the floor, as if in slow motion, going down on one knee and hunching over. He clamped a hand over the wound in his side, blood dripping onto the dirty floorboards, obscenely red against the years-old grime. Cary couldn't see his face, but judging from Ty's expression, he didn't really want to.

The purple and silver vortex above the altar quivered, and the window grew entirely opaque, the otherworldly scene no longer visible behind the veil. With no readily available magic to hold it stable, it began to break apart, plumes of smoke tearing away and drifting to the ground like chunks of shredded fabric. The entire structure around them seemed to convulse at the release of the unstable energy, shaken violently as if by a powerful earthquake.

"No!" Vincent pushed himself up, but his look of horror was directed at the disintegrating portal rather than his partner in crime bleeding out a few feet away from him. He cast about, his look wild, almost deranged. Cary tightened his grip on the gun, but Vincent's attention wasn't on him at all.

Ty rushed to Cary's side and hauled him to his feet. The feel of his warm, solid body pressed against his own nearly made Cary faint with relief, and he had to bite back unexpected tears. He was trembling, and the words "I just fucking shot someone" blazed in his mind's eye like a neon sign, making it difficult to focus on anything else.

"I got you, baby," Ty whispered, though he was hardly in a better shape. He put his arm around Cary's shoulder, steadying them both. Cary was grateful when he took the gun away from him, because he couldn't have pointed that thing at another human being even if his life depended on it.

They nearly stumbled as another shock wave ripped through the ground. There was a high-pitched, keening sound, and a part of the roof near the barn door caved in, showering them with dust and splinters and effectively cutting off their escape route.

"Fucking shit," Ty breathed.

Cary closed his eyes. He was too exhausted to care. If this was the end, at least they would face it together, and that was more than he'd had any right to hope for.

"Come on." Ty pulled him away, going to the back of the barn, keeping to the walls and ducking when pieces of the roof fell down around them. Cary had no choice but to open his eyes and follow him reluctantly. It was pointless. His entire body was wracked by agony, and he wanted nothing more than to lie down and go to sleep.

He saw Vincent picking up Leland and carrying him, slung across his shoulder. The sorcerer's head was lolling from side to side and his blood was staining Vincent's shirt, but from this distance, Cary couldn't tell if he was still breathing. But the illusion of loyalty only lasted the number of seconds it took Vincent to reach the steps to the altar and haul Leland's unconscious body onto the stone, as if it were a game carcass. He waved his hands desperately through the thinning smoke, frantically paddling it toward Leland's half-open mouth.

"Work, damn it!"

He's insane, Cary thought. But the realization was dull and distant. Ty dragged him, almost bodily, around the altar toward the far wall, where he left Cary standing under the flaking sigil. Cary sagged to his knees, watching in apathy as Ty leaned against the altar and, with all his strength, pushed his foot between the stairs. It took him a couple of tries, but then something clicked, and a portion of the stairs moved apart, revealing a square hole in the floor with a steep stairway running down into the damp-smelling darkness below.

Cary stirred, blinking at the sight. A secret passageway was like something out of an action flick—an unexpected twist in a contrived plot, but hell, he wasn't complaining.

There was a loud crack, like a tall tree snapping after being hit by a bolt of lightning. The purple and silver vortex collapsed on itself, sending out billows of smoke that immediately turned black and putrid. The ground shook, and two upper beams broke in half. Another portion of the roof came down, burying Rossi's body under the wreckage.

"No, no, no!" Vincent wailed, and clawed at the air where the portal had been. "I need to go back! I want to go home!"

Cary stared, fascinated by the display of utter frenzy, but Ty grabbed his good hand and pulled him down the secret stairway before Cary had the chance to see what Vincent was going to do next. It probably wouldn't be much, considering the barn was coming down right on top of them. Cary ducked as the wall behind them burst outward, and skidded down the stairs, Ty following right on his heels. He heard Vincent's final cry of despair as the remnants of the roof crashed down with a deafening roar, sealing the opening above their heads.

Chapter Twenty-Four

TY COUGHED AS a cloud of dust from the barn's collapse followed them underground. The earth above them vibrated with the aftershocks as he led Cary down the rickety flight of wire mesh stairs, groping blindly at the rail in complete darkness. It was freezing cold and the air was dank and musty, filled with the vapors of decay.

The end of the stairs came rather abruptly, and he steadied himself, his arm slung around Cary's shoulders. Cary's labored breathing underscored the pain that radiated from him. His skin was cold and clammy, and he was shivering uncontrollably—unsurprising, considering he'd nearly missed being bled dry to feed the forces that had ripped apart the very fabric of reality to create a portal to another world.

"We're safe now," Ty told him, doing his best to sound matter-of-fact. His voice echoed in the silence, which Ty had to convince himself was nothing like that of a grave.

He whispered a short spell, and a tiny light, barely the size of a firefly, appeared above his outstretched palm. That was the best he could do under the circumstances, but it was enough to make out Cary's dirty face, gaunt with exhaustion, and the way he was clutching his broken arm to his chest. The silver pendant gleamed dully on a chain around his neck, the etchings standing out in dark sharp lines.

This wasn't how either of them had envisioned getting it back. As far as Ty was concerned, Cary was welcome to keep it. There was no way in hell he would ever touch the damn thing again, no matter how big a reward someone might promise him.

The curved ceiling was mere inches above their heads, and hairlike cracks ran through the cement. Ty hoped it would all hold long enough for them to reach the exit. He'd only been there once in the past, but he remembered the passageway wasn't all that long, merely connecting the barn with the basement of the farmhouse.

Cary grasped his hand, and Ty halted, turning to him in concern.

The feeble illumination painted Cary's face with a deep, sharp-edged stain of shadow. But he wasn't looking at Ty. Instead, he brought the tip of his finger to the tiny light and uttered the same spell that Ty had cast moments before. The light grew, almost blinding in its sudden intensity, until Ty was holding a glowing orb of pure incandescence that banished the surrounding darkness into nonexistence.

A wholly unfamiliar sentiment curled beneath Ty's breastbone, a jumbled tangle of tenderness, warmth, and fierce pride. He was watching Cary coming into his own, stepping up to his abilities like he'd always known he could. It was humbling and awe-inspiring at the same time, and he knew that even if Cary wanted nothing more to do with him after all this was over, it was something he'd cherish for as long as he lived.

"Showoff," he said with a smile, unable to keep the affection out of his voice. His feelings must have been written clearly on his face, but he didn't care. If they weren't too busy running for their lives at the moment, he would scoop Cary up into his arms and let him know just how much he cared for him.

Cary smiled back at him, his eyes twinkling with the same emotion. He squeezed Ty's hand briefly, and then they hurried along the narrow tunnel.

"The hell is this place?" Cary asked when they reached the other end and climbed the stairs up to the basement door, which Ty had made sure to unlock in preparation for the possibility of them taking this route.

"I'll tell you later," Ty muttered, reluctant to go into the gory details after all the shit Cary had already had to endure. He opened the metal door cautiously, peering inside first, but the 350 square-foot concrete basement was blessedly empty, save for the miasma of death and ghostly crying only Ty could hear.

"Come on," he told Cary, tuning out the prickling of his skin over the voices of the dead. If he never saw this basement again, it would be too soon.

The staircase leading up to the main house was rotten almost through, as was the floor of the living area, but they managed to emerge outside without further injury. Ty allowed himself to take a full breath for the first time since he pulled up the driveway with Bas. He couldn't believe it was only hours ago. An entire lifetime seemed to have ended and begun anew during the course of the night.

The pinkish glow of predawn colored the eastern portion of the sky. Birds chirped in the trees that swayed in the gentle breeze, and the ducks were bustling down at the pond, probably only just returning after all the commotion had died down.

A thick cloud of dust hung in the air above the barn, or more accurately, where the barn used to stand. It was no more than a heap of ruins now, the roof completely caved in, the jagged scaffold timbers sticking out like broken bones. As far as Ty could see, nothing moved among the wreckage.

A horrible stench wafted from the few charred bodies strewn in the tall grass, which was eerily untouched by whatever fire had engulfed them. But apparently, not all of Giordano's men had fallen victim to Leland's rampage, because the three SUVs were gone, the only evidence of their presence the deep tire marks left in the dirt. Ty's precious Chevy was missing as well, which meant Bas had managed to get away, too, much to Ty's relief.

A white Honda, which he assumed belonged to either Leland or Vincent, was parked some distance away, close to the remnants of the fence. It was the only vehicle in sight, and Ty was infinitely grateful it was there. The last thing he wanted to do was hike eight or so miles to Diamond Springs on foot.

He closed his fist, killing the light, and made another quick survey of the surroundings before helping Cary step off the porch. They hobbled down the driveway, clinging to each other like a pair of train wreck survivors. If this had been an action movie, this would be the moment Vincent blocked their path, mangled and zombie-like. But this was real life, and Ty doubted anyone could have survived that crash. No one was coming for them, except maybe the pissed off ducks.

Cary leaned heavily on his arm as Ty steered him toward the orphaned Honda. It took him five whole minutes to break into the car and wire it, which served to prove exactly how drained he was.

"Can you drive?" Cary asked, watching from the sidelines. The faint morning light emphasized the deep dark circles beneath his eyes and the grayish cast to his usually tawny skin.

Ty would have driven the fuck away even if both his arms had been cut off, but he didn't say it. He only nodded wearily and then helped Cary into the passenger seat.

"You're hurt," Cary insisted, indicating the blood that was crusted on Ty's forehead. His eyes met Ty's with concern. "You might have a concussion or something."

"I'm okay," Ty said. He was shaking with fatigue and the traces of adrenaline that coursed through his bloodstream, but he could still function well enough to drive. He had a thick skull. Nothing could get through, except perhaps that soon he'd have to say goodbye to the only person he'd been willing to lay down his life for since he'd left Leland's apprenticeship.

He probably should be feeling something, now that Leland was dead. He should be hurting because of his mentor's betrayal, or grieving his loss. He should be trying to make sense of what had happened. But he was just too damn tired, and too numb. The only thing that mattered now was getting Cary the medical care he needed, and distancing him from any police or media attention that would eventually be drawn to what had happened. He had to keep Cary safe until it was time to let him go forever.

Ty cast a last look at the barn before slamming the car door and heading down to the main road. Even though there had been no way for him to know about Leland's involvement, he couldn't help but feel a twinge of guilt. Whoever Leland had been, whatever he'd become, he didn't deserve to die like that, his body a broken mess in a makeshift grave. Ty would venture to say neither Rossi, nor even the weird Vincent guy, deserved that, but there was nothing he could do for either of them.

Cary slumped in his seat. His injured left arm rested in his lap, the swollen flesh straining against the fabric of the shirtsleeve, and he was touching the amulet that still hung around his neck with his other hand. His long graceful fingers traced the interwoven lines of the pattern, a wistful expression on his face.

Ty wanted to ask if he was okay, but it was a stupid question. Of course Cary wasn't okay. Killing a man, even in self-defense, or in someone else's defense, as the case was, was never easy, and the kinder the person, the worse it affected them. So he clamped down on his urge to fuss and smother Cary with his sympathy, and kept quiet as he followed the curves of the road. Cary needed his space, and they both needed to put as much distance as they could between themselves and the farmhouse before the break of day.

THE SUN ROSE behind them, but soon the weather changed, and heavy gray clouds covered the sky. They'd been driving for about an hour, and Ty thought Cary had fallen asleep, when he suddenly sat up and said: "Pull over, please."

Ty complied and brought the Honda to a stop on the shoulder. Sparse trees flanked the road, but to their right, they could see a small lake, or rather a pond. The wind was sending ripples over the surface of the water.

Cary got out of the car and limped toward the pond. Ty followed, leaving the engine running, and joined Cary by the edge of the pond, where the water was licking the muddy bank. Distant thunder rolled, and the first drops of rain landed on their heads and shoulders. But Cary didn't seem to notice. He took the necklace off with his right hand, clutching the metal disk so hard his knuckles went white.

"Baby," Ty said quietly, but Cary didn't answer. He was looking at the water, his gaze distant and unseeing. Ty wondered what it was that was playing in front of his eyes.

"It's all I ever wanted," Cary said suddenly. "To be good enough. I thought that with this, I would be. That I'd finally get that break, that I'd make something of myself like

Granddad wanted. But not like this. Not at the price of…" He looked at the amulet in his hand.

Ty took a step toward him.

"You're good enough," he said. "You're everything."

His voice shook, and he had to bite his lip to hold himself together.

Cary looked at him, his eyes big and bright and full of emotion. His mouth twisted, and it seemed like he was going to say something, but he turned back to the pond. He took a deep breath and then swung his arm. The amulet traced a graceful arc in the air, the chain trailing behind it like the tail of a comet, before hitting the surface and disappearing with a loud *plunk*.

Cary's face crumbled and a sob tore out of him. Ty caught him before he could sink to his knees, holding him close, stroking his hair. He might have said things, too—silly, soothing things he'd be embarrassed to recall later. But Cary probably didn't hear them anyway. He was crying—the ugly, convulsive crying of a heartbroken child, and Ty's heart was breaking right along with his.

The rain poured down, soaking clothes that were already beyond filthy, but neither of them cared. Cary's sobs finally subsided, and he shuddered in Ty's arms, sniffling. He started to pull away, but Ty held him tight, careful not to put pressure on the injured arm, and after a few tense minutes, Cary relaxed, leaning against him and burying his face in Ty's tattered jacket.

"It's okay, baby," Ty whispered and planted a ghostly kiss on his head. "Or it will be."

Cary shifted to look up at him and nodded. Despite the bone-deep weariness etched into the lines of his face and the puffiness around his red eyes, he looked calmer. He wiped his eyes in a jerky motion and stepped back to pull the gold ring off his finger.

"I understand now why you wanted it back so badly," he said as he handed it to Ty with a wry smile. It didn't quite reach his eyes; they were still full of shock and grief.

Ty took the ring. It glinted in his palm—a simple thing, but it had saved Cary's life when Ty had been powerless to do so. He took Cary's right hand and slipped the gold band back on his ring finger. It was both an apology and a promise Ty wouldn't let himself utter out loud.

"Keep it," he said, gently squeezing Cary's hand shut. His voice was too raw, and he swallowed to stop it from cracking. "That way I'll know you'll never be harmed by magic again."

"Protecting the silly little 'common'?"

"You're anything but common. You're the bravest person I know," Ty said, the words spilling out before he could clamp down on them.

"For throwing that thing out?"

"For believing you can do without it."

There was a slight pause as Cary digested that.

"We would never have had a moment's peace with that thing," he said finally and sighed. "Giordano would never let it go, and others might have become too interested if I kept using it. I don't want us to go through this kind of hell again."

"But that's not why you got rid of it," Ty said.

"No," Cary agreed.

They stood there in silence for a while, still holding each other as they got soaked through.

Ty didn't fail to notice that "us," but even as his heart leapt with joy at the short word, he knew hope was futile. With the amulet gone, there were no more conflicting interests, no more hidden agendas, no more games. Similarly, there also was nothing holding them together anymore. Ty was stupid enough to have fallen in love with the man he'd planned to con, but there was no way Cary would feel the same for someone who'd tried to rob him and led him on with every intention of completing the task. Not to mention it was Ty's fault Cary had been taken hostage and nearly killed by a mad sorcerer. Cary would have to be mad himself not to harbor a grudge, let alone return any feelings Ty might have. Once the adrenaline haze dissipated and Cary realized that Ty had inadvertently fucked up everything he had going for himself, any attraction he may have been feeling would turn to resentment.

It would be better to save himself the heartache. He'd see to it that Cary was returned home safe and sound, say his goodbyes, and pretend like none of this had ever happened. He'd already done enough damage, and, frankly, he wasn't sure his current shaky mental state would allow him to bear the inevitable scorn and rejection stoically.

Ty was a mess, and Cary deserved so much better and so much more than he could ever hope to give him.

"Come on," he said, letting his hands fall from Cary's shoulders and schooling his face into a neutral expression. He'd said enough sentimental crap already. "Let's get you to a hospital."

Chapter Twenty-Five

TWO MONTHS LATER

Cary stood in front of the basement apartment door, chewing on his lip. The decision to come had been brewing in his head for quite some time, but now he was suddenly hesitant to follow through.

He hadn't seen Ty since the day they returned to San Francisco—in a rental car. Ty had insisted on wiping down and dumping Leland's Honda while Cary was being treated at the Sacramento Medical Center for his broken arm and bruised ribs. Ty flat-out refused to be checked despite Cary's insistence. But by the time Cary was done with filling all the forms, waiting, getting X-rays, waiting, getting his arm in a cast, then waiting some more for his pain meds and antibiotics prescriptions, Ty had reappeared wearing clean clothes, with the gash in his forehead neatly taped, and carrying takeout. Cary was nearly out of it with fatigue and medication, but he inhaled the meatball sub and soda before falling asleep in the car.

Ty drove him all the way to his apartment, which still looked like it had been in the path of an elephant stampede, and deposited him at the door. He wore a stony expression the whole time, and Cary was too damn hazy to ask any questions. Later, he was furious at himself for not doing anything, for not asking Ty to come in and stay the night, even if it meant sleeping together (or rather, passing out) on a slashed mattress. As it was, he'd fallen asleep, curled up in a ball on the couch, as soon as the door closed after Ty, fully expecting to have a much more meaningful talk with him the next day.

But Tuesday came and went, and there'd been no sign of Ty. Cary waited for him to call, or pick up his phone, or drop by, or...do something. But there'd been nothing. Every time Cary called Ty's cell phone, it went straight to voice mail. It was as if he'd disappeared off the face of the earth without a word.

The memory of the next few days was somewhat blurred, but there was no doubt they'd been hell. Cary had trouble sleeping, but when he'd finally manage to doze off, he'd dream of that night in the barn. He'd hear the gun going off, and see Leland toppling. There was smoke in his lungs, suffocating him. He'd watch helplessly as Ty swung in his chains, and he'd wake up either thrashing or soaked in cold sweat.

The physical pain of his injuries could be dulled by the analgesics, but the pain that had settled deep down in his chest was constantly there, twisting and gnawing at his insides. He wondered what he'd done to make Ty leave him. When Cary had broken down by that lake somewhere along Route 50, Ty had looked at him like he'd gladly trade his soul for Cary's happiness. There was simply no way a man who was indifferent could look at someone the way Ty had looked at him then.

He'd been wrong about so many things before in his life, but he couldn't have been wrong about that.

That was what he'd been telling himself for the last two months, while slowly piecing his life back together. He was on the last stretch of his savings, but he'd gotten his agent to work things out with the Garland to book more shows starting next week and sort out the cancelled shows.

Eventually, the bruises had faded, and his arm healed. Even the nightmares became less frequent. But the real ache had never gone away.

He had to find Ty, to ask him why he'd split. Ask him if he'd been wrong in his assumptions... But Ty wasn't an easy man to find, and Cary had absolutely no means of contacting him.

However, there was someone who could.

He took a deep breath and knocked on Sebastian Monroe's door.

It swung open immediately, startling Cary just a little, and Sebastian peered out, giving him a critical once-over. Strands of dark hair, which he was obviously growing out, fell haphazardly around his face, and his fingernails were once again painted bright red.

"Darling," he said, opening the door wide to let Cary in. "What in damnation took you so long?"

Cary walked inside and halted in indecision. At Sebastian's gesture, he perched on the edge of the silk sofa while Sebastian poured them both fragrant tea from a chipped porcelain teapot. Cary fidgeted with the ring on his finger, the band smooth and cool under his fingertips—a promise he was almost afraid to believe anymore. Perhaps he'd been reading too much into it. Perhaps it had only been a gesture of apology, a payoff. It was difficult to tell what was real and what wasn't. Maybe he was clinging to something that had never been there, to a ghost reflected off his own confused emotions.

"So, you want me to get in touch with Ty for you?" Sebastian adjusted his long silk dressing gown, gold with flying herons embroidered in purple, around him as he took a seat across from Cary.

"How did you know?"

Bas just shook his head with an expression of utter pity.

"Please, darling. Now, stop fretting. I'll talk to him for you, and I'll even do it for free."

"Why would he listen to you?" Cary asked. Now he felt a bit stupid for coming, asking for Sebastian's help. It felt so pathetic, like something a desperate lovestruck high-school student might do. Surely, Ty had the right to call quits on him if he wanted to.

"Ty has this annoying little habit of actually caring for his friends, no matter how he tries to convince himself to the contrary. Works every damn time."

Cary grimaced. He wanted to see Ty again, but it kind of rankled that he'd rush to Sebastian's aid at the drop of a hat, and dismiss *him* so casually. The thought did little to boost his confidence.

"He cares about you," Bas said, much more gently. His pale gaze was sympathetic as it rested on Cary. "In fact, I think it's more than just caring, God help him. He's doing that stupid 'protecting himself by disassociation' thing."

"Protecting himself?" Cary said incredulously. "Against what?"

"Being hurt. Nothing hurts like love, does it? You know what I'm talking about," Bas said. At Cary's silence, he added: "Now you go on. I'll make sure you lovebirds get your happy reunion again."

IT HAD BEEN a good show. Granted, Cary was making almost no money since he was still paying the Garland for his willful breach of contract, but he was very close to eliminating his debt and starting to turn a profit. Either way, he was slowly building a name for myself while learning to subtly weave his magic into his performance. Even the slightest touch of it produced amazing results. He had to admit that even the most intricate illusions in the world could not compare to the real thing when it was done right.

He kept it simple, though, sticking to the classic illusionist repertoire. He was still finding his footing, figuring out what he could do, what he'd be best at. There was plenty of time for him to tweak things before he ventured on to greater things.

Cary took off his top hat (he really needed to invest in a better stage outfit) and opened the door to his dressing room. And stopped dead.

It was like *déjà vu*, watching Ty get up from the old oversized armchair at the back of the dressing room. Only this time, there was no gun in his hand. He stood, silently regarding Cary, his face partially obscured by shadow. He was wearing a leather jacket, very similar to the old one that had been ruined on that memorable night at the farm. His sun-bleached hair was cut even shorter, and a thin white scar, about an inch long, crossed the side of his forehead.

Cary's heart surged and then plummeted as he reminded himself not to get his hopes up. It had been two weeks since his visit to Sebastian, and despite the sorcerer's grand promises, Cary had already convinced himself it had been a fool's errand. He closed the door behind him with a soft click and tossed the hat on the vanity.

"So, um, hi," Cary offered, immediately hating himself for being a doofus.

"Hi," Ty said. Cary thought he sounded a touch apprehensive, but he must have been imagining things. What reason did Ty have to be apprehensive?

Cary took a deep breath. It was just like when he'd thrown his grandfather's amulet into the lake—throwing his hopes and dreams and yearnings out there, and hoping that somehow everything would be all right.

"I'm sorry for making Bas call you, but I had to see you," Cary said, searching Ty's blank face for some sort of reaction. "Because I missed you like crazy, and I don't understand why...why you'd disappear like that. I thought we had something going. Maybe I was wrong about that, and hey, maybe it was only the adrenaline talking, because how can you fall in love with someone you've only known for two weeks? It was one hell of a ride, and if that's all it was for you, that's okay. I'll never bother you again. But if I am wrong, please, just tell me."

Cary fell silent, swallowing hard. There was no easy way to say it, no way of letting Ty know what was in his heart without laying it bare and bleeding before him. But he had to. He owed it to Ty as much as he owed it to himself.

Ty took a step forward, coming under the bright fluorescent lighting of the mirror bulbs. His eyes burned with intensity.

"I'm sorry too, Cary." His voice was hard. "For bailing on you. I've been stupid and cruel. Thought I could forget about you and go on with my life, but I can't, because it's a damn lie. I'd been telling myself I was doing the right thing by staying away, especially after everything I'd done, and everything I'd planned on doing. How could you ever love someone like me? But I won't go on being afraid any longer, because that would mean losing you, and I can't do that. God help me, I've tried."

Cary didn't remember moving, but suddenly they were in each other's arms, kissing so hard their teeth clashed, needy and impatient, as if they could cram months of separation into a few seconds.

"I missed you so much," Ty gasped when they finally broke apart for air. He was holding on tight, as if Cary would disappear if he let go even for a moment.

"Whose fault was that?" Cary asked, but he couldn't hide the stupid grin that spread on his face. During the last two weeks, he refused to let himself think about Ty. So what if the world seemed less joyous, the colors around him more muted? Time healed all wounds, even a broken heart.

But, looking into Ty's eyes again, Cary realized how wrong he'd been. He loved him, and that made all the difference between living and existing.

"I'm sorry," Ty repeated. "Baby, I'm so fucking sorry."

"Then show me just how much."

Instead of an answer, Ty lifted him up, and they were kissing again, all the way back to the armchair. They landed on it so heavily the poor thing creaked and shuddered beneath them. Cary leaned back and spread his legs, making room for Ty while he was busily taking off his jacket and shirt. He bent down, kissing the side of Cary's neck, more slowly now, taking his time to taste and bite and nibble, and Cary threw back his head, giving him as much access as he could. He bucked against Ty, both his desire and need evident without words.

They fumbled as they divested each other of various articles of clothing, barely managing to stay on the chair in the process. They moved against each other, legs, arms and lips in a messy tangle, yearning for that closeness beyond the slide of skin on skin.

It was like their first time all over again, with neither of them having come prepared. But it didn't matter. There was no time for preparations or for prolonged foreplay—only the desperate mutual pleasure that ensured this was indeed real, that this was the first step in a long journey they would be making together.

They rubbed their hard cocks together, striving for that delicious friction as Ty wrapped a hand around them both and leaned into Cary's embrace. Cary dug his fingers into

Ty's hips and heard his grunt, but didn't relent. There was no space between their bodies, nothing that would separate them. Pleasure pooled at the base of his spine, and every stroke, every kiss, every breath brought him closer and closer to that dangerous edge with dizzying speed.

I love you. He closed his eyes against the imminent incandescent whiteout, but maybe he'd said it out loud, because it worked as surely as a spell. He heard Ty's sharp intake of breath as he stiffened in his arms, and then hot wetness splashed across his stomach.

Ty's lips brushed against his cheek, his breathing broken and ragged.

"I love you too." His words were soft, barely audible, like ghost traces on his skin—a touch of magic that tipped him over into an infinite abyss, spiraling out of control in the spasms of climax, knowing he would land safely in Ty's arms.

"SHIT." CARY SURVEYED the shards of a green glass lamp that were scattered all over the floor. The thing had been perched precariously on a wobbly side table, and they'd definitely not been careful. "They're gonna make me pay for that."

"With all the piles of junk you have in here, I hardly think anyone would notice," Ty reasoned and pulled him closer. They were snuggled on the armchair, naked, sweaty, and sticky, and so ridiculously content it was probably illegal somewhere.

"So what were you up to these past months? Working?"

"Nah," Ty said. "Took a break for a while. I've got a lot of things to figure out."

"What kinds of things?"

Ty shrugged. "All this stuff with Leland. Being stolen to Faerie as a baby. Maybe I'll try finding my family. I'm good at finding lost things."

"I know. I was one of them." Cary stroked his hand. Ty snorted in amusement and planted a quick kiss on his temple.

"You're not so bad at it yourself," he said in a playful tone that was somewhat belied by his earnest expression. "And you're damn persistent when you want something."

"That's one way to call it," Cary said. He pushed himself up on one elbow, looking down at Ty's flushed face. "Maybe...we could figure out all these things together?" When Ty didn't answer right away, he added in a rush, "I mean, you could teach me how to use my magic properly, and that could be useful, right? We could be a team—"

"What about your show?"

"I would still do that. It's going rather well, actually."

"As long as you don't overdo it," Ty said gently.

Cary sighed. "I know, I know. I'll be careful."

The temptation to explore his newfound powers was great, but he'd witnessed too much horror not to realize he had to tread that path very carefully. The last thing he wanted was to draw the attention of another overambitious sorcerer or mob boss. From what he'd heard (after inquiring very discreetly), Tony Giordano had moved to Washington, DC with his sister, but that didn't mean there weren't other people on the prowl with the idea of a magical boost to their aspirations.

Ty cupped the side of his face and leaned in for another kiss that left them both a little bit breathless. When they finally drew apart, there was laughter in his warm hazel eyes—laughter and something so profoundly tender Cary's heart melted all over again.

"Well then, Incredible Mr. Mars. I think we're going to make an excellent team."

About the Author

A voracious reader from the age of five, Isabelle Adler has always dreamed of one day putting her own stories into writing. She loves traveling, art, and science, and finds inspiration in all of these. Her favorite genres include sci-fi, fantasy, and historical adventure. She also firmly believes in the unlimited powers of imagination and caffeine.

Email: info@isabelleadler.com

Twitter: @Isabelle_Adler

Website: www.isabelleadler.com

Other books by this author

Adrift (Staying Afloat, book 1)
The Castaway Prince

Also Available from NineStar Press

Connect with NineStar Press

Website: NineStarPress.com

Facebook: NineStarPress

Facebook Reader Group: NineStarNiche

Twitter: @ninestarpress

Tumblr: NineStarPress

www.ingramcontent.com/pod-product-compliance
Lightning Source LLC
Chambersburg PA
CBHW060539190726
48283CB00003B/790